GRIGORY'S GADGET

BOOK 1 OF THE GASLIGHT FRONTIER
SERIES

E. A. HENNESSY

Copyright © 2016 E. A. Hennessy

All rights reserved. Printed in the United States of America. No part of this book may be used or reproduced in any manner whatsoever without written permission except in the case of brief quotations embodied in critical articles or reviews.

This book is a work of fiction. Names, characters, businesses, organizations, places, and events either are the product of the author's imagination or are used fictitiously. Any resemblance to actual persons living or dead, events, or locales is entirely coincidental.

For information contact:
eahennessy.com

Cover and map design by Deranged Doctor Design

ISBN-10: 0-9971943-0-8
ISBN-13: 978-0-9971943-0-2

First Edition: March 2016

Emerald Owl Publications
Buffalo, NY

Dedicated to Mohua and Rotem, who have inspired and supported my writing throughout our friendship.

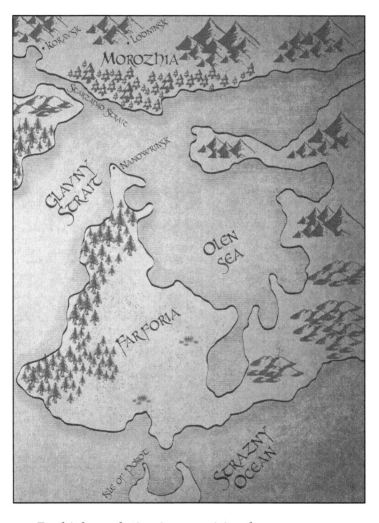

For high resolution image, visit eahennessy.com

CHAPTER ONE

Zoya Orlova's mind was a manic, swirling fog as she scurried around her apartment, moving clothes from her now-bare bed into the two leather suitcases on her floor. Those suitcases were all she'd have once she and her friends left Lodninsk.

A steady knock on the door startled Zoya.

Zoya looked around her bedroom, trying to spot anything she'd missed. She had already packed the few decent blouses, bodices, corsets, and pants she owned. The dresser was empty now, except for a brass clock with an ivory face that read a quarter after six. Zoya played nervously with a strand of her violet hair. The hair, along with her gray eyes and freckled skin, reminded Zoya of her mother and grandmother.

Another knock, this time frantic.

"Zoya! Are you ready?" Zoya's friend Lilia Alkaeva shouted, knocking again rapidly. Zoya walked into the tiny living room and opened the door with a smile.

"Almost," she said. "I'm waiting for my landlord to come by, and I need to grab one more thing."

Lilia shuffled in and sat on the small sofa. She pulled back her fur-lined hood and unwrapped her scarf. Her tan skin was flushed from the cold. Lilia's soft round face hadn't changed since childhood, when she and Zoya first became friends. She reminded Zoya of simpler times when they were young, before they'd experienced so much tragedy and loss. She was a comforting presence for Zoya, and Zoya knew the feeling was mutual.

Lilia regarded Zoya with sleepy eyes as she tucked a piece of her thick black hair behind her ear and adjusted her glasses.

Zoya closed her door and walked into the room that had been her grandmother's. Grandma Orlova's clothes still hung in the closet. They, like Zoya's, would be distributed to needy folks in the city. As worn as those clothes were, they would likely be the nicest donation received in quite some time. Zoya knelt and rooted around in the bottom drawer of her grandmother's dresser until her fingers found the small box she'd hidden there. The box held a family keepsake: a small sphere, the size of a grapefruit, composed of tightly packed gears and wires. Zoya thought it looked as though the parts should be able to move, but never had been able to make them budge. As Grandma Orlova lay on her death bed, barely able to speak lest she go into a horrible coughing fit, she'd told Zoya this keepsake was particularly important.

GRIGORY'S GADGET

"If you protect it," she'd said, "it will protect you."

Zoya had nodded and promised her grandmother she'd keep it safe. She'd assumed her grandmother's mind was going or clouded by medication. Grandma Orlova had never mentioned that particular keepsake before, but it obviously meant something to her. Zoya grabbed the little gadget and packed it into the corner of one suitcase as a sentimental token to bring to her new home.

"Has your landlord paid you yet?" Lilia asked as Zoya returned to the living room.

"I haven't seen him," Zoya said, shrugging in annoyance. "He's been busy, brushing me off every time I bring it up."

"He knows you're leaving today, right?"

Zoya shrugged again then fastened her suitcases closed.

"I still can't believe it," Lilia said, grinning as she glanced out the small window. There was nothing to see but ice and the stone of the next building. "It feels so surreal. We're finally leaving!" She smiled broadly at her friend. "We'll start our brand new, wonderful life in Mirgorod soon!"

"I didn't get any sleep last night," Zoya said. "I'm just so nervous. What if something goes wrong?"

"Don't talk like that," Lilia told her. "Only I'm allowed to talk like that." Lilia winked, but her fidgeting hands betrayed her nerves.

A series of hard, steady knocks sounded on the door. Zoya opened it and smiled politely at her landlord. He was a tall, malnourished man with yellowed eyes and teeth. "Enjoy your new perfect life, Miss Orlova. Here's the money for the furniture." He shoved a small stack of bills into Zoya's hand. Zoya stared at it and wrinkled her brow.

"Is this it?" she asked.

"Tough economy," her landlord said simply then turned to leave.

"Wait just a second," Zoya objected. "This isn't even half of what these things are worth!"

The landlord turned back around, frowning and rolling his eyes.

"The dresser in my grandmother's room is an antique," Zoya went on. "It's at least a hundred twenty years old, and in perfect condition! And the brass bed frame dates back to the rule of King Vassiliy II!"

"Yes, it's old," the landlord grumbled. "I was generous." He turned and walked away before Zoya could object further.

"Gosh," Lilia said as Zoya closed the door. "Well, it's better than nothing, I suppose. On the bright side, that's the last time you'll have to deal with him ever again."

Zoya frowned as she glanced around the small apartment. Lilia stood and patted Zoya's shoulder.

"Come on," Lilia urged. "Everyone else is waiting downstairs. We'll miss the train if we don't hurry!"

"Am I the only one who had trouble fitting my entire life into two suitcases?" Anya Filipova asked as Zoya and Lilia arrived in the lobby of the apartment complex. She was fussing with her golden-brown hair, which was a mess about her head from the wind outside. "I barely had room for all of my craft supplies, let alone clothes!" Tall and skinny, Anya always moved with an easy grace such that the simple act of fixing her hair seemed like a flourish.

"She didn't let me sleep at all," Lilia teased. "I can just buy new fabric there, right? Oh, but I love this fabric! Which beads should I bring?"

"Shush, you," Anya replied with a playful shove. "These are important decisions."

"Demyan and I had it easy," Nikolai Polzin responded. He leaned casually against the wall and grinned. Fresh snowflakes still dotted his black dreadlocks and melted against his mahogany skin. "We split our archeology books and tools between the two of us. The only downside is we'll need to share." Demyan Volkov playfully shoved his friend, his green eyes sparkling. He was nearly a head shorter than Nikolai, with a small frame.

"Lucky," Lilia told them. "I had so much trouble narrowing down which books I wanted to bring."

"My issue wasn't space so much as weight," Zoya said. "Screwdrivers and wrenches get heavy fast. I could pack only the most basic tools." Zoya walked over to Demyan and hugged him, kissing him on the cheek.

"I don't need much," he told her, "as long as I have you." Zoya stuck her tongue out at him.

"You're so sweet," she said.

"Sickeningly sweet," Nikolai added.

"Anyhow, friends," Lilia said with urgency. "We really do need to get moving. We don't want to be late!" The friends nodded and bundled up to head outside.

The city of Lodninsk, Morozhia was a dreary place surrounded by coal mines and filled with factories. Soot stained the stone and brick buildings. The only saving grace was the near-constant falling snow that made the city seem somewhat clean.

"Where are you off to at this hour of the morning?"

A platoon of soldiers stood in the friends' path, their hands placed firmly on the metal batons strapped to their belts. The friends cast their eyes to the ground.

"We're going to the train station, sir," Zoya said. "We're heading to the port in Koravsk."

"Tickets," the leader commanded. The friends complied, handing over their tickets.

"Mirgorod?" the leader asked. "What is there for you in Mirgorod?"

"We're students, sir," Anya said, "transferring to the Grand University of Mirgorod for our final year of studies."

"What's wrong with Lodninsk University?" the leader asked. Anya opened her mouth to answer and froze. She glanced at her friends.

"Absolutely nothing, sir," Zoya said. "We have been taught that living through hardship builds character. What better hardship than to endure being far from this great city, sir?"

GRIGORY'S GADGET

"Indeed," the leader replied. After he looked at each ticket, he nodded and returned them to the group.

"On your way," he said. He and the rest of the platoon resumed their march down the street. The friends sighed and continued on their way.

The wind howled through the streets as the friends made their way to the train station. The large, stone building was one of the grandest in the city. Thick glass filled its facade, reaching almost to the top of its domed roof. Zoya and her friends smiled at each other then entered.

The lobby was huge with high ceilings made of a brown stone. The marble floors laid out a warm geometric pattern trimmed with gold. In the center of the lobby sat a fifteen-foot clock tower.

"Wow," Nikolai said. "I've never been in here before."

"Neither have I," Demyan agreed. "Who knew there was anything this colorful in Lodninsk?"

"A sign of good things to come," Zoya said, smiling.

They lumbered toward the signs labeled *Baggage Check* and showed their tickets. The woman behind the desk glanced at each ticket and frowned.

"You didn't reserve baggage space," she told them. "You'll need to bring your bags with you to your seats."

"Could we pay for the space now?" Zoya asked.

"No more space left," the woman said, handing back the tickets. The friends bowed their heads and continued toward the boarding platform.

"I could have sworn I reserved baggage space," Demyan said.

"She's right, though," Nikolai replied, putting one of his suitcases down and pointing to his ticket. "These don't say anything about baggage."

"I guess we'll have to squeeze in together," Lilia said.

"I don't have a problem with that," Demyan said, nudging Zoya with his elbow.

"You two need to behave." Anya rolled her eyes. Demyan and Zoya laughed.

The friends walked onto the station's platform, sheltered by stone and glass. Smoke billowed out of the large locomotive and filled the platform area. The train's whistle blew.

"Hurry," Lilia pleaded to her friends. "We need to get to our seats." She rushed ahead to where the conductor collected tickets.

"Third car," the conductor barked, shoving the ticket back to Lilia. The group of friends walked down the platform until they found the car marked *Three* and boarded.

A narrow hallway extended down the length of the car. Gas sconces lit the dark wooden walls and deep red carpet.

"Alright, compartment numbers," Zoya mumbled, looking at her ticket. "I have 313."

"Me too," Lilia and Anya said in unison.

"Wait," Demyan said. He glanced at Nikolai's ticket. "We both have 313 as well."

GRIGORY'S GADGET

They walked until they found 313. Anya opened the door to find two velvet benches within. Each bench could comfortably seat two people, uncomfortably three.

"How long is our train ride?" Anya asked.

"Ten hours," Zoya replied.

Nikolai sighed. "Let's get cozy." He stepped into the small room.

Nikolai and Demyan hoisted each of their suitcases onto shelves above the benches. Demyan stowed Zoya's bags as well, filling the remaining available space.

"We can put our bags on the floor," Anya said, shoving her suitcases between the benches. "It will be like a table."

"Make sure our suitcases are stable up there," Zoya said. "I don't want to get hit on the head when the train starts moving."

Demyan tapped the suitcases and smiled when they didn't budge. He and Zoya sat together on one bench, while Nikolai, Lilia, and Anya sat opposite them.

"Ow!" Lilia shouted. "Nikolai, what's in your pocket?"

Nikolai felt around his pockets then pulled out a drawing compass.

"Er, sorry," he muttered, and tucked the compass into the side of his suitcase.

"Who keeps a compass in their pocket?" Lilia asked.

Nikolai shrugged and laughed.

A moment later, the train whistle blew again. Slowly, the locomotive chugged away from the platform. The early morning sun peeked through the clouds, splashing the inside of the car with a rosy hue. The friends stared out the window as the train left their home town behind.

"Goodbye, Lodninsk," Zoya mumbled. "We won't miss you."

Nikolai and Demyan fell asleep almost immediately once the train started moving. Lilia pulled out a large, leather-bound book to read, while Zoya and Anya contented themselves to watch the snowy scenery pass by outside. Zoya tried to shut her eyes for a nap, but sleep evaded her. After about an hour, Anya pulled out some yarn and a crochet hook. Lilia looked up from her book and furrowed her brow.

"Are you really knitting right now?" she asked.

"No," Anya replied. "I'm crocheting."

Lilia rolled her eyes, closing her book. "What are you, eighty years old?"

Anya looked at Lilia through the corner of her eye. "Fine," she said. "You don't get a scarf for your birthday this year."

Lilia laughed. "Good, I won't need one," she said, teasing. "Mirgorod is going to be warm and sunny, and I'll never need a scarf again!"

"They still get snow sometimes," Zoya said. "For, maybe, a month out of the year."

"See?" Anya said to Lilia. "And that will be one month you'll wish you had a scarf."

GRIGORY'S GADGET

Lilia stuck her tongue out then reopened her book.

Another hour passed when they heard a knock at the door. Zoya reached past the still-sleeping Demyan to open it. A server stood next to a cart full of breakfast plates. Each plate had a piece of dark bread, a small cup of butter, a sausage link, and a bowl of porridge. Zoya shook Demyan awake, and Lilia did the same for Nikolai. The friends then eagerly took their breakfast. Nikolai glanced into the hall.

"Don't we get anything to drink?" he asked.

"Looks like they poured our drink into the porridge," Lilia replied, watching the watery slop fall from her spoon.

"The sausage tastes like newspaper," Anya said after taking a bite.

"They really serve the high-quality fare on these trains," Demyan said.

"We should be thankful we're being fed at all," Zoya said. Her mouth twitched into a smile, and she burst into a laugh. "The food is terrible."

After the friends finished their breakfast, they stacked their plates and shoved the pile to the edge of the suitcase nearest the door. Nikolai shifted in his seat, squishing Lilia in the process.

"What are you doing?" Lilia complained, pushing Nikolai toward the wall.

"I'm sitting on something," he replied.

"Another compass?" Lilia mocked. Nikolai stood and looked down at his seat.

"Oh, it's a newspaper," he stated, pulling the crumpled papers out from under him. He sat back down as he neatened them.

"How did you not notice that before?" Demyan asked.

"I was sleeping," Nikolai told him, "and then I was eating." Nikolai smoothed out the newspaper and looked at the front page.

"Uh-oh," he uttered. He turned the newspaper around to show his friends. The image on the front of the paper was of three soldiers standing in front of a large, armored tank. The text above it read *War Brews in the South*. The word "war" was larger than the rest of the headline.

"Well," Zoya said, "we knew it was coming, one way or another. Does it say if Starzapad has attacked Morozhia yet?"

Nikolai skimmed the article. "It's nothing we haven't already heard. The Queen of Starzapad continues to offend Our Great Leader with embargoes, insulting accusations, spying, et cetera." Nikolai put the paper down. Lilia snatched it up and read it.

"It says Starzapad attacked Morozhia because of the disappearance of the Princess Rozaliya." She looked at her friends, puzzled. "Starzapad blames Morozhia for the disappearance. Why would we kidnap a princess?"

"Who knows?" Demyan said.

"Who cares?" Nikolai added. "We're leaving. It's not our problem anymore."

GRIGORY'S GADGET

Lilia's eyes went wide. "What about our ship?" she asked. "We have to sail right by Starzapad. Will they attack us?"

"I doubt it," Zoya replied.

"Me too," Demyan said. "There will probably be Starzapadian spies on the ship, so if anything they'll ensure the ship reaches Mirgorod safe and sound."

Zoya jabbed Demyan in the side with her elbow. He yelped and glared at her.

"You know you can't say things like that," Zoya told him in a hushed tone. "We're not out of Morozhia yet."

"Calm down," Nikolai said. "No one's listening. Besides, it's not as if we said *we're* spies."

"Is there a problem?" a muffled voice asked through the door. Zoya tilted her head and stared at Nikolai, who only shrugged in response. Demyan opened the door. Standing in the hall was the man who had served them breakfast and the conductor.

"No trouble at all, sirs," he said. "We were just reading the paper, that's all."

"Horrible mess," Anya said. "Starzapad is always trying to start trouble."

"They're foolish to think they stand a chance against Morozhia," Nikolai added.

"Indeed," the conductor replied. He nodded to the server then headed down the hallway. The server turned to follow.

"Excuse me," Nikolai said before the server had gone very far. "Could we get anything to drink? Tea, perhaps?" Lilia slapped him on the arm.

"Do shut up," she whispered.

"I'm thirsty," Nikolai whispered in response.

"Yes, right away," the server said with a nod.

"Thank you." Nikolai smiled.

"Now keep your mouths shut," Zoya told Nikolai and Demyan after the server had left. "I think we all just need to be quiet and inconspicuous. We still have eight hours before we get to Koravsk."

"Agreed," Anya said, picking up her crochet project again. Lilia opened her book.

"Well, aren't you prepared?" Nikolai grumbled.

With a smirk, Demyan stood and started digging through one of his bags. He pulled out a small brown box and presented it to his friends.

"That doesn't look inconspicuous to me," Anya said.

"Yes!" Nikolai cheered. Lilia slapped his arm again. Nikolai lowered his voice and chanted, "Durak, Durak, Durak!"

"As if we'd play anything else," Demyan replied, opening up the box to reveal a stack of cards. The backs of the cards were covered in a geometric design of brown and teal. Most of the cards were bent or creased, but they always insisted they didn't know which cards were bent in which ways.

"Are you sure this is a good idea?" Lilia asked. "We get pretty intense playing this game."

"We'll be quiet," Demyan replied. "We promise."

"How about this," Anya said. "Anyone who speaks above a whisper has to pick up a card."

"I can live with that," Nikolai whispered.

GRIGORY'S GADGET

Demyan shuffled the deck and offered it to Nikolai.

"Get out of here," Nikolai whispered, shooing the deck away with his hand. Demyan sighed and dealt each of them six cards. He pulled out one of the remaining cards and placed it face up on a suitcase.

"Trump card is a ten of hearts," Demyan said, keeping his voice low. He placed the remainder of the deck facedown next to the trump.

The server knocked on the door. Nikolai opened it.

"Here's your tea," the server said, lowering a tray with five small teacups. Nikolai took his cup and sipped the hot tea. He leaned back and sighed.

"Thank you," he called as the server left.

"Pick up a card," Anya whispered to him with a smirk. Nikolai opened his mouth to protest and closed it again. With a huff, he scooped up an extra card. His friends laughed softly as they began their game.

The game of Durak went on for over an hour until only Demyan was left with cards in his hand and dubbed the Fool. Anya had been the first to win, promptly returning to her crocheting. When Zoya emptied her hand, she rested her head against the back of the seat and closed her eyes. Demyan wrapped an arm around her, letting her rest on his shoulder. Zoya's exhaustion finally caught up to her, and she fell asleep.

It felt as though only minutes had passed before Demyan shook her awake.

"We're here," he told her, smiling as she opened her eyes. Her friends were standing and grabbing their suitcases.

"That went by fast," Zoya commented as she followed suit.

"Lucky you," Nikolai replied.

"I told you," Lilia said, "you should have brought a book or something."

Nikolai mocked her silently when she looked away.

"Well," Anya said, "let's head to the Koravsk port!"

The sky was clear as the friends disembarked. The red sun sat on the distant horizon. Its reflection glittered along the surface of the ocean. The buildings of Koravsk were made of concrete and steel and shone in the fading sunlight.

"Wow," Lilia said. "I've never seen the ocean before."

"None of us have," Anya replied. "It's beautiful."

Zoya smiled. "I'll take this as a good omen." Her friends nodded in agreement.

"I can't wait to swim in the ocean," Demyan said. "When we get to Mirgorod, of course."

"I bet swimming in the ocean is far better than swimming in that pool at school," Nikolai said.

"We won't have to worry about freezing when we get out of the water," Zoya said.

As they spoke, they made their way toward the harbor. Small pine trees lined the streets. Their green combined with the red sun to create the most colorful landscape Zoya had ever seen. She spotted their ship immediately. It was a huge, colorful sidewheel steamer.

GRIGORY'S GADGET

Its top deck rose well above the two and three story buildings of the port. A tall staircase connected the ship's deck to the docks below. Light smoke rose from three blue smoke stacks. There were large paddle wheels on the port and starboard sides of the ship, encased in brass and wood. Its windows and portholes were framed by reds, golds, and oranges.

Zoya's mouth fell open. "Wow."

"That'll be our home for the next two weeks," Nikolai said.

"Hopefully we'll have better quarters on the ship than on the train," Anya said, casting a look at Demyan. Zoya patted him on the shoulder and laughed. Demyan grunted and continued toward the docks.

"Papers," a guard dressed in dark gray stated curtly as they approached the security counter. Anya handed him hers first, and he waved her by. Lilia and Demyan then did the same.

"Open your suitcases," the guard said when Nikolai presented his documents.

"What? Why?" Nikolai asked before he could stop himself.

"Open them, now," The guard said, coming around from behind the desk. Another guard appeared to accompany him. Silently, Nikolai obeyed, clenching his jaw. One guard eyed Nikolai as he shuffled through the assorted maps and sketches in the bags. Then, abruptly, they shoved the bags back at Nikolai and waved him on.

"It will be better in Mirgorod," Demyan told him as he closed his suitcases.

"Why did you need to look in his bags?" Zoya asked in spite of herself.

"Zoya," Nikolai said, "it's fine."

"Feeling bold today, are we?" the guard said with annoyance. "Open your bags." Zoya sighed but obeyed.

"And what is this?" the guard asked, holding up Grandma Orlova's keepsake. "Looks a bit suspicious to me." The guard grinned smugly.

"It's just a knickknack from my grandmother," Zoya explained, reaching for it.

"I think it needs to be confiscated," the guard replied. "And I think you and your friends should be questioned." Zoya's heart raced, and she stared wide-eyed at her friends.

"Hey! You! Stop!" The yells of other guards echoed through the building. An older man with a rucksack ran past the security lines toward the dock. The guard holding Zoya's keepsake dropped it on his desk and followed the other guards to tackle the man. Zoya quickly grabbed the object and shoved it back in her bag.

"Let's go!" she urged her friends in a hushed tone. "Come on!"

The friends walked briskly away from the commotion and toward the line of passengers waiting to board.

"Crazy old coot," another passenger grumbled, watching the old man attempt to evade the guards. The passenger wore a long brown coat and mottled top hat.

GRIGORY'S GADGET

He itched at his unkempt beard. "Every other day there's some idiot rebel thinks he can scare the government with a bomb threat. I bet that rucksack is just filled with rocks." He huffed and boarded the ship. As she and her friends boarded the ship, Zoya watched the guards corner the old man. As soon as she set foot on the deck, a horrendous boom sounded on the dock. She turned to see smoke rising from one corner of the security building.

"Would you look at that," the scruffy passenger said with amusement. "This one actually had a bomb. Poor fool." He laughed and walked away.

"I'm so happy we're leaving," Lilia said. Her friends nodded in agreement.

The passenger ship had finally departed several hours past schedule, after security searched the vessel from top to bottom. Zoya and her friends had enjoyed large, if bland, dinner in the meantime.

"I call top bunk!" Nikolai shouted as he ran into his cabin. Demyan shook his head and followed. The cabin had one bunk bed and a single bed. An elderly man was already asleep on the single bed, snoring loudly.

"I don't want the top bunk," Lilia said as the girls headed into their cabin next door.

"I'll take the top," Anya offered. Lilia smiled and put her luggage and coat on the bottom bunk.

"You sure you don't want the single?" Zoya asked.

"You can have it," Lilia replied. "To make up for being cheated by your landlord."

"What did he do?" Anya asked. Zoya sat down on her bed and removed her coat.

"He hardly gave me anything for the furniture in my apartment," she said. "Half the things in that apartment are from before the Revolution. But all that means to him is that they're old."

"What a chump," Anya grumbled. "At least you're done with him now."

"Exactly!" Lilia said. "We're done with everything in Lodninsk. We can focus on our new life in Mirgorod."

"By the way, Zoya," Anya said. "What was that thing the guard pulled out of your bag?"

Zoya dug the gadget out of her suitcase and showed it to Anya. The gears in it shimmered in the light of the sconces on the wall.

"It was my grandmother's. I'm not sure what it is, but it seemed important to her. So I decided to bring it."

"Oh!" Demyan said, popping his head in the doorway. "That's nifty. What is it?"

"Why don't you tell us, Mr. Archaeologist?" Zoya replied with a smirk. Demyan picked the object up and turned it over in his hands.

"Let me see," Nikolai said as he snatched it out of Demyan's hand and looked at it.

"I've already figured out what it is," Demyan said proudly. He paused and looked around at his friends.

"No you didn't," Nikolai replied lazily.

"Yes I did." Demyan said. "It's a little ball of gears!"

GRIGORY'S GADGET

"Thank you for that insight," Anya said. Zoya took the gadget back from Nikolai and put it in her bag.

"I wonder what the Grand University will be like," Lilia wondered, lying back on her bed. "I bet the library is huge."

"I bet their trowels aren't chipped!" Nikolai laughed.

Anya picked up a booklet from the table by the beds. "Look, here's a whole brochure for Mirgorod." She opened it and displayed it for her friends. The brochure contained numerous engravings depicting elaborate architecture, crowds of well-dressed people strolling by the ocean, and images of the latest models of carriages, even the new horseless carriages.

"Zoya, you're an engineer," Demyan said. "How do those horseless carriages work?"

"I'm not an engineer yet." Zoya stuck out her tongue. "I can tell you about boilers, but horseless carriages? You'll have to wait until after I've studied at the Grand University." Demyan pulled Zoya into a hug and kissed her temple.

"Look at those clothes," Anya said. "They look so light. It must be so warm there!"

"They have such a short winter," Zoya mused. "I can't even imagine what it will be like to be so warm."

Zoya and her friends sat huddled together in the cabin poring over the brochure as the reality of moving set in. After so much planning and waiting, they were finally on the ship headed to Mirgorod.

"So," Nikolai said, "that old man in the port. You don't think he was a Starzapadian, do you?"

"Of course he was," Anya replied, putting down the brochure. "No Morozhian would be dumb enough to blow up a building. I mean, what does that even accomplish?"

"Terrorist," Demyan spat.

"Do you think he was alone, or…" Nikolai trailed off, studying his friends.

"No, you don't think…" Zoya replied.

"What?" Lilia asked. "If he's not alone, then what?" Her eyes opened wide as she stared at Nikolai.

"No," Lilia said. She stood, wagging her finger at Nikolai. "Nope. No. I don't like where you're going with this, Nikolai."

"I wasn't going anywhere," Nikolai defended. "You're the one going somewhere with it."

"No," Lilia replied. "No, we're going to be fine."

"Of course we'll be fine," Zoya told Lilia, placing her hand on her shoulder. "We're on a Vernulaian ship now, not a Morozhian one. So even if there were more terrorists, they wouldn't target this ship."

"Right," Lilia said, still looking at Nikolai. "See? She's right."

"And don't forget all we learned in our lessons," Anya said.

"What, dance lessons?" Demyan asked. "What good would dance lessons do?"

Anya exchanged grimaces with Zoya and Lilia.

"Maybe if you took the lessons with us, you'd know," Lilia said, crossing her arms. Demyan and Nikolai merely shrugged.

"Ok," Zoya said to her friend with a smile. "Now that that's settled, why don't we go get dinner?"

"Yes," Anya said, standing. "That sounds good to me."

CHAPTER TWO

Nikolai stared at the ceiling of the cabin, listening to Demyan and the elderly man snore. *This is my luck,* he thought unhappily. He rolled onto his side and picked at the golden wallpaper. Above, he heard the sound of rushed footsteps. *At least I'm not the only one awake.*

A few seconds later, a loud boom echoed through the ship. Nikolai felt the bed and walls shake.

"Nikolai, what are you doing?" Demyan asked sleepily. Nikolai heard a second boom, and Demyan jerked awake. "What was that?"

"I have no idea," Nikolai said, jumping down to the floor. The girls appeared in the doorway.

"Is the ship being attacked?" Anya asked.

"Are you all alright?" Zoya added.

The elderly man stirred from his sleep.

"Sir, the ship is being attacked," Nikolai told him, offering a hand to help him out of bed.

"Go back to sleep," the man said grumpily. "The guards will take care of it. Silly kids." He pulled his

GRIGORY'S GADGET

blanket back over his head and rolled over. Another boom sounded, and the ship shook especially hard.

"What do we do?" Lilia asked her friends. "Should we just stay in our cabins?"

"I'd say that's a good idea," a strange voice said behind her. The girls jumped and turned around. A lean young man with dirty blond hair and blue eyes grinned at them while drawing his pistol. A multitude of necklaces hung about his neck, and his ears were dotted with golden earrings. "I suggest you go back to your cabins and hand over any valuables."

"We don't have any valuables," Zoya lied. The young man seemed surprised by her and stepped back eying her quizzically. It took less than a few seconds for him to compose himself. He stepped toward Zoya with his pistol aimed at her head.

"You look pretty valuable to me." A second man with black hair and almond eyes appeared next to the first, similarly covered in gold jewelry with pistol drawn. "We're in need of more crew, right Alexi?"

"That's right, Fyodr," Alexi, replied. "You and your friends have two minutes to grab anything you can carry. Then you're coming with us."

"We're not going anywhere with you!" Nikolai said defiantly. Alexi stepped toward Nikolai, now pointing his pistol at Nikolai's head. Anya stepped forward, placing herself between Alexi and Nikolai.

"Two minutes," she said, staring the pirate in the eye. He smirked, nodded, and lowered his pistol.

"Anya!" Nikolai said, glaring. Anya returned his look then turned and walked into her cabin.

"What did I tell you kids?" the elderly man growled from within Nikolai and Demyan's cabin. Nikolai glanced back at him and stepped to block the doorway. When the man saw Alexi and Fyodr, he furrowed his brow in annoyance.

"What are you, now? Pirates?" He spat in Alexi's direction. "Bunch of lazy crooks. The guards will put you down in a second."

"We've disposed of the guards already," Alexi said. "We can dispose of you, too, old man, unless you give us whatever valuables you have."

"Do I look like the sort who owns any valuables?" He gestured to his raggedy clothes. He wore a dingy, ill-fitting vest and a button-down shirt that may have once been white. His trousers were covered in salt stains and worn through in one knee.

"Well, if you have nothing of value, maybe we should just put you down," Alexi said, raising his pistol and aiming at the old man.

"Don't you dare!" Nikolai shouted, rushing toward Alexi. Fyodr turned his pistol on Nikolai and drew a sword. Alexi drew his sword as well. Zoya and Demyan moved to Nikolai's side, guarding his body with their own.

"Your two minutes are almost up," Alexi told the group. "I'd get moving if I were you."

"You can't just kill an innocent man!" Lilia protested. "He hasn't done anything wrong!" Fyodr

GRIGORY'S GADGET

sheathed his sword and grabbed Lilia by the arm, shoving her toward the girls' cabin.

"Get packing, miss!" he ordered. "This doesn't concern you!"

Zoya took the opportunity to grab for Fyodr's gun. He twisted around and slammed her into the wall, his forearm pressed against her neck. Zoya gasped and clawed at his arm. Demyan yelled and charged toward him, knocking his arm away from Zoya's throat. Alexi shot his pistol into the air.

"Enough!" he shouted.

"That's right, enough!" A third pirate appeared. This pirate was older, with scarred tan skin and black hair that was turning gray. The pinky and ring finger of his left hand were missing, as was half of the middle finger on his right. His eyes were large, and Nikolai thought he saw a kindness in them.

"Pavel," Alexi said. His face flushed red and he lowered his pistol.

"Stop acting tough, Alexi," Pavel said. "This old man hasn't done anything wrong, let him be. The captain is almost ready to leave." Pavel then regarded the group of friends. "Recruiting, are we?"

"Pavel, this bunch says they have no valuables," Fyodr said. "They look pretty valuable to me."

"So, try not to damage them." Pavel smirked. "Let's go. The captain is waiting."

Pavel's presence seemed to pacify Alexi and Fyodr, who watched silently as the friends gathered their things. Nikolai and Demyan packed quickly then joined the girls in their cabin to help them. Anya, having already packed her bags, stood in the doorway and glowered at the pirates.

"Zoya, what do we do?" Lilia whispered as she fastened her suitcase.

"I don't know," Zoya admitted. "They have guns and swords. I've got wrenches and screwdrivers. I don't think we stand a chance."

Nikolai watched as Zoya dug out her gloves. Her shaking hands knocked her gadget out of the bag. It rolled halfway to the door before she caught it. Fyodr and Pavel weren't looking, but Alexi saw it and looked at Zoya coolly.

"It's nothing," Zoya muttered quickly, fumbling to hide the object.

"Put that away and hurry up," Alexi replied. "We don't have all night." Zoya exchanged a concerned look with Nikolai as they finished packing and stood.

"Alright!" Pavel announced with a smile. "Let's go introduce you to your captain!"

"Well, what have we here?" a middle-aged man bellowed as Zoya and her friends reached the main deck of the ship. "New recruits!" He wore an array of mismatched and mottled, though grandiose, clothing that Zoya assumed he'd collected through years of pillaging. His light brown hair was neatly-trimmed, and his eyes were a piercing blue. His right leg was missing from the knee down, and in its place stood a prosthetic leg made of wood and brass, which shone just above the top of his boot.

"I'm Captain Edmund Sokoll the Savage!" he boomed. "Happy to have you!" The captain gestured to his men, who shoved their captives into a line for his inspection.

"Thought you were going to Mirgorod?" the captain asked as he looked over his new recruits. "Change of plans! For the best, trust me." The captain let out a hardy laugh. He paused and observed Zoya's hair.

"Interesting color," he remarked. "Afraid we don't keep hair dye on the ship."

"It's my natural color," Zoya replied, fidgeting with her braid. Captain Sokoll squinted at her and nodded.

"And what do you do, Violet?" he asked, grinning.

"I'm an engineer, sir." She looked the captain in the eye and said, "And my name is Zoya."

"Did she say engineer?" Pavel asked. "Perfect! Tonia needs more help in the boiler room."

Zoya's face flushed. "Well, I'm still a student," she said. "I'm not licensed yet."

"Poppycock!" the captain shouted. "A license is just a new way to pay the government money! We need your skills. What of the rest of you? What do you do?"

"I can sew and solder," Anya said. Demyan, Nikolai, and Lilia exchanged worried glances. Captain Sokoll watched them and waited.

"We study archeology," Demyan said, gesturing to Nikolai.

"I study history and literature," Lilia added.

"Well, we'll find plenty of use for you," the captain said with a smile. "We always need more hands on deck." He gestured to his men again, who pushed the recruits toward a rope ladder connecting the passenger ship to a smaller pirate ship below. As she crossed the deck, Zoya saw that many of the ship's guards lay dead on the deck. Other members of the ship's crew nursed superficial wounds.

"They'll be fine," Pavel said. "Trust me, we did this ship a favor by taking out the guards. Everyone else will make it safely to Mirgorod." He paused and then clarified. "Well, if they don't make it safely, it won't be our fault."

Anya shivered in the cold as the pirates moved their confiscated goods on to their ship. Pavel stood guard over the recruits by the ship's center smokestack. Anya noted how different the pirate ship was from the larger passenger ship. The smaller ship had two wooden masts carrying white sails and a small set of paddle wheels on the port and starboard sides. Toward the bow of the ship the deck was raised to house the captain's cabin. Toward the

GRIGORY'S GADGET

stern, the deck was raised for the saloon and galley. The pilot house perched above that. A black flag waved atop the mainmast, emblazoned with a white skull surrounded by a violet ring. Its colors glowed in the moonlight.

"She's called the *Ocean's Legend*," Pavel said. "She's a good ship, sturdy. Though she isn't quite as comfortable in this cold." Pavel shivered, hugging his jacket tight. Anya noticed it was far too thin for the frigid weather.

"What are you going to do with us?" Lilia asked, her voice shaking. Tears rimmed her eyes.

"Oh, we'll put you to work," Pavel explained cheerily. "Swab the decks mostly; maybe help cook if you're any good at that." He turned to smile at Lilia, but his smile fell as he looked at her face.

"Oh, none of that, dear!" he said sweetly, putting his hand on her shoulder. "It'll feel like home on this ship in no time!"

"We don't want our home to be a ship!" Nikolai said. "We were on our way to Mirgorod. That's where we want our home to be!"

"Why did you take us?" Anya asked. "Why us, specifically?"

"You're young," Pavel replied. "You're healthy. Which is more than can be said of most people on that ship. And you've got some fight in you, which is always welcome on a pirate ship, so long as you follow the captain's orders."

"What if we don't?" Zoya asked. "What if we don't want to be a part of your crew?"

"Too bad," Alexi spat as he walked up to them. "You are part of our crew now. Best get used to that. The captain doesn't take kindly to those suggesting mutiny."

"Now, Alexi," Captain Sokoll said as he approached. "That's no way to talk to our new friends. I'm sure they need time to adjust. Pavel, show them to their cabin." Pavel nodded and gestured for the group to follow him. Anya watched Alexi as she passed him. He was staring at the captain with raised eyebrows. When he caught Anya's eye, his expression changed to a scowl and he walked away.

They walked toward the stern of the ship and into the saloon. A burst of warm air greeted them, filled with the scent of bread, salted meat, and ale. They followed Pavel to the left, down a narrow staircase below deck.

A hallway stretched before them with cabins on the right and portholes on the left. Pavel showed the group into the first tiny room. It was windowless and filled with crates.

"It doesn't look like much," Pavel admitted with a shrug. "No doors on the cabins, that's by order of the captain. We've got some extra hammocks you can hang to sleep in and maybe a cot somewhere too." He glanced at the friends' suitcases, which they were still carrying.

GRIGORY'S GADGET

"Looks like you over packed," he said and chuckled. "The captain seems to be in a generous mood lately. He may let you keep the things you absolutely need. Anything else we will sell at the next trading town. It'll earn you some respect with the captain if you give up your valuables willingly." Pavel eyed Anya's fingers, which wore several rings. Anya clasped her hands nervously.

"These aren't worth anything," she said. Her voice shook. "Just little things I made myself out of copper. The stones aren't special or precious."

"Copper is quite valuable," Pavel said, shrugging. "You have until we get to the next trading town to decide if you'll give them up willingly or not. I'll go get those hammocks for you." With that, he politely nodded and walked away.

Anya stared at her rings. She wore five, though only three truly mattered to her. She'd made two of them with wire and small pieces of gravel in honor of her father and brother. They had died in a huge cave-in in the Lodninsk mines. She'd made the third ring with two beads from a necklace that belonged to her mother, who had died from the plague.

With a nervous sigh, Anya placed her suitcases along the side of the room and sat down on a crate.

"We were just kidnapped by pirates," Zoya said, her eyes wide. "We *actually* were just kidnapped by pirates."

"This is just our luck," Nikolai said, leaning against a crate. "Of course this happened to us. Why not?"

"Stop it." Anya sighed in frustration. "We can't start this *woe-is-me* act again. We'll get through this like we've gotten through everything else."

Lilia buried her head in her arms and sobbed. Zoya put an arm around her.

"It'll be ok," she cooed. "We'll be ok. Like Anya said, we'll get through this. We always do."

"This isn't the same!" Lilia shouted, raising her tear-streaked face. "How can you think this is the same?"

"I knew we should have taken the airship," Nikolai grumbled. Demyan jabbed his friend in the ribs. Nikolai glared in response.

"You know why we didn't take the airship," Demyan hissed at him.

"No, you're probably right," Lilia said, wiping her face dry. "If we'd taken the airship, we'd still be on our way to Mirgorod."

"Lilia, we understand why we couldn't take the airship," Anya assured her. She glared at Nikolai, who sighed and looked away. As angry as he was, Anya knew he understood. They were all there at the hospital when Lilia's father and brother had died. They'd made it out of the zeppelin crash alive, but later succumbed to their wounds.

GRIGORY'S GADGET

"You know," Demyan said after a few awkward minutes of silence. "Pavel said something about this ship not being comfortable in the cold."

"Yeah, I've noticed there's no heat in this room," Anya said with a shiver.

Demyan nodded with a laugh. "Well, yes, true. But, I think that also means we're heading someplace warmer now. That is to say, this is farther north than they normally sail."

"That makes sense," Anya said. "So at least we'll be warm, even if we're not in Mirgorod."

"Wait," Zoya said, standing and checking that no one was outside the door. "If we're heading some place warmer, we're probably still going in the general direction of Mirgorod." She looked at her friends, waiting. When she was met with only blank stares, she sighed.

Lowering her voice to a near-whisper, she said, "We can play along, be part of this crew for now. Then, at some southern trading town, we can escape. Find some other passage to Mirgorod!"

"I'm a bad liar, Zoya," Lilia said. "Actually, so are you."

"We're all pretty terrible liars," Demyan said.

"So don't say anything," Zoya replied. "We keep our heads down and do as we're told. We're used to that, right?"

"No way," Nikolai said. "That's a ridiculous suggestion."

"Do you have a better plan?" Anya asked.

"This plan will get us arrested, or killed," Nikolai replied. "What if a navy ship attacks this one? Do you think they'll believe us and spare us if we explain we were kidnapped?"

"Maybe," Lilia said. "We still have our documents."

"The pirates are going to take our things any minute now," Nikolai said. "Pavel's trying to ease our nerves, to pacify us, but they are pirates. They steal and they kill. How do you expect to play along with that?"

"Nikolai, honestly," Anya said. "Do you have a better plan?" She studied his face. Nikolai pursed his lips and squinted his eyes before throwing his hands in the air.

"No, no I don't."

"Good," Anya said with a smile. "So, we have a plan."

"What plan?" Pavel asked, appearing in the doorway with a handful of fabric.

"We figured out where each of us will sleep," Anya said quickly. "There's only room for four hammocks to hang in here, so Nikolai is sleeping on the floor." Nikolai glared at Anya and opened his mouth to protest. Before he could, Pavel chortled loudly.

"Well, good thing I found that cot, then." Pavel handed the fabric to Demyan and Zoya, then lifted a folded cot into the room.

GRIGORY'S GADGET

"I hope you'll be able to get some sleep tonight," Pavel said. "I know the first night can be hard especially in this weather."

Pavel stepped out briefly as the friends tied up their hammocks. He returned with a handful of wool blankets.

"Breakfast will be served at sunrise," he said. "One of the crew will come by to make sure you're awake." Pavel glanced at the walls of the room with a frown. "Sad to say, we only have bland food. Stale bread and tough meat. But we have some decent tea, and we always get the finest ale!" He snickered and headed upstairs.

"So much for being bad at lying," Anya said proudly with a wink.

"Yes, good job," Zoya said, staring out the doorway. "Does anyone else find it odd how kindly Pavel is treating us?"

"I was thinking the same thing," Demyan said.

"You catch more flies with honey than with vinegar," Anya said. "He's treating us nicely so we cooperate. And let's make sure we do just that. Who knows how vicious these pirates might become if we don't."

The friends nodded as they sat down and bundled themselves up for the long, cold night ahead.

Zoya and her friends were unable to sleep that night. They each huddled under the blankets, their coats thrown on top for extra warmth. They were used to being cold in Lodninsk. Some nights a roaring fire wouldn't keep the biting cold at bay. However, the cold was the least of their worries.

For the first hour, they simply sat in the room, watching the doorway and listening. Wind whistled, waves crashed, and the wood of the ship creaked. Somewhere below deck, the steam engines hissed and puffed. A few pirates snored loudly down the hall.

Zoya's eyelids became heavier and heavier, and she lay back and tried to sleep. She heard Nikolai toss and turn on his cot, which creaked and groaned with every movement. Zoya had finally dozed off, albeit fitfully, when there was a knock at the door.

"Wake up," Fyodr grumbled, rubbing his eyes. "Breakfast."

The friends sat at their own little table in the saloon alongside Pavel. The warmth of the room was a relief after their chilly night. The saloon was packed full with the crew, except for Fyodr, who had continued outside to man the wheel. As the crew had filed into the saloon, many members acknowledged their new mates with a smile or a handshake. They met Lev, with a gray braided beard, and Ira, who had short platinum hair. Olya and Oleg were fraternal twins who looked identical, their only distinguishing feature being that Olya was missing her left hand, while Oleg was missing his right. They each wore brass prosthetics. Zoya thought she saw the metal fingers moving, but convinced herself it was a trick.

Samuil, tall and muscular, glared at the friends when he entered the room, huffing as he passed by. Pavel stood and whispered in his ear. The man flashed a quick smile and muttered a rushed introduction before continuing on his way.

"Don't mind him," Pavel said. "He's always worried about running out of food, but we have enough. He'll warm up to you."

"I hear this is our new engineer," a dark-skinned woman announced as she patted Zoya on the shoulder. Her hair was piled high atop her head and braided tightly with golden ribbons. "I'm Tonia. I'm in charge of the boiler room."

"Nice to meet you," Zoya said, cautiously extending her hand.

"So formal," Tonia said, shaking Zoya's hand. "Best get them some ale, Pavel! They need to relax."

"Food first," Pavel replied. Tonia nodded and walked away. More members of the crew filed in, skipping introductions as they hurried to get their meal.

Pavel wasn't lying about the food. The bread was hard as a rock, and the meat so tough that the dulled knives they had barely cut through it. Zoya was starving after the long and eventful day and night, and ate as quickly as she could. The tea was decent, as Pavel had told them, and hot.

"Crew!" the captain shouted after everyone had gotten their plates of food. "I say we should raise a toast to welcome our new mates!" There was a roar of agreement as the crew raised their cups. Zoya exchanged a glance with Demyan and smiled awkwardly at the warm reception.

"Well someone doesn't seem so happy about kidnapping us," Nikolai whispered to Demyan, gesturing toward Alexi. Zoya followed his gaze. Alexi sat with his arms folded and a sour expression on his face, staring out a window. Before anyone else could see what Nikolai was talking about, Captain Sokoll nudged Alexi, who then raised his cup.

"Welcome aboard the *Ocean's Legend*! Demyan, Nikolai, Lilia, Anya, and Zoya!" The crew cheered and drank to their new crewmates.

"Seems like they're happy to have us," Anya remarked, tilting her head.

"Except Alexi," Nikolai replied.

Across the room, Alexi stood and walked toward the door. Nikolai stood to follow him.

"What are you doing?" Demyan asked with a knowing look.

"Don't get us in trouble the first day we're here," Zoya told him. Then she mouthed the words, *Remember the plan.*

"Don't mind Alexi," Pavel said, lightly grabbing Nikolai's arm. "He's a troubled boy, is all."

Nikolai sat back down, still staring out the door.

"Now," Pavel said, gesturing to Oleg. "Time to celebrate! Drink up, my friends. It will ease your nerves and drive off the cold." Oleg walked over with cups of ale for the friends.

"It's barely eight in the morning," Zoya whispered to Demyan. Demyan shrugged and took the cup of ale offered to him.

"Seems as good a time as any," he said.

Zoya took the ale and drank it, pleasantly surprised by the taste.

"What did I tell you?" Pavel said with a smile. "We always get the finest ale!"

After breakfast, the crew of the *Ocean's Legend* got right to work. Zoya could tell at a glance which pirates' jobs required them to be outside. Before bundling up in their coats, gloves, and hats, they had downed an extra cup or two of ale. And they all wore frowns.

"Alright," Pavel said as the dishes were cleaned up. "Zoya, you're needed in the boiler room below. Anya, Lilia, Demyan, and Nikolai will start cleaning the saloon and galley."

"Works for me," Demyan replied. "Glad to stay inside." Zoya noted that Demyan was swaying back and forth. She wondered if it was because of the waves, the ale, or both.

"You can follow me, Zoya," Tonia said, appearing next to Pavel.

"You all seem very excited about having a new engineer on board," Zoya remarked as she followed Tonia below deck. "I'm a little afraid of what I'm about to find."

"Well we haven't exploded yet," Tonia replied with a smirk. Zoya forced a laughed and nodded.

"I have some of my own supplies," Zoya said. She stopped in front of the room where she and her friends had slept. "Goggles, gloves, a few tools."

"Excellent," Tonia replied. "Go get them."

Zoya opened up one of her suitcases and grabbed her grandmother's gadget. She folded a shirt over it and buried it under the blanket on her hammock. Then she dug out her tools and goggles.

"It'll be nice having a real engineer on board," Tonia said as Zoya rejoined her in the hall. Zoya put on her gloves and hung her goggles around her neck.

"Wait," Zoya said. "Are you saying you don't have a real engineer now?"

"Afraid not," Tonia said, leading Zoya around a corner and down another hall. "I've worked with boilers often enough, but was never formally trained. Like I said, we haven't blown up yet, but that might just be luck."

"I don't know if the Captain told you," Zoya said, fidgeting with the tools in her hand. "But I'm not—"

"Licensed, yes, yes," Tonia interrupted with a wave of her hand. "You're on a pirate ship, kid. We

GRIGORY'S GADGET

don't care about papers. We care about what you can do."

Zoya nodded. The two women continued below deck, down another flight of stairs, before coming to the boiler room. The air was filled with the roar of the furnaces and the whir of pulsing pistons, as well as significant amounts of smoke and soot. Lev and Samuil shoveled coal into the furnace. The heat was almost unbearable.

"I don't think it should be this smoky in here," Zoya said, coughing. "Maybe we could start with that?"

"Works for me," Tonia replied.

Lilia, Anya, Nikolai, and Demyan collected the plates, cups, and silverware from around the saloon, stacking them all in a small sink at the front of the long narrow galley.

"What do we clean them with?" Lilia asked. The sink had a drain, but no faucet. Pavel gestured to a bottle of clear liquid sitting nearby.

"That liquor there," he said. "It's strong stuff, but tastes like kraken ink. So, we use it to clean." Lilia grabbed the bottle. She poured the alcohol over the dishes and began to scrub.

"There are more bottles in here," Pavel said, opening a small closet. "Seems everyone up north stocks it on their ships. I suppose if you can get past the taste, it warms you up pretty well." He handed a bottle to Nikolai and one to Anya, along with a few rags.

"It *is* made from kraken ink," Anya said. "I recognize it."

"Well that explains the taste," Pavel replied.

"It is vile," Anya said, "but it does seem that everyone in Morozhia drinks it." She and Nikolai wet their rags with the liquor and began cleaning the tables.

"You don't look well, Demyan," Pavel said. Demyan leaned against a table, his eyes glossy and skin pale. He didn't reply.

"If you're going to get sick, go outside," Anya told him, backing away. Her advice came too late. Demyan stumbled away from the table, dropped to his knees, and retched on the floor. Anya groaned, clutching her stomach as she turned away.

"It's alright," Pavel assured Demyan. "Bundle yourself up and get some air." Demyan nodded and headed below deck to grab his coat.

"We've got a mop and a brush," Pavel told Anya and Nikolai. "I'll let you decide who uses which to clean that up."

"I'm already cleaning dishes," Lilia said. She refused to look at the mess on the floor, the thought of it making her own stomach churn. She heard Anya and Nikolai sigh.

"You can have the mop," Nikolai said. "I'll take the brush."

GRIGORY'S GADGET

"Are you sure?" Anya asked. "Who knew you were such a gentleman." Lilia chuckled. Sighing, Anya and Nikolai went to work.

"May I ask a question?" Anya asked Pavel, trying to keep her mind off the half-digested food she was pushing with the mop.

"Of course," Pavel replied.

"What are pirates doing this far north?"

"Curiosity," Pavel said. "The Olen Sea is much warmer and has much more gold to be sure. But all the pirates know that. There're so many pirates in that area now, it's a wonder merchant ships dare to sail. It's not a question of if they will be attacked by pirates, but how many pirates will attack them at once. For a pirate, there's too much competition."

Lilia stopped scrubbing dishes suddenly and glanced around. She heard a scratchy, fizzing noise.

"What's that sound?"

Everyone fell silent and listened.

"Ah, the telegraph," Pavel replied, pointing to a small speaker on the wall in the corner of the room. "The signal comes in and out, depending on where we are."

"A telegraph?" Nikolai asked. "In the middle of the ocean?"

"It's wireless," Pavel replied. "Don't you have wireless telegraphs in Morozhia yet? Don't ask me how they work, but they're pretty common nowadays."

As Lilia listened to the sound she began to discern short and long beeps.

Nikolai spoke up, trying to translate the code. "Five-hundred something this morning, something about Starzapad, to meet the force of the Queen's mighty ships." He paused and squinted. "It's going by too fast, I can't catch it all. Oh wait, Morozhia still denies accusations of abducting the princess? It's far from the only tension between Starzapad and Morozhia."

"You picked a hell of a time to satisfy your curiosity," Anya told Pavel. "I'm guessing it's easier to fight another pirate ship than a fleet of warships."

"Don't worry too much about that," Pavel said. He reached into his shirt and pulled out a small brass pendant. It was too small for any of the friends to make out its shape.

Pavel brought the pendant briefly to his lips and whispered something under his breath.

"Vestnik will steer us clear of their ships, I'm certain." He walked to the other side of the saloon, scrubbing another table with kraken ink liquor. Lilia leaned toward Nikolai and Anya.

"Who's Vestnik?" she whispered. Her friends shrugged and continued cleaning.

"Maybe it's like a Skarbnik," Nikolai said.

"Aren't those the rock fairies you read about?" Lilia asked. "They don't actually exist."

"True," Nikolai replied. "I guess it wouldn't make sense for him to invoke one of those."

"Is he praying to someone?" Anya asked. "I've never met someone with religion before."

"Me neither," Lilia said. She resumed scrubbing the dishes. "It must be nice, believing someone out there will help you…"

"That's probably why religion wasn't allowed in Morozhia," Anya said. "Our government probably believes thoughts like that are dangerous."

"I'd support anything Morozhia thinks is dangerous," Nikolai said. "Dangerous to them, that is."

"Me too," Lilia replied. She smiled. "It's sort of liberating to say that out loud."

Demyan wrapped his scarf tightly around his neck after pulling on his coat. He could feel the ship swaying in the choppy waves and struggled to keep his balance. His stomach felt heavy, like there was a stone in his gut. It churned with every rock of the ship. After pulling up his hood, he took a deep breath and headed back above deck.

"You alright?" Nikolai called as Demyan cut through the saloon. Demyan didn't reply, heading straight for the door and out onto the deck.

Icy wind slapped him in the face as soon as he emerged, nearly knocking him off balance. The sails snapped loudly above, though most were pulled up and secured. The paddle wheels rolled steadily, churning the already choppy water below.

Only a few pirates were on the deck, securing the remaining sails and fastening anything on the deck that may blow away in the wind. Demyan walked toward the bow of the ship. Its figurehead, a woman clad in elaborate armor carved out of wood, bobbed up and down and around with respect to the horizon. Demyan's stomach churned again. He stared straight down at the dark ocean below and focused on his breathing.

"How are you holding up, pal?" Nikolai asked as he approached several minutes later. He was bundled up so that only his eyes were visible.

"Fine," Demyan replied. "Seasick."

"Pavel says it will pass," Nikolai told him. "He's a nice guy. Not the kind of pirate we've read about in books."

"Mm," Demyan muttered. "That's good." Nikolai watched his friend for a moment, wrinkling his brow. Then he turned away.

"Oh no," Nikolai said, looking off to the south. Near the horizon, he glimpsed masts and smokestacks. The low, orange sun reflected off the metal ships.

"No need to worry ourselves over warships," Captain Sokoll declared, approaching and clapping a hand on Nikolai's shoulder. "We'll lower that Jolly Roger, and raise one of the other flags we've got in stock." He grinned and winked.

"Other flags?" Nikolai asked.

GRIGORY'S GADGET

"Yes," Captain Sokoll replied. "I think Chereplazh's colors should do. That country never gets involved in these conflicts." The captain smiled, then shivered. "Best get back inside," he said. "No sense being out in this weather if you don't have to."

Nikolai looked at Demyan, waiting. Demyan nodded and walked toward the stern, holding on to the railing of the ship for balance. The waves appeared small from up on the main deck. Demyan wondered how awfully the ship would rock in a storm.

"Having a rough time?" Alexi emerged from the saloon, looking at Demyan with disdain.

"He's just a little seasick," Nikolai said. "It'll pass."

"Not everyone is cut out for this life," Alexi told Demyan, ignoring Nikolai. "Maybe we should have left you on that passenger ship."

"Yes, maybe you should have," Demyan replied. His eyes were still fixed on the waves below.

Nikolai ushered Demyan back inside, glaring at Alexi.

"What's wrong with you?" he asked the pirate.

"We didn't bring you on this ship to babysit you," Alexi said. He glanced around the deck then turned back to Nikolai. "Just get to work."

Before Nikolai could respond, Alexi climbed the stairs to pilot house, disappearing inside.

CHAPTER THREE

Zoya stepped out of the boiler room, coughing as she lifted her goggles. She'd spent most of the day making adjustments to the ship's engine, maintaining the water levels, and changing the speed at which Lev and Samuil added coal to the furnace. Once conditions in the boilers seemed to stabilize, Tonia gave Zoya leave to take a break.

"It'll be dinner time soon," Lev told Zoya. "Clean yourself up, unless you like the taste of soot." Zoya nodded, then headed to her cabin.

Demyan was asleep in his hammock when she entered. Zoya leaned down and kissed him lightly on his forehead, frowning when she realized she'd left a lip-shaped soot smudge on his skin. She turned one of her gloves inside-out, and used the clean fabric to wipe it off.

"What are you doing?" Demyan asked groggily as he opened his eyes.

GRIGORY'S GADGET

"I was going to ask you the same thing," Zoya replied. "Are you feeling alright?"

"Just seasick," Demyan said. Zoya glanced around at the windowless room.

"It'll probably just get worse in here," she said. "Maybe there's a window you could sit by. In the saloon, probably?"

"I'd rather not," Demyan replied. "I'm out of the way here." His voice was slow and sad.

"You won't be in anyone's way in the saloon," Zoya insisted, rubbing Demyan's shoulder. "It's almost dinner time anyway." Demyan didn't reply, but rolled over to face the wall.

"Alright," Zoya conceded. "I'm going to clean myself up. Then I'm coming back here, and we're both going up to the saloon. I'll sling you over my shoulder in your hammock if I have to." She smiled and laughed, but Demyan still gave no reply.

The ship had two small bathrooms: one near the bow and one near the stern. Zoya headed to the one that was aft, looking herself over in its tiny, rusted mirror. She grabbed a rag soaked in liquor and began to scrub her face. The spirit made her skin tingle and stung her nose. After using the rag to wipe the soot smudges from her fingers, Zoya headed back to her cabin.

Demyan was standing when she returned, his face pale.

"Do you need help?" Zoya asked, noting how weak Demyan looked.

"No," he replied. "I can get myself upstairs." He stumbled out of the cabin, taking his time as he climbed the steps up to the saloon.

The sun was low in the sky, casting bright oranges and reds across the choppy ocean. It cast a warm hue through the saloon. Lilia, Anya, and Nikolai were helping Pavel to prepare dinner. They smiled as Zoya and Demyan entered.

"Feeling any better, Demyan?" Pavel asked as he stirred.

"Not really," Demyan admitted.

"Here," Zoya said, leading Demyan to a chair by a window. "Watch the horizon. It'll help."

"You're a mess, Zoya," Anya said, observing the soot stains covering Zoya's clothes.

"Yes," Zoya said. "It is what it is. What have you done all day?"

"Cleaned," Lilia replied. "And now I'm cooking."

"Followed by more cleaning, I'm sure," Nikolai said. "And then bed."

"Not as exciting as stories you've read," Pavel said. "Life at sea can be pretty mundane sometimes."

"Fine by me," Lilia muttered.

"That doesn't look mundane," Zoya said, pointing out a starboard window. White sails and shining metal reflected the light of the setting sun along the horizon. "Are those warships?"

Captain Sokoll walked in then, followed by Alexi, Fyodr, and Samuil.

"Aye, those are warships," the captain confirmed. "But nothing for us to worry about." Zoya glanced at her friends. Nikolai shrugged.

"The stew smells as good as ever." The captain bellowed to Pavel, "How are your new helpers?"

"Best sous chefs I've ever had," Pavel replied, smiling.

"When they're not vomiting," Alexi said to Fyodr and Samuil. The men laughed.

"Now, now," the captain said, "a little seasickness is normal."

"They tell me they're from Lodninsk," Pavel added. "Tiny landlocked town, it's a wonder they aren't all seasick." Across the room, Demyan groaned.

The rest of the crew began to trickle in, pouring themselves cups of boiled water for tea. Some pirates still wore heavy jackets. Zoya assumed they were the unlucky souls who worked outside. Regardless of the number of layers the pirates wore, the entire crew was shivering.

"You're not really used to the cold at all, are you?" Anya wondered aloud.

"There's cold, and then there's *cold*," Fyodr grumbled.

As the pirates huddled over their cups of tea, Zoya poured a cup for herself and Demyan. She sat across from him and placed their cups on the table.

"You're probably dehydrated if you've been getting sick," Zoya said, nudging his cup of tea toward him. Demyan didn't touch it, but looked up.

"I know how to take care of myself," he said, glaring. "Stop trying to play doctor; you're an engineer. And you're not even that, technically."

Zoya stared at Demyan with her mouth agape. *Demyan's never talked like that, to me or anyone else.* She leaned back in her chair and looked out of the window.

"I was just trying to help," she said at last. Then she stood and crossed the room to join their friends.

"We're not looking for a mother on this ship," Alexi told Zoya as she passed him.

"I would hope not," Zoya replied. "Last thing I need is a bunch of grown men with mother issues." She turned away, hoping she hadn't sounded too abrasive. *You're supposed to keep your head down, remember?* To her relief, Alexi just scoffed and returned to conversation with Fyodr and Samuil.

"He's just being a curmudgeon," Anya told Zoya, nodding toward Demyan.

Nikolai leaned in and whispered, "And thinks he's making himself look weak. Most everyone has been really nice to us, but we need to remember we're on a pirate ship."

"I know," Zoya said, staring down at the table. She sighed.

The pirates ate their dinner in near silence, aside from the slurping and chomping as they scarfed down their food. Partway through the meal, Demyan returned below deck. *He can take care of himself*, Zoya thought. *He has to take care of himself.*

Toward the end of the meal, the Captain raised a toast once more to the new crewmates. Some pirates switched from tea to ale, while others tried spiking their tea with liquor. Zoya watched as their faces puckered in disgust after taking a sip of the rancid combination. But they downed the drink all the same. Pavel laughed, shouting something about kraken ink.

After the toast, Alexi grabbed his coat and headed outside, alone.

"What a brute that guy is," Nikolai grumbled as Alexi left. His friends followed his gaze as he stood. Lilia grabbed his arm and tried to pull him back into his seat.

"What are you doing?" she asked.

"I just want to chat with him," Nikolai said, wresting his arm free and walking toward the door.

"I'll follow him," Anya said, standing. "Make sure he doesn't do anything stupid." Pavel just laughed and took a swig of ale.

"But it's freezing out," Lilia complained to Zoya.

"Hey!" Nikolai shouted over the whistling wind as he followed Alexi outside. Anya hurried after him. She wrapped her arms around herself and shivered as the cold air hit her. Alexi turned around, looking annoyed when he spotted Nikolai.

"Why are you being such a brute toward us?" Nikolai asked him.

"I don't know what you're talking about," Alexi replied with a shrug.

"I saw you," Nikolai said. "You didn't want to toast to welcome us; you were glaring at us. All you've done is glare and insult us all day. Honestly, you're the only one behaving the way I thought a pirate would behave. But why? Why is the entire crew so thrilled to have us on board except you? You're the one who kidnapped us!"

Alexi laughed. "Kidnapped," he huffed. "Don't be melodramatic."

"What exactly would you call it?" Nikolai's voice rose in annoyance.

"Nikolai, stop," Anya said as she caught up to him.

"Listen to your girlfriend," Alexi spat.

"She's not my girl—" Nikolai stopped mid-sentence, overcome with his frustration. He shivered, regretting not taking his coat with him.

"Nikolai," Anya said. "Just go back inside. Please." Nikolai threw his hands up and walked back to the saloon.

"At least one of you has some common sense," Alexi mumbled. He turned to walk toward the pilot house.

"What is your problem with us though?" Anya asked him. She folded her arms, partially in reproof, partially due to the cold. Alexi stopped and turned around.

"Nikolai has a point. Everyone else seems really happy to have us," Anya explained, teeth chattering, "and they've been nothing but nice."

"Yes," Alexi responded simply. "And don't you find that odd?" Before Anya could ask what he meant, he entered the pilot house and closed the door.

At the end of the night, Zoya and her friends sat in their hammocks. Once again, they found themselves unable to go to sleep. Demyan was the exception. Curled into a ball in his hammock, he snored softly.

"I hope he feels better tomorrow," Zoya said.

"I'm sure he'll be fine," Nikolai replied. "I think we'll all be fine as long as we stay away from Alexi."

"What did he say to you?" Lilia asked, looking to Anya. Anya was staring off into space, fiddling with one of the rings on her fingers.

"Anya, aether-head," Lilia cooed. "Come back to us." Anya snapped back, looking at her friends.

"What?"

"I asked what Alexi said to you, after Nikolai came back inside?"

"Nothing, really," Anya replied.

Nikolai turned toward her, brows furrowed. "No, he said something. I know that look. That's the one you always got when you were in trouble with an aide at the orphanage."

"He's right," Lilia said. Then she tilted her head and eyed Nikolai. "Since when are you so observant?"

"I'm always observant," Nikolai said, crossing his arms over his chest. "Maybe you're just too unobservant to notice." He stuck his tongue out.

Lilia turned back to Anya. "So, what did he say that's bothering you so much?"

"He thinks it's odd that everyone is being so nice to us," Anya said at last.

"Oh, that's just because he's an unpleasant idiot!" Nikolai shouted. Zoya smacked him in the arm, bringing a finger to her mouth. Nikolai grimaced, looking out the door. Zoya listened. Above the sounds of the waves and creaking wood, loud snores echoed through the ship.

"Everyone's asleep," Nikolai whispered. "It's fine."

Zoya regarded Anya. "I don't know though. It is odd, isn't it? Why *are* they being so nice to us?"

"Because we're part of the crew," Lilia said, wringing her hands. "Why would they be mean to us?"

"You're right," Nikolai said. "The plan is working. I think we're doing perfectly fine. We'll keep our heads down, do as we're told, and hope we don't get

GRIGORY'S GADGET

arrested. Eventually we'll find our way to Mirgorod."

Zoya lay back in her hammock, shutting her eyes to try and sleep. She rolled to face the corner and pulled out her gadget.

Moonlight shone through the porthole across the hall, illuminating the cabin with a pale blue glow. Zoya lifted the gadget and watched it sparkle in the dim light. She turned it over and over in her hands idly as her mind raced. *Are we going to be ok? Will we make it to Mirgorod? Is it strange that the pirates are nice to us, or are Lilia and Nikolai right? How long are we going to be on this ship?*

Demyan shifted in his hammock, rolling over to face the room. Zoya put her gadget down and closed her eyes, listening. She heard Demyan get up and tiptoe out of the room then tucked the gadget back into her suitcase and followed him.

As Zoya exited the cabin, she saw Demyan climb the stairs to the saloon. Zoya waited until he was out of sight then followed, careful to make her steps soft. Her effort was in vain; every other step creaked loudly as she shifted her weight onto it.

Demyan was alone in the saloon. He sat at a table watching as Zoya entered.

"I can leave if you want to be alone," she said.

"No, I was counting on you following me." He smiled, and Zoya returned it as she joined him at the table.

"You know me too well," she said.

"I wanted the chance to apologize," Demyan said. "All of this...it's overwhelming in and of itself. And then I got seasick."

"It's ok," Zoya told him, grabbing his hand. "We all have our bad moments. And if it takes being kidnapped by pirates and getting sick for you to have yours, I'd say that's pretty good."

Demyan laughed. "It is really absurd," he said.

Zoya agreed and felt a wave of relief as she laughed. Then she turned serious again. "That's why we need to stick together. That means playing tough in front of the pirates. And it means making sure we don't take our anger or frustration out on each other."

"Agreed," Demyan said. "We're a team. You, me, and the others." He stood and walked around to Zoya, hugging her and planting a kiss on her forehead.

"I love you," he said.

Zoya grasped Demyan's face softly in her hands, then brought him close for a kiss.

"I love you, too," she said.

The next morning, Fyodr jolted everyone awake by pounding on the door frame.

"Wake up, you're needed on the main deck."

"What's wrong?" Zoya asked, rubbing her eyes as she climbed down from her hammock.

GRIGORY'S GADGET

"Move it," Fyodr grumbled. "Quickly. Don't keep the captain waiting!" The friends exchanged nervous glances as they bundled up and followed Fyodr up the stairs.

"I'm worried," Lilia whispered to Zoya. "This doesn't seem good."

"I'm sure it's fine," Zoya lied.

As they emerged from the saloon, Lilia saw that the sun was just rising over the ocean. The air was warmer, suggesting the temperature might rise above freezing later in the day. Almost the entire crew of the ship was standing around on the main deck, with Captain Sokoll at the center.

"What's going on?" Demyan asked. The captain looked past him toward Fyodr and simply nodded. Without warning, Fyodr roughly shoved Nikolai toward the center of the ship.

"Hey, what—" Nikolai started.

"Can you catch?" Fyodr asked. He was holding a cutlass in each hand.

"I—Yes, I can," Nikolai replied, glancing around. Fyodr tossed one of the swords to Nikolai, who clumsily caught it by the hilt.

"Whoa," Demyan protested. "What do you think you're doing?"

"Time we put you all to the test," Captain Sokoll said. "We let gave you time to settle in, now we need to see what you're made of!"

"I'll start easy," Fyodr said, circling Nikolai. Nikolai hesitantly assumed a fighting stance, staring at Fyodr with wide eyes. He gulped.

"Nikolai's never handled a sword before," Demyan whispered to his friends. "Unless you count one time in the archeology laboratory, but that was to analyze the metal content of a five-hundred-year-old broken blade."

Fyodr lunged at Nikolai, who barely reacted in time to parry the blow. He stumbled, turned, and nearly lost his balance. Fyodr laughed and continued to circle Nikolai, lackadaisically twirling his sword in the air.

Fyodr lunged again, this time swinging the sword overhead and immediately following with a blow to Nikolai's side. Again Nikolai clumsily blocked the attacks, this time falling to one knee. He hurriedly got back to his feet.

"Not too promising," Fyodr said to the crew. They laughed in reply.

"Leave him alone!" Zoya shouted, stepping forward.

"If he can't prove his worth," Alexi replied, "we'll be sure to leave him alone. Marooned, on a deserted island!"

Samuil, who sat next to him, guffawed and clapped his hands. "That's right, boy!"

Taking advantage of the pirates' gloating and threatening, Nikolai charged. Fyodr blocked the strike effortlessly, shoving Nikolai backwards and

GRIGORY'S GADGET

knocking him over. The sword flew out of Nikolai's hand and landed a few feet away near his friends.

Without hesitation, Lilia picked up the sword and pointed it toward Fyodr.

"Think you can do better?" he asked with a smirk. Lilia didn't respond, but simply stared him down from across the deck.

"Let's see," Fyodr said, walking toward her nonchalantly. Lilia moved so as to keep facing him, but did not step away. Fyodr lunged, and she spun around and elbowed him in the back.

Fyodr, stunned, stumbled forward before turning back around.

"Clever," he said. Before he could resume his stance, Lilia thrust her sword toward him. She delivered a flurry of blows, chopping and stabbing continuously, driving Fyodr back toward the railing of the ship.

Just before he reached the edge, Alexi appeared and deflected Lilia's blow, sending her twirling backwards. She leapt back, resumed her fighting stance and eyed the two men.

"That's not fair," she protested, breathing heavily.

"Pirates," Fyodr stated, lunging forward again. Lilia tried desperately to fend them off, but she slipped on a patch of ice and fell as they surrounded her. Before she could stand up, Alexi held his sword to her throat.

From the edge of the main deck, Captain Sokoll clapped. A moment later, the rest of the crew joined in.

"Very good!" the captain proclaimed. "Good to see you have some experience!" Alexi put his sword down and extend his hand to help Lilia up. Lilia watched him warily as she stood.

"So this was a test?" she asked. She crossed the deck to rejoin her friends, breathing heavily.

"I thought you said you took dance lessons," Nikolai said, raising an eyebrow.

"That was code," Lilia said. "Civilians aren't supposed to have experience with weaponry. Better safe than sorry."

Nikolai and Demyan glanced at Zoya and Anya.

"And you two," Demyan said, getting defensive. "Did you take these 'dance' lessons as well?" Zoya and Anya nodded.

"Why didn't anyone tell us about them?" Demyan protested. Zoya blushed, looking away.

"Well, well!" the captain exclaimed while approaching the group. "You three will be very handy, then." He gestured to the girls then looked at the boys. "And you can teach these two how to fight starting today."

"Wait," Zoya said. "Come in handy? For what?"

Captain Sokoll pointed past the bow of the ship. Beyond, the ocean flowed into a wide channel framed by two land masses.

GRIGORY'S GADGET

"That's the Starzapad Strait," he explained. "Lots of merchant vessels pass through there from the Glavny Strait and Olen Sea. A golden opportunity for you. Now get to work!" The crew cheered and then dispersed, resuming their chores.

"You just had to show off," Nikolai mocked after the captain walked away.

"They're going to force us to be pirates," Lilia said staring out at the Strait.

"I guess they have room for more loot," Demyan said. He patted Zoya on the back. "Have fun with your thieving. Nikolai and I will be relaxing below deck, decidedly not committing crimes with a death sentence."

"Your empathy is touching," Zoya replied. "But you heard the captain. We're going to have to teach you to fight. In a single day, no less."

"I guess we should go grab some more swords," Anya said. "You boys have a rough day ahead of you." She smiled wickedly and headed inside.

As the morning promised, the day was a particularly warm one. Ice melted off the shrouds and sails, dripping and trickling onto the deck below. Zoya and her friends, still bundled in their coats, began to sweat as they practiced their swordplay.

"Stop slouching!" Anya called to Demyan. He responded with an exasperated sigh.

"I'm still a little seasick," he said. Anya feigned a pout and lunged at him. Demyan stumbled aside, slashing flimsily with his sword.

"Let him take a break," Nikolai shouted. He lifted his own sword and pointed it at Anya, who happily engaged with him.

Zoya and Lilia stood to the side, practicing their stances and familiarizing themselves with the swords.

"These are heavier than Isaak's," Lilia said.

"And in worse shape," Zoya replied, noting the nicks and rust on her blade. "But I guess that's to be expected on a pirate ship."

Zoya and Lilia engaged in a mock battle, slowly at first then picking up speed.

"Alright, I'm taking a break," Anya called to them. "Nikolai, spar with Lilia for a bit." Nikolai and Lilia obliged, laughing as Nikolai exhibited wild hand gestures and twisted facial expressions as he lunged and parried.

"This is fun," Anya told Zoya as they leaned against the railing.

"Yeah, it is," Zoya admitted.

"Until we have to fight for real," Demyan added, bracing himself on the railing beside Zoya.

"Zoya!" Tonia emerged from the saloon. "Take a break from swordplay. You're needed in the boiler room."

"Is something wrong?" Zoya asked as she sheathed her sword.

GRIGORY'S GADGET

"Nothing's wrong," Tonia replied. "Just need the man power."

Zoya nodded and followed Tonia below deck, stopping in her cabin to grab her goggles and gloves. As she did, she bumped the gadget out of her suitcase. It rolled across the floor and stopped near the doorway. Before Zoya could fetch it, Alexi appeared and snatched it up.

He rushed into the room with the gadget, his eyes wild.

"Put this away!" he demanded in a hushed tone. "Now!"

"Ok," Zoya replied, grabbing the gadget. "Sorry." She stared at Alexi, hugging the gadget to her chest. *What in the world is going on?*

"Bury it," Alexi told her, his hushed voice frantic. "You hear me? Bury it and don't let anyone see it."

"Yes, fine, ok," Zoya stammered. She turned to put the gadget back in her suitcase, but looked up as Alexi rushed out of the room.

"Hey, wait a second!" she called after him. She looked out of the doorway and saw him run up to the saloon. With a frustrated sigh, she reentered the room. She stopped after wrapping her grandmother's gadget in a blouse. Her hands shook.

Why was he blowing a gasket over this gadget? Protect it and it will protect you. What did you mean by that, Grandmother? What is this thing? She shoved the gadget to the bottom of her bag. Then she collapsed onto the floor, closing her eyes and directing her attention inward. Her breathing was shallow, and she shuddered with every rapid beat of her heart. Tears filled her eyes as she covered her face with her hands.

It's alright. We'll be alright. She repeated the thought like a mantra, letting her lips mouth the words.

I'm sure it's nothing. We'll be alright.

A few moments passed before Zoya calmed down. *Just overwhelmed. We are trapped on a pirate ship after all. We'll figure it out. We'll be fine.* She wiped her eyes, grabbed her goggles and gloves, and stood. She passed a small closet in the hall that contained spare swords and knives. She grabbed a knife and stuck it in her boot before continuing to the boiler room.

The sun approached the horizon by the time Lilia decided to take a break from swordplay. She realized she had missed the rush of the dance, the feel of heavy metal and wood in her hand, and the sense of power and strength. At times while she practiced, she could hear Isaak's voice taunting her in good humor.

Watch your footwork! You move your feet so quickly, but your sword moves through molasses! Keep your head up! Not that far up!

She missed Isaak. It pained her to remember the last time they had seen him. She, Zoya, and Anya had escaped into the alley as the soldiers arrived.

GRIGORY'S GADGET

They had lingered by the door, listening to the interrogation for as long as they'd dared. As they ran away, they could hear the screams of a woman and a child and then of Isaak himself. It was a wonder they'd made it back to the apartment, tears frozen around their eyes.

Lilia pushed the memory from her mind and entered the saloon.

"Did the captain dismiss you from your swordplay?" Pavel asked happily when he saw her.

Lilia's face flushed. "Well, no, he didn't. I was hoping I could take a break to help cook." She stood by the doorway and fidgeted with her hands.

Pavel smiled. "Start preparing the broth. I'll go ask the captain if you may assist me with dinner preparations."

"Will that be alright?" Lilia asked. "I don't want to cause any trouble."

"Don't worry, my dear. I won't get you in trouble. Next time, though, ask the captain before taking a break." Pavel clasped Lilia's shoulder and winked then strolled toward the captain's cabin.

Lilia started the fire on the stove and grabbed a pot to fill with the salty stock. She stirred idly and took deep breaths to calm herself. Pavel entered the saloon a moment later.

"You have been given permission by the captain to assist me in the kitchen." Pavel stood beside Lilia and began cutting strips of meat. Lilia eyed his hands warily.

"I hope this isn't rude to ask," she said, staring at his missing fingers. "But you didn't lose...those aren't from..."

Pavel looked at his hands and laughed. "From cutting meat? Vozh be good, of course not!" Pavel put down the knife and pointed to his left hand, where he lacked his pinky and ring finger.

"Do you want the interesting story or the embarrassing truth?"

"Both," Lilia replied with a shrug and a smile. Pavel chuckled.

"The story I like to tell," Pavel said, "is that I lost these two fingers by wrestling a Gibel Crab while vacationing on the Isle of Pokot in the Strazny Ocean. My skill and bravery earned me the adoration of everyone on the island, especially the ladies." Pavel winked then guffawed. "But, sadly, that is not the truth. The truth is, I was young, stupid, rash, and clumsy. I was a new recruit in the Starzapad Navy, learning to use a sword for the first time. My reflexes and instincts were very poor, and, well—" He made a slashing motion across his left hand, accompanied by a *swooshing* noise. Lilia grimaced.

"Don't worry," Pavel assured her. "I've come a long way since then."

"Did you say the Starzapad Navy?" she asked. Pavel nodded.

"And a fierce navy it is," he said, his tone dark. "And a fiercer army. You and your friends are lucky

GRIGORY'S GADGET

to be leaving Morozhia now before you got trapped in this war. I'd even say you're lucky we grabbed you off that passenger ship. War creates a lot of gray areas, diplomatically speaking."

Lilia gazed into the pot, still stirring, thoughts spinning in her head. Pavel patted her on the shoulder.

"Ah, but this hand," he said, his tone lightening. "This injury is a mark of pride for me. Proof of loyalty and camaraderie. You see, I was taken into custody, questioned about my dear captain. They poked and prodded and cut off the top half of this finger." Pavel held up his right hand, wiggling the stump of his middle finger. "My own fault, really. I presented them with this finger one too many times."

"How did you escape?" Lilia asked, feeling slightly nauseated. She'd never had a strong stomach for gore.

"The brave captain rescued me," Pavel said. "Burst in with the crew, pistols waving, and got me out. That was back in the day before the world got anxious and posted armed guards at every door and window."

"Now that sounds more like the stories I've read in my books," Lilia said with a small grin.

"Oh, we've got the stories," Pavel said. "Sometimes they seem few and far between, but they more than make up for the mundane interim."

CHAPTER FOUR

That night, Anya lay awake in her hammock, restless. The others had fallen asleep quickly especially Demyan and Nikolai who were sore from swordplay. Practicing with swords had the opposite effect on Anya. She could hardly bear to put her sword down at the end of the day; fire raced through her veins. While they ate dinner, Anya bounced one leg repeatedly, fidgeting with her fork once she had finished her food. When her friends decided to call it a night, Anya conceded, grumbling.

So there she lay, staring out the porthole across the hall at the sparkling silver ocean. Frost crept in from the edges of the glass, creating a frame of sorts. Once the sun had gone down, the bitter chill returned, slowly refreezing everything that had thawed.

With a huff, Anya stood and grabbed her coat and gloves. As she left the cabin, she first turned toward the stairway then stopped. *I've seen the deck, but not much down here.* She turned and headed down the hallway.

Every few feet there was another doorway that led to rooms filled with sleeping pirates. One was lit by a lone candle. Next to it, Ira lay in her hammock, eyes closed, an open book hugged to her chest. Anya tried to read the title, but it was obscured by the woman's hands.

Anya turned a corner at what she believed was the stern of the ship and paused at a door. She peered through the window in the door and saw a room with giant floor to ceiling windows at its rear. She tried the door: locked. Dim candlelight filled the room with a warm glow. Anya could make out maps and parchment on a large oaken table. She heard whispers inside, but couldn't see who was speaking or hear what they were saying.

Anya continued on, following the hall which turned to head toward the bow. She tripped over a pile of cannon balls stacked next to a cannon. She leaned against the wall as she rubbed her foot, squinting to see down the dark hallway. No candles or sconces were lit on this side of the ship. She could hear pirates snoring in their cabins.

Partway down the hall, Anya found the stairs that must have led to the boilers and cargo. Warm, foul-smelling air drifted up, convincing Anya to move on without exploring that lower level.

Markedly bored below deck, Anya climbed the stairs to the saloon. The room was empty, lit by two small sconces on the back wall. The air still smelled of ale and salty stew. Anya bundled up in her coat, lifted her hood, and headed outside.

The *Ocean's Legend* was passing through the Starzapad Strait. Jagged land masses rose up, Morozhia to the north and Starzapad to the south, separated by the sparkling gray water. Anya watched through the shrouds as the hills rolled slowly by, marked by clusters of light where small towns resided.

Anya paced the deck, trying to find the best view of either continent. No matter where she stood, ropes, pulleys, masts, and sails blocked her view. As Anya looked through a gap in the shrouds, she grinned. She grabbed the rigging, hoisting herself up to stand on the ship's railing.

The waves below were a moving, mottled mix of black and silver, crashing lightly on the ship's hull. Anya steadied herself, gripping the rigging with both hands. Her right foot slipped on the icy railing, sending her twirling into the ropes of the shrouds. She reached for the shrouds with both hands, her heart racing. Slowly, she lifted her right foot to rest on a rope then did the same with her left. The shrouds were notably less slick than the wooden deck.

Anya tested the sturdiness of the rope beneath her feet then tugged at the ropes in her hands. She peered over her shoulder, letting go of the ropes with her left hand. Slowly, carefully, she pivoted to

GRIGORY'S GADGET

look out at the ocean. With a satisfied sigh, Anya leaned back into the shrouds and relaxed.

"Fancy yourself a rigging monkey?"

Anya grabbed the ropes tightly and turned around. Alexi stood by the pilot house, watching.

"Excuse me?" Anya replied. Alexi laughed and walked down to the main deck.

"It's a nautical term, not an insult," he said. "It's what I am."

"I was beginning to wonder exactly what it is you do," Anya replied. "Other than bother and insult people. Heckler monkey is more like it."

Alexi grasped his chest and frowned. "Your words wound me so," he said. Then he chuckled. "Just promise me you won't fall into the ocean. The captain would give me forty lashes and then some if I let one of you go on my watch."

"Let one of us go?" Anya asked. She started climbing down the rigging. "What does that mean?"

Alexi turned and walked toward the saloon. "You know, get lost to sea, die." He waved his hand. Anya hurried after him, grabbing his arm before he opened the door.

"What's going on here?" Anya asked, forcing him to face her. "Stop being so cryptic."

"Cryptic?" he replied. "I'm not being cryptic. You're just being apprehensive. I guess that's a normal response; it is your first time on a pirate ship." He tried to continue into the saloon, but Anya kept her grasp tight on his arm.

"You told me it's odd that everyone else is being nice to us," Anya said. Alexi opened his mouth to respond, but Anya continued. "Now you tell me you'll get in trouble if you *let one of us go* on your *watch*? Are we members of the crew or are we prisoners? And if we're prisoners, why?" Alexi turned to face her, glancing toward the captain's cabin with a wrinkled brow.

"You're members of the crew," Alexi said in a hushed tone. "But, yes, you are also prisoners, in a way." He grabbed Anya by the arms and looked her in the eyes. "But you do not know that, alright? And you certainly didn't hear it from me. As far as the captain is concerned, you're welcome members of the crew who are treated well. He's trying to build your trust." This time Anya let him go into the saloon. She followed him.

"But why?" she whispered before he headed below deck. Alexi paused, thinking.

"Just keep an eye on your things and your friends," he said. "Especially Zoya."

"I've been told you have an affinity for climbing," Pavel said to Anya the next morning at breakfast. "We could use some more hands in the rigging if you're up for it?"

Anya was taken aback. She hadn't expected her escapades on the rigging the night before to be common knowledge. Alexi had obviously told Pavel, but to what end? Regardless, Anya nodded with a wide grin. She had enjoyed climbing the rigging. Returning the smile, Pavel headed out on deck.

"What are you, crazy?" Lilia asked. "Everything's icy; you'll slip and fall!"

"I'll be fine," Anya said.

"No you won't. You'll die!" Lilia replied.

Zoya placed a hand on Lilia's arm. "She'll be fine. She's in Pavel's hands. He won't let her do anything too dangerous." Lilia sat back thinking about Pavel's stories of how he lost his fingers. Before she could object further, Anya stood and headed outside.

"Anya, over here!" Pavel shouted from the pilot house. Anya glanced around as she climbed the stairs. It was a dreary day and snow fell steadily. The continents on either side of the ship lurked like massive gray monsters.

"So," Pavel said. "I hope you aren't afraid of heights." He waved his hand toward the mizzenmast where one of the sails was torn. Anya hesitated for a moment.

"You can't take it down to repair it?" she asked slowly.

"We don't have the space for that," Pavel said. "Or the time, or an extra sail. So, we have to repair them where they fly. But don't worry; Alexi will help you." As he heard his name, Alexi stepped out of the pilot house.

"Good morning, Anya," he said with forced courtesy. "How are you this morning?"

Anya raised an eyebrow at him. "I'm fine, and you?"

"I'm splendid," he said. "Ready to be a rigging monkey?"

"That's what we call—" Pavel started.

"I know," Anya interrupted. She blushed at her rudeness and turned to Pavel with a smile. "I've heard the term before."

"Good, good," Pavel replied. "Alexi will show you the ropes." He headed back down to the main deck.

Alexi stepped back into the pilot house briefly, then reemerged with a bundle of rope in his hand.

"This is how we get up there," he explained, smirking. "You'll get fastened with this, and I'll lift you up to the sail. Sound fun?"

He held out the bundle to her.

"Step your legs through here," he instructed. "Then this part goes over your shoulders."

Anya stepped into the tangled mess and eyed Alexi.

"Don't try anything," she told him.

"Wouldn't dream of it," Alexi replied as he tightened the contraption around her torso. "Nice and snug. Are you ready?" He grabbed some sewing supplies from the deck and handed them to her. Anya took a deep breath.

"I suppose I am," she said. "Don't you dare drop me."

"Why would I do that?"

"How should I know? With how strangely you've been acting, is it really that much of a stretch to think—"

"I am not going to drop you," Alexi said. "I promise." He looked her in the eye, his face sturdy and stoic.

"Fine," Anya replied. "Then let's get this over with."

"Fine," Alexi mocked. He grabbed a long piece of rope that was tied to the cords now strapped around Anya's body. Pointing to the nearest shroud, he said, "Climbing that is the easiest way up." He traced a path up the rigging with his finger then pointed to the first horizontal piece of wood that held the sail. "Climb that way, then up to the first yard. You can sit on that while you work."

"Doesn't seem too hard."

She walked to the base of the shroud and grabbed on to a rung. The ropes were frayed, but still felt sturdy. She climbed. The first few feet seemed easy, but as she climbed higher she began to feel dizzy and out of breath.

"You ok up there?" Alexi asked. Anya closed her eyes for a moment and took a deep breath. When she opened them, she focused her gaze out around the ship, rather than down. The scenery was gray, mottled between land and sea and sky. Its monotony was oddly calming.

"Yeah, I'm fine," she replied at last. She finished her ascent to the yard and hoisted herself onto it.

"Hard part's over!" Alexi said.

Anya quickly got to work mending the sail. The tear was at least a foot long, but in a spot that was easy to reach. Halfway through sewing, Anya felt a wave of vertigo and gripped the sail tightly. But after a moment, her fear turned to excitement, and she continued. After Anya finished her work, she looked around then down at Alexi.

"Do I get down the same way?"

Alexi nodded and pointed back to the shroud. Carefully, Anya stood up on the yard, holding the sail for balance. She inched herself toward the shroud slowly, trying not to look down. Just as she was about to reach for a rung, her foot slipped, and she tumbled through the air.

The ropes tightened in a painful jerk, leaving Anya suspended halfway to the deck. She groaned and pulled herself upright in the ropes.

"You alright?" Alexi asked, holding on to the other end of the rope tightly. Anya nodded.

"Ok," he said. "I'm going to lower you to the deck." Anya nodded again.

Less-than-gracefully, Alexi lowered Anya until she landed with a thump in front of the saloon. He then hurried to help her up.

"Could have been a bit gentler," Anya said as he helped her to her feet.

"I'm sorry," he replied. "I've probably frightened you now."

GRIGORY'S GADGET

Anya laughed. "Frightened? That was the most fun I've had in a long time!" She winced as she pulled the rope harness off.

"I might have some bruises, though."

Laughing, the two of them returned their supplies to the pilot house.

"Anya," Alexi said as Anya began to leave the pilot house. He gestured for her to come closer.

"I saw that object Zoya has in her suitcase," he whispered. Anya furrowed her brow.

"She's not going to let you sell it," Anya replied. "It was her grandmother's. It means way too much to her. She'd die before she let anyone take that from her."

"Good," Alexi said. "Tell her to keep it hidden. Do not let anyone on this ship see it." Anya stared at him blankly.

"What?" she said at last.

"I shouldn't have even brought it up," Alexi said, waving his hands. "Just keep it hidden. That's all I'm going to say." He walked toward the door of the pilot house, then stopped. "Pavel needs you for some less-exciting sewing," he said. "Apparently, Fyodr ripped his pants." He smirked, then left.

Zoya and her friends got their first taste of real piracy that afternoon.

The *Ocean's Legend* sailed furiously toward a merchant vessel as the sun rose steadily in the sky.

Pavel supplied Lilia, Zoya, and Anya with sheathed swords.

"You likely won't have to do much fighting," he assured them as they buckled the sheaths on. "Unless you want to, of course." He winked at Lilia, who blushed. Then he headed below deck.

"I wish I didn't pick up that sword," Lilia said. "It was just instinct, I guess."

"It'll be alright," Zoya replied. "I can't imagine we'll stay at sea much longer after this. How much room for loot can they possibly have on this ship?"

"That's true," Anya said. She placed a hand on Lilia's shoulder. "Just survive today."

"Good luck with that," Nikolai said as he and Demyan approached. "As much as I'm still upset that you never invited us to your dancing lessons, I won't complain about relaxing below deck."

"Is that what you think?" Pavel laughed, appearing again. "Just because you won't be wielding a sword doesn't mean we don't have use for you. You'll be helping with the cannons." He pointed below deck then headed toward the captain's cabin.

"Still better than fighting," Demyan said. "That's what you get for not telling us about your dancing classes!"

"We were going to tell you!" Lilia said. "But, the timing was never right."

"We started taking lessons right before the plague hit," Zoya explained sadly. "Nikolai was grieving for his mom, Demyan for his dad." She placed her hand on Demyan's shoulder.

"And not long after," Anya said, "the guards found our instructor. They shot him in his home. He didn't even have a chance to defend himself."

"We barely managed to escape out the back door before the guards busted in," Lilia said.

The pirates then interrupted their remembrance, rushing around the deck. They were wild-eyed, yelling and shouting and pointing toward the merchant ship.

"We're closing in on the ship," Zoya said, glancing at Demyan. "You better get to those cannons."

"And you better get ready to fight," Demyan replied solemnly. He pulled Zoya into a tight embrace and kissed her. "Be careful." After a second, lingering kiss, he headed below deck with Nikolai.

Their hands on the hilts of their swords, the girls crossed the main deck. Zoya could see that the merchant vessel was almost close enough to board, and its crew looked panicked. Captain Sokoll stood nearby, grinning hungrily.

"We don't want any trouble!" a man, presumably the ship's captain, shouted to the pirates. "We ain't got much on this little ship!"

"Perfect!" Captain Sokoll replied. "We have only so much storage on our ship! Now, if you don't want any trouble, you can surrender right now! We'll kindly take the loot and be on our way!"

"Please surrender," Lilia whispered.

"We'll never surrender!" a young man shouted from the merchant ship. The captain shushed the boy and pushed him away.

"So be it!" Captain Sokoll laughed. "Prepare to feel the wrath of Captain Edmund Sokoll the Savage and the pirates of the *Ocean's Legend*!"

Lev, Samuil, Oleg, and Olya hoisted planks of wood toward the merchant ship. The planks clattered onto its deck, connecting it to the *Ocean's Legend*.

Captain Sokoll raised his arm and signaled his crew. With a roar, they boarded the other ship. Some crossed over via the planks while others swung to the ship on loosed ropes.

"Ready for your big debut?" Tonia asked as she approached. "Don't worry, I don't think this fight will last very long." She clapped Zoya on the shoulder then with a shout followed the rest of the crew onto the other ship.

"Ok, I guess," Zoya sighed. "Here we go." Drawing their swords, the three women headed toward a plank.

It quickly became apparent that the pirates vastly outnumbered the crew of the small trading ship. By the time Zoya, Lilia, and Anya had crossed over, every member of the merchant ship's crew was engaged in a fight with a pirate.

"I guess we're just backup," Lilia said.

"Well that's no fun," Anya said with a grin.

GRIGORY'S GADGET

"What are you talking about?" Lilia asked. "I'm not looking for fun here, I want to stay alive."

Anya didn't respond and instead rushed into the center of fighting.

"Anya!" Zoya called. "Stop!"

Before Anya could swing her sword, Captain Sokoll's booming laughter echoed across the deck and the fighting came to a halt.

"Do you surrender?" he asked with a big grin.

"Yes," the other captain replied sadly. "We surrender." The young man who had protested defiantly moments earlier lay dead at the man's feet in a pool blood. The captain had tears in his eyes as he looked at Captain Sokoll, defeated.

"Good," Captain Sokoll told him. "And now you know it's better to surrender to Captain Edmund Sokoll the Savage, isn't it?" The man nodded silently.

Lilia turned away from the scene, her hands over her face. Zoya wrapped an arm around her shoulder, unsure what to say.

"You'd think we'd get used to things like that," she said at last.

A few members of Captain Sokoll's crew stood guard over the merchants as everyone else gathered the loot. The girls followed Pavel as he crossed the deck.

"What will happen to the other crew?" Zoya asked Pavel as they returned to the *Ocean's Legend*.

"We'll let them be," Pavel replied to the girls.

"More people to spread the legend of the great pirate Edmund Sokoll," Alexi muttered, coming to stand next to Pavel. "More people to inflate his ego."

"Watch your mouth," Pavel warned. Alexi mumbled something unintelligible, then headed toward the other ship. He whispered something to Samuil, who guffawed and patted Alexi on the back.

"Does he just go around trying to cause conflict?" Lilia asked Pavel.

"He's just troubled," Pavel replied.

"Yes," Nikolai said. "You've said that before." He and Demyan were above deck again, covered in black from the gunpowder. Anya tilted her head as she examined their blackened clothes.

"I didn't hear the cannons go off," she said. Nikolai and Demyan looked at each other.

"We don't want to talk about it."

The friends helped bring crates full of fine porcelain dishes and gilded bric-a-brac below deck as Captain Sokoll shouted orders at the merchant crew. As the last of the boxes and bags were carried over, the pirates drew their pistols and pointed them at their victims.

"We'll be on our way now," the captain boasted. "Thanks very much for the supplies. Now you stay put until me and my crew have disembarked this lovely vessel."

The pirates headed back to the *Ocean's Legend* waving their pistols in the air. Captain Sokoll turned

GRIGORY'S GADGET

and looked over his crew, while Alexi removed the planks connecting them to the merchant ship.

"Not yet, Alexi," the captain said, still eying his crew. "Where's Lev?"

"I saw him go below deck, sir," Alexi replied, removing the last plank.

"No," Captain Sokoll said. "I commanded Lev to report to me immediately."

"Well, he didn't," Alexi said.

"Are you giving me attitude, boy?" As the captain spoke, Lev appeared above deck on the other ship.

"Captain!" he called as the merchant crew rose to their feet. Alexi hurried to drop a plank again, but it was too late. The captain of the merchant ship and several members of his crew surrounded Lev. They grabbed him and his sword and cut him down. Alexi stared at the scene, hands shaking.

"Alexi!" Captain Sokoll's angry voice echoed around the ships. Alexi looked up at the Captain and dutifully walked toward him. He made no eye contact with anyone.

Brusquely, Captain Sokoll grabbed Alexi by the throat, and slammed him into a wall.

"What kind of imbecile are you? Are you just constantly looking for more ways to disappoint me? To make me embarrassed to call you son?"

"What?" Anya whispered to her friends. Captain Sokoll turned to Fyodr and Pavel.

"Ten lashes!" he roared. "And make them count!" Fyodr and Pavel obediently grabbed Alexi and dragged him over to the mainmast. They shoved him face-first into the mast and ripped open the back of his shirt. In all of the commotion, Ira grabbed a whip. And it began.

Horrified, Lilia turned and hugged Zoya, whose gaze was fixed on the brutal scene before them.

"I don't want to watch this," Anya said, turning around as well. The whip cracked, and Alexi let out a stifled grunt.

"Let's go back below deck," Zoya suggested. Nikolai and Demyan stood in the doorway of the saloon, stunned silent by what they had seen. The whip cracked again. The five friends hurriedly descended below deck.

Anya rushed into their cabin then walked out again. She clutched her stomach, her mouth quivering, then headed down the hall to where the toilet was located. Lilia sat on the floor in the corner and stared off into space. The other three paced around the tiny room.

"This is all too real," Demyan said at last. "This is exactly the kind of thing I was hoping we'd avoid."

"He should have waited, like the captain said," Nikolai said. "His poor judgment just got Lev killed! He was murdered, right in front of us!"

With an exasperated sigh, Zoya joined Lilia on the floor. "We're in over our heads," she said.

Anya stumbled back into the room. "His son? He's the captain's son?"

GRIGORY'S GADGET

"I don't think that's the most important point, right now," Lilia said. "We just saw a child and then Lev murdered, and now there's a flogging going on!"

"But at least they aren't going to kill him," Zoya said.

"Because he's the captain's son," Anya said. She knelt on the cot. "This means something. It's connected, somehow."

"Connected to what?" Nikolai asked.

"To why he was acting strangely," she replied. "His warning about the gadget. He knows something."

"Wait, what?" Zoya asked. "He warned you about the gadget, too?" Anya stared at her, mouth agape.

"What, that ball of gears?" Demyan asked.

"He probably just wants to take it from you and sell it," Nikolai said. "What could he possibly warn about? No offense, Zoya, but it looks like a piece of junk." Zoya glared at Nikolai.

"Nikolai, shut up," Lilia growled. Anya stood, determined, and stormed back above deck.

As she entered the saloon, intent on grabbing a cup of ale, Alexi stumbled in. His shirt, or what remained of it, was in tatters that fell to the floor. Exhausted and weak, he fell into the nearest seat and rested his head on the table. Anya stood still and silent, wondering if he had noticed her. A moment later, Pavel entered with a leather bag. Out of it he pulled a glass vial and clean strips of fabric. He began tending to Alexi's wounds. As quietly as she could manage, Anya walked toward the cupboard.

"Pour Alexi a cup as well," Pavel told her. Alexi winced as Pavel placed a soaked piece of fabric onto his broken skin. Anya poured two cups of ale and walked to the table.

"Are you ok?" Anya asked as Alexi downed the entire cup.

"This is nothing," he told her. "I'm surprised it wasn't worse. He could have thrown me into the ocean." Anya contemplated his words for a moment.

"How many..." she started, then paused. "Has this happened before?"

"Accidentally abandoning a crew mate to die?" Alexi asked, looking into her eyes. "No. My father getting angry and having me whipped? Now that's a regular occurrence." He winced again from the pain on his back.

"Well," Pavel said as he began packing up his leather bag. "Take it easy, Alexi. Best stay out of the captain's sight for the rest of the day." Alexi nodded as Pavel left the saloon.

"So, you're the captain's son?" Anya said.

"You don't need to sit here and babysit me," Alexi grumbled. "Making small talk. I'm fine." As he spoke, Tonia, Oleg, and Olya entered the saloon.

"He should have killed you, boy," Oleg spat. "You're lucky you're his brat."

"So they tell me," Alexi replied, groaning as he stood. "I'll leave you alone."

GRIGORY'S GADGET

"Wait," Anya said. "It's not his fault. He didn't mean to strand Lev on that ship."

"Oh, he didn't mean it," Olya replied. "Good, then that will bring Lev right back to us." Olya's prosthetic hand formed into a fist. Anya stared at it. *How did she do that?*

"You don't know this boy like we do," Tonia said. "He's always been trouble. Mouthing off, disobeying orders. Give him an inch and he'll take a mile. No mistake goes unpunished for this one."

"It's fine, Anya," Alexi said. The three pirates glared as Alexi slowly walked by them, hunched over in pain. He gripped the railing as he limped below deck. Anya followed him.

"I'd stay away from that kid," Tonia warned her. "You saw how he was today. He's too rash and doesn't appreciate all his father's given to him."

"I'll keep that in mind," Anya replied and continued below deck after Alexi.

"Can I help you with something?" Alexi asked sarcastically, turning to face Anya as they passed her and her friends' cabin.

"I just want to talk," Anya replied.

"Well, I've got nothing to talk about," Alexi said with a nasty tone. "Certainly not to you."

"Hey," Nikolai said, walking out of the cabin. "Do we have a problem?"

"We will if you don't turn back around." Nikolai scowled at him and stood his ground.

"You don't get to boss me around," he said. "Not after you just got someone killed! Exactly how much trouble do you think you can get in before daddy decides you need to get what's really coming to you?"

"Nikolai," Anya said.

"No, he's right," Alexi said simply, turning to face Nikolai. He walked up to him and stared him down. "Exactly how much trouble do *you* think I can get in before my father gives me *what's coming to me*?"

"Are you threatening me?" Nikolai asked, unflinching.

"I simply restated your own observations," Alexi replied. "Make of them what you will." Nikolai pushed Alexi away from him.

"Nikolai, stop," Anya protested. Nikolai ignored her and walked toward Alexi, who was laughing.

"You're going to pick of a fight with me?" Alexi asked through his laughter. "Oh, big tough man you are! Fighting a man who's just been flogged! How do you find such bravery?"

"You son of a—" Nikolai shoved Alexi again, this time hard enough to knock him into the wall. Alexi let out a groan of pain, but continued to laugh. Nikolai punched him square in the face.

"Nikolai!" Demyan shouted as he grabbed his friend by the arm. Nikolai struggled and spat at Alexi as Demyan pulled him away.

"You stay away from us," Nikolai said, turning back to their cabin.

GRIGORY'S GADGET

"Gladly," Alexi responded, wiping blood from his nose. He turned and lurched down the hall. Lilia and Demyan walked back into the cabin.

"Let him be," Zoya told Anya, who followed Alexi with her eyes. "For now." Anya nodded, and the two of them joined their friends in the cabin.

CHAPTER FIVE

Breakfast the following morning was interrupted by a startling shout from Fyodr.

"Something's in the water!"

Zoya and her friends followed as half the crew headed outside at his call, walking to the port side of the ship. The *Ocean's Legend* had left the Starzapad Strait, entering the much wider Glavny Strait. Morozhia and Starzapad were faint gray phantoms on the horizon behind them.

Zoya gazed into the open water and spotted dark shapes floating ahead.

"I'm going to get a better look," Anya said. She walked to the shrouds and began to climb.

"What are you doing?" Lilia asked. "You're going to fall!"

GRIGORY'S GADGET

"No I won't!" Anya replied while smiling. She leaned forward, gripped the ropes tightly, and scanned the waters below.

"I think it's a ship!" she shouted to the crew. Then she recanted. "Er, it looks like it *was* a ship."

Captain Sokoll plodded out of his cabin and strode toward the bow.

Small pieces of wood, cracked and burned, began floating by the *Ocean's Legend*. As the ship slowly neared the center of the wreckage, a strong smoky odor filled the air.

A large piece of charred wood floated by, with the words *Hello Eddie* scratched on it.

Captain Sokoll snarled and slammed his fists into the railing.

"Sir," Pavel said slowly. "You don't think—"

"Of course it's her," the captain said. "Who else would it be?" Turning in a fury, he stomped toward the pilot house.

"Fyodr!" he shouted. "Change course! Whatever the nearest town is. We'll make a short trip of it." He turned to Zoya.

"Go find Tonia in the boiler room. I want the engine operating at full speed," he commanded. Without a word, Zoya ran down to the boiler room. There she found Tonia, along with Olya and Oleg, covered in soot and out of breath.

"What happened in here?" Zoya asked.

"Nothing you need to worry about," Oleg replied.

"Crisis averted," Olya added. She held her prosthetic in her right hand, then twisted it onto the end of her left arm until it clicked. The mechanical fingers twitched. Zoya watched with interest.

"How do those work?" she asked, glancing at Oleg's matching mechanical hand.

"Magic," Olya replied, winking.

Zoya frowned. "Ok, well, the captain wants the engine at full speed."

"Why?" Tonia asked.

"We just passed a wrecked ship, and the captain seems really upset by it. We're changing course to get to land sooner. Whoever attacked that ship, the captain seems to want to stay far away from them."

"Well, good," Olya stated. "We're running low on coal. Better to get to a town as soon as possible, anyway."

"We'll get her going as fast as she can go," Tonia said with urgency, picking up a shovel.

Zoya nodded, grabbing a shovel as well.

"Do you know who it is?" Zoya asked as she shoveled coal. "Who the captain is afraid of?"

"The captain isn't afraid of anyone," Olya and Oleg retorted in unison. Tonia nodded in agreement.

"He's not scared," she said. "But some people are simply problematic. Especially when they're family."

"Family?" Zoya asked.

"If I'm assuming what the captain's assuming," Tonia replied, "the crew that attacked that ship is led by the captain's sister."

"Brother and sister, rival pirates," Zoya mused. "Sounds messy."

"You have no idea."

"You know," Lilia called after Anya, who was rushing below deck. "Other members of the crew may be able to tell us what's going on." Anya ignored her and continued down the stairs. She weaved her way to Alexi's cabin.

"Now what do you want?" Alexi asked as Anya entered. "Can't you just let me rest?"

"Your father's upset," Anya said.

Alexi laughed. "Yes, I'm aware."

"No," Anya said. "Not because of you. We just passed a wrecked ship. He was livid and ordered Fyodr to change course." Anya studied Alexi's face.

"So?" Alexi responded after a moment. "We've got a ship full of goods, we're running low on coal, and the crew is tired. We don't want to challenge another pirate crew right now."

"Really? That's why your father is so mad? Alexi, he was absolutely furious!"

"Residual anger at me, I'm sure," Alexi said. "And he hates to be inconvenienced."

"Sorry," Anya said, sitting on a crate by Alexi. "But I don't believe you."

"Sorry, but that's your problem." Alexi lay down in his hammock with his back to Anya.

"Why did you tell me that Zoya needs to keep her gadget hidden?" Anya asked.

"Well, if she doesn't want us to steal it..." Alexi said.

"Will you stop lying?" Anya shouted in frustration. She grabbed a necklace that she wore around her neck, and pulled Alexi over to face her.

"This necklace is solid gold," she said. "With three large pieces of solid opal that my father snuck out of the Lodninsk mines for me. I wear this in plain sight. You haven't said a thing about it."

"Sorry I didn't notice your pretty necklace," Alexi replied, shaking Anya's hand off his arm.

"Something about that object is different," she said. "Somehow. It means something. Doesn't it?"

"Keep your voice down," Alexi said.

"Why? Because you don't want anyone to know what we're talking about? Because it needs to be kept a secret?"

"Because you are loud and I'm tired!" Alexi shouted at her. "So shut up! I don't know what you're going on about. Just leave me alone!" Anya slapped him across the face then stood and hurried out of the room.

"Let me guess," Nikolai said when he saw her. "You just tried to talk to Alexi?"

"Shut up, Nikolai." Anya climbed the stairs to the main deck.

GRIGORY'S GADGET

Zoya slid her goggles to the top of her head. She wiped sweat from her brow and turned to follow Tonia out of the boiler room. The engines whirred as they slowed to idle.

Zoya stopped in her cabin to grab her coat and gloves before climbing the stairs to the main deck.

"I wonder where we are exactly," Lilia said as Zoya appeared. The *Ocean's Legend* was docked at a small town. It was filled with buildings made of brick and stone and had well-kept cobblestone streets. A heavy, wet snow fell, melting as soon as it touched the ground.

"I have no idea," Zoya replied.

Demyan turned to them, whispering. "Is this our chance? Is this where we, you know…" He looked around to make sure none of the pirates was within earshot.

"We should come up with a plan," Zoya said. "And quickly. Who knows when we'll get another chance, and if we're caught…"

"This looks like as good a town as any," Anya said. "It actually looks pretty well-to-do."

"This doesn't seem like a town that would welcome pirates," Zoya said, eying the crew.

"That's why we're not staying long," Pavel said, appearing next to them. "Nanowrinsk is a very prosperous town and treats pirates less kindly than towns farther into the Olen Sea. We need to find a place to sell as many of our goods as we can and stock up on supplies before we raise any serious suspicions."

Just then, Captain Sokoll stepped out of his cabin. He wore a splendid blue jacket with gold fringe and a matching captain's hat.

"If I didn't know any better," Anya said, "I'd say he looked like a real captain."

"Don't you say that to him," Pavel said. "He'll be quick to correct that he *is* a real captain."

Captain Sokoll barked orders to his crew, who then retrieved goods from below deck. When he approached the five friends, a big smile spread across his face.

"You five will help watch the ship! Guard it and help us load and unload throughout the day. Fyodr will secure the pilot house, so don't get any ideas of running off with my ship!" He let out a hearty laugh, and the five friends laughed along awkwardly. "Samuil and Ira will keep watch above deck. Alexi will also stay on the ship. He shouldn't bother you though. Seems he's decided to stay moping below deck."

"We have the worst luck," Lilia grumbled as the pirates disembarked.

"No, not the worst" Zoya said. "We just have to wait until the crew goes into town. As for Fyodr, Samuil, and Ira, I'm sure we can devise a distraction."

GRIGORY'S GADGET

Zoya gestured for her friends to follow her to their cabin. She rested on her hammock and grabbed the gadget.

"We'll wait and listen until they leave the ship," she said. "Then we can discuss a plan."

As the friends sat in silence, Zoya heard a series of soft thumps in the hallway. She tucked the gadget into her coat, glad her outerwear was already bulky. Alexi appeared in the doorway. He leaned on the frame, wincing.

"You want off this ship?" he asked.

Zoya glanced around at her friends. "W-what? No, of course not."

Alexi smirked. "You don't need to lie. You want to escape and I want to help you."

"We're not going to fall for that," Nikolai said. He turned to his friends. "It's a trap. He wants to get us in trouble so he can watch someone else get whipped."

"It was a mistake to bring you on this ship," Alexi said. "It was my fault, my poor judgment. So I want to help you escape. I'll distract Fyodr and the others."

"Why?" Anya asked. "Why was it a mistake?"

Alexi looked at Zoya. "You still have the gadget, that ball of gears? Keep it hidden, and safe. It's too much to explain right now, but I can't let my father take it. Now grab your things and prepare to run."

Alexi hobbled up to the main deck.

"Well, you heard him," Anya said. "Let's grab our things and go."

"I'm not going anywhere," Nikolai said. "This is definitely a trap."

"Nikolai, this is our chance," Zoya said. "This is the best we can hope for."

"It does seem a little too convenient," Demyan said.

"I'm going," Zoya said, lifting her suitcases. "I'm done dealing with pirates. Who's coming with me?"

"I am," Anya said.

"Me too." Lilia held her suitcases and stood by the door.

Demyan sighed and picked up his bags. "Fine, me too."

Nikolai threw his hands in the air and grabbed his things. "Don't be angry with me when I say I told you so."

"If you're right, we'll be dead," Anya said. "So it won't matter."

The five friends hurried up to the main deck. As they exited the saloon, they stopped dead in their tracks.

"Hello there," said a woman with short brown hair and a blue eye. A black patch covered her left eye. She held a knife to Alexi's throat. "It's a pleasure to meet you. My name is Snezhana Krupina, née Sokoll. I'm Alexi's beloved aunt." She patted her nephew on the shoulder.

GRIGORY'S GADGET

Four men flanked Snezhana. Two were tall and obscenely muscular; one had fiery red hair, the other black. The third man had a slight build emphasized by well-tailored clothes and wore brass spectacles. The fourth man was barely a man at all. He was young, eighteen years old at the most, and lanky.

At their feet lay the bloody bodies of Fyodr, Samuil, and Ira.

Zoya drew her sword. The four men drew pistols in response.

"Now, let's not make this messy," Snezhana cooed. "You'll all be coming with me on my ship, the *Hell's Jewel*. I think you'll find it's a much more impressive ship than my brother's." She gestured across the docks, to another sidewheel steamship that was notably larger than the *Ocean's Legend*. It had three masts and two smoke stacks, and the paddle wheels looked almost twice as large as the ones on Captain Sokoll's ship.

Not sure what other option they had, Zoya sheathed her sword. Her friends did the same.

"See? Nice and simple," Snezhana said. "And so nice of you to grab your things already! Boys, won't you lead our guests back to my ship? And relieve them of those pesky swords." She looked at Alexi. "I've missed you, nephew. We have so much catching up to do once you're on my ship."

Snezhana's men surrounded the group and held out their hands. Zoya and her friends handed over their swords. The tall muscular men grabbed suitcases, while the other two kept their pistols drawn. Snezhana lowered the knife from Alexi's throat and pushed him toward the other hostages. Then, they dutifully followed her onto the *Hell's Jewel*.

"Show them where they'll be staying, won't you?" Snezhana said once they were on board. Her crew brought them below deck and past the boiler room. They turned the corner and entered a cramped room which contained three cells, one on each wall, surrounded by iron bars.

"You're putting us in the brig?" Alexi asked, his face red.

"Captain's orders," said the bespectacled man.

"Gotfrid, come now," Alexi said. "My aunt shouldn't treat me like this." Gotfrid didn't respond, and simply pushed the friends into cells. Nikolai and Demyan were shoved to the left, Zoya, Anya, and Lilia to the right. Alexi was put into the center cell by himself. Without another word, Snezhana's crew left the room.

"I knew it was a trap," Nikolai said.

"Not one I set," Alexi replied. "Not one I saw coming."

Nikolai glared at him.

"Sorry about the accommodations," Snezhana said as she entered the room. "Space is tight, you understand."

GRIGORY'S GADGET

"What is this about, Snezhana?" Alexi demanded boldly. "Shouldn't we have a happy reunion? I thought you were—"

"Dead? Well, your father can't always get what he wants."

"No, he can't," Alexi said. "What is this, a lesson for him?"

"Of sorts," Snezhana said. "Now, Alexi, let's not be rude. You haven't introduced your friends to me."

"We're not his friends," Nikolai said. Demyan jabbed him in the ribs with his elbow.

"Careful," Demyan said, watching Snezhana out of the corner of his eye. Snezhana laughed.

"I see you still need to work on your people skills, Alexi," Snezhana said. She turned to Nikolai and Demyan. "What are your names, boys?" They introduced themselves curtly. Snezhana turned to the girls and posed the same question.

"Lilia."

"Anya."

"Zoya."

"That's some interesting hair you've got, Zoya," Snezhana said.

"I hear that a lot," Zoya said, raising an eyebrow.

"Runs in your family, I bet?" Snezhana asked. Zoya eyed her suspiciously.

"Yes," she said. "It does."

Snezhana looked back toward Alexi. "Very interesting."

"We'll speak again soon." She left, closing the door behind her.

"Gotfrid!" Snezhana called as she returned to the main deck of the *Hell's Jewel*. "Igor! Pyotr! Adam!" The four men marched to her side.

"We'll be setting sail for a new destination," Snezhana told her men. "A city we haven't dared venture to for a long while. A city especially dangerous for pirates. But the time has finally come. So, we'll need to find someone with more extensive and precise navigational knowledge. No offense, Igor."

"None taken, Captain," Igor replied. He had pale green eyes and red hair that matched his fiery personality. Since the true navigator of the *Hell's Jewel* perished in a battle with a Morozhian warship, Igor had taken over navigation. Snezhana's ship hence had gone in circles, as she learned Igor's eye for landmarks was not particularly keen.

"We need someone who can find a covert way into Mirgorod," Snezhana said. "I've spent plenty of time in jail and don't intend on returning."

"You want us to get you a new navigator?" Adam asked. He was as large as Igor. His slick black hair was showing signs of gray, and his eyes were small and narrow.

"Yes, quickly," Snezhana replied.

GRIGORY'S GADGET

"Aye, Captain," Gotfrid said with a small bow. The men walked toward the dock, then Pyotr turned around. He was the youngest of the four men, with light blond hair and sea green eyes.

"Captain, where *are* we going?" he asked. Snezhana smiled.

"We're going to Mirgorod."

Snezhana's crew strolled down the quaint streets of Nanowrinsk, reading the signs on each of the doors.

"Blacksmith. Jeweler. Cafe. Tailor."

"Pyotr," Adam growled. "Shut up." The boy blushed and looked down. Igor patted him on the back.

"Ah, here we go," Gotfrid said, stopping in front of a dark wooden door. "Cartographer."

"We need a navigator," Adam replied. "Not someone who makes carts." Gotfrid rolled his eyes and opened the door.

The shop was filled with maps and charts. Several wooden desks were covered in telescopes, astrolabes, and compasses. A huge globe sat in the center of the room with continents outlined in gold.

"All this will fetch a pretty penny," Igor said, looking around greedily.

"We are here for one specific purpose," Gotfrid replied. "We need to get our navigator and get out of here quickly and inconspicuously."

"Can I help you?" a man asked, entering the room from a back office. He had golden tan skin, and short, well-kept black hair. His mouth was framed by a neat mustache and goatee. Small, brass glasses balanced on his nose.

"I should hope so," Gotfrid said with a polite smile. "You see, our crew is hoping to get to Mirgorod. We haven't been out that way for a long while, so we are in need of a navigator."

"Ah, I'm sorry," the cartographer replied. "I don't do navigation work anymore. I've retired to cartography. I'm settling down, you see."

"You must have found a woman," Gotfrid said.

"Yes, I have. Oh, please excuse my manners. My name is Yeremiy Robertov. Now, there is a young man who works for me who has been itching to get on a ship. He's on a holiday right now, but will be back in two days' time."

"I'm afraid that won't work for us," Gotfrid said. "We're in a bit of a hurry." Adam and Igor stepped toward Yeremiy, smirking. Then they grabbed him by the arms and dragged him into his back office.

"Hey! What's this about?"

Gotfrid and Pyotr followed into the office, closing the door behind them. Adam and Igor held Yeremiy restrained against a wall filled with books.

"You can't just barge into my place of work like this!" Yeremiy shouted, struggling.

Gotfrid looked around the room, feigning confusion. "Oh, well, it seems we just did, didn't

GRIGORY'S GADGET

we?" Gotfrid took off his glasses and began cleaning them with a rag he pulled from his pocket. "Now, you can come with us willingly, or we can force you. It's your choice."

Yeremiy shoved his arms back, jabbing his elbows into Adam's and Igor's abdomens then ran to his desk. He picked up a letter opener and pointed it as if it were a dagger. The pirates pulled out their pistols.

"You won't shoot me," Yeremiy said. "You need me, for some reason, apparently. So you won't shoot me."

"Oh, quite the contrary," Gotfrid replied. "We only need you alive. I suppose you need your dominant arm. But what use are your legs, really?"

"You're bluffing," Yeremiy insisted, still pointing the letter opener. Adam shot a hole in the desk inches from where Yeremiy stood. Yeremiy jumped.

"The next shot will be in your right leg," Adam told him. Yeremiy dropped his faux dagger and lifted up his hands in surrender.

"Very good," Gotfrid said, stepping toward him. "Now, if you'll just come with us."

Yeremiy grabbed a potted plant from the floor and hurled it at the pirates. They stumbled back, coughing and momentarily blinded by flying dirt.

"After him!" Gotfrid shouted as Yeremiy ran out the door. The pirates ran back into the front room of the shop and looked around. The room appeared empty, and the front door was still closed. Gotfrid gestured toward the door, and Pyotr stood guard next to it.

"Up for a game of hide-and-seek, are we?" Igor shouted. "We know you're in here!"

"I think we got off on the wrong foot," Gotfrid said, walking around the edge of the room. "Why, we didn't even introduce ourselves! My name is Gotfrid. These are my crewmates, Adam, Igor, and Pyotr. We would be honored to have you as our new navigator."

Igor walked by a tall, intricately carved desk that stood in the far corner, and was about to peer underneath it when Yeremiy leapt out, wielding an astrolabe. He hit Igor over the head with the device, sending the pirate sprawling to the ground. Yeremiy then made a run for the door, but was intercepted by Adam. Pyotr ran over, and he and Adam tackled Yeremiy to the ground. Pyotr grabbed the astrolabe from Yeremiy's hands and knocked Yeremiy unconscious with it.

"Are you alright, Igor?" Pyotr asked.

Igor sat up, rubbing his head. "Yeah, great," he grumbled.

"Good. Now, let's bring our new friend back to the ship."

"Ok, what is going on?" Zoya demanded looking at Alexi. Alexi shrugged.

GRIGORY'S GADGET

"My aunt decided to kidnap us," he said. "She and my father have a complicated relationship."

"But what about me?" Zoya asked, her voice getting frantic. "Why did she seem interested in me? Why are you concerned about my grandmother's heirloom? You need to start explaining right now!" Lilia put her arms around Zoya.

"You have no idea what you're dealing with." Alexi laughed, shaking his head.

"So enlighten us!" Demyan said.

Anya walked over to the side of the cell and looked Alexi in the eye. "You need to stop lying," she said softly. "Whatever you were trying to hide from us, whatever you thought you were protecting, you need to let us in."

Alexi looked at Anya, silent, then nodded.

"Do you have the gadget?" he asked Zoya.

"Yes." Zoya glanced at the door, then pulled the gadget out of her coat. It was still wrapped in a shirt.

"Let me see it," Alexi said.

"Why?" Demyan asked.

"Because I need to see if it's really what I think it is," Alexi responded, annoyed.

Hesitantly, Zoya unwrapped the gadget and walked toward the side of her cell. Alexi reached toward it.

"No," Zoya said. "You can look at it, but I am not handing it over."

"Fine," Alexi replied, leaning down to look at the gadget. After a moment, he said, "It looks so insignificant. But that's it, alright."

"That's what?" Zoya asked. "What is it?"

"I don't remember what it's really called," Alexi said. "Usually it's just referred to as the gadget or the device. But both my father and my aunt have been hunting it for as long as I can remember. Supposedly it holds great power. Who knows if that's really true, but they seem pretty convinced. The amount of trouble this thing has caused…"

"How did your aunt know I have it?" Zoya asked.

"He told her, probably," Nikolai said. "This is all a setup, Zoya, don't be stupid. He just convinced you to take your gadget out. Now they know you have it, and they're going to take it from you."

"Shut up, Nikolai," Alexi said. "Zoya, put the gadget away. I'm not working with my aunt. I don't want anything to do with any of this."

"You didn't answer my question," Zoya said as she tucked the gadget into her jacket.

"It's your hair," Alexi said. "This gadget, whatever it is, is protected by the family of the man who created it. Apparently they all have purple hair." Zoya played with a lock of her curls.

"So then, your father knew who I was, too? But he didn't say anything?"

"He's got a hell of a poker face," Alexi replied, leaning back on the wall and sinking to the floor. Zoya and her friends sat in contemplative silence.

GRIGORY'S GADGET

"You catch more flies with honey than with vinegar," Anya said at last. "So we were right. It was strange that your father's crew was being so nice to us." She tilted her head and stared intently at Alexi. "It would have been helpful to know *why*."

"Really?" Alexi asked. "What would you have done so differently that would change the position we find ourselves in now?"

"I would have thrown the gadget overboard," Zoya said, fidgeting with her hands.

"And the moment my father found out, you'd be whipped, beaten, maybe killed," Alexi said. "Sure, we did actually need more crew, especially an engineer. But if you destroyed that piece of junk he's been searching for his entire life, you could kiss any semblance of kindness goodbye."

"So why didn't he just take it? He had plenty of opportunity to search our bags."

"He did search your bags," Alexi said. "He found the gadget, then put it back. My father enjoys manipulating people to get what he wants. He didn't want to take the gadget from you. He wanted to build your trust; he wanted you to offer the gadget to him."

"That's messed up," Nikolai said.

"You'll get no argument from me," Alexi replied.

Zoya sighed and let her head fall back against the wall, closing her eyes. The captives fell into a tense silence.

A few moments later, the door to the room swung open. Adam and Igor rushed in, holding on to a barely conscious, well-dressed man. Gotfrid and Pyotr followed behind them. They opened Demyan and Nikolai's cell and shoved the man in to join them. Without a word, they left.

Groaning, the newcomer pushed himself up and leaned back against the wall. His black hair was an absolute mess, and both lenses of his small brass spectacles were cracked. He groaned and held his head in his hands.

"Who are you?" Demyan asked. The man glanced around trying to piece together where he was.

"Am I in jail?" he asked slowly.

"You're in the brig of a pirate ship," Nikolai said.

"Pirates?" the man said. "Pirates! Oh, those bloody pirates!" He winced and raised a hand to his head. "They came into my shop, and they kidnapped me."

Zoya stood and walked to the front of her cell. "Why did they kidnap you?"

"They said they needed a navigator. I told them I don't do navigation work anymore. I'm just a cartographer. But they didn't care." Alexi stood up, looking alarmed.

"A navigator?" he asked. "Why? Where are they going that they need a navigator?"

"Mirgorod," the man replied.

Zoya gasped and looked at her friends with wide eyes. "Are you sure?" she asked him. "We're going to Mirgorod?"

GRIGORY'S GADGET

The man nodded. "I'm Yeremiy, by the way," he said. The others introduced themselves in turn.

Yeremiy looked curiously at Alexi. "Why are you in a cell by yourself?" he asked.

"Because he can't be trusted," Nikolai said. "Because he's a pirate, just like them."

"You know you're all pirates now, too?" Alexi said, folding his arms.

"Only because we were kidnapped," Nikolai replied angrily. "You kidnapped us! All of this is your fault. It's all on you."

"Nikolai, stop!" Anya shouted.

"No!" Nikolai shouted. "He says he wants nothing to do with the gadget? But he must have known when he first saw Zoya. He knew who she was; he knew she might have it. And he decided to kidnap us. He brought us on his father's ship. And now he's gotten us kidnapped by his aunt."

"Who's bringing us to Mirgorod," Zoya said.

"I feel a bit confused," Yeremiy said. "And I don't think it's the concussion I likely have. What is this gadget you're talking about?"

"It's nothing," Alexi said. "None of your concern."

Snezhana entered then, smiling widely.

"Yeremiy Robertov, is it?" she asked. "I'm Captain Snezhana Krupina. It's lovely to meet you."

"The feeling is not mutual," Yeremiy replied. "You need to return me to town at once. I have a shop to run, and a fiancée. I'm to be married this weekend!"

"Oh, my boys left a note. Your lovely fiancée will know that you've been employed for a bit. The wedding will have to be postponed, but you'll get back to her. If you cooperate, that is."

Yeremiy spit at Snezhana's feet.

"Everyone always wants to do things the hard way," Snezhana sighed. "Just as well, that's more fun." She pulled out her pistol and pointed it at Yeremiy.

"Stand up," she said. "Put your back against the bars with your hands together. We'll bring you up to our pilot house, so you can give us a heading." Yeremiy didn't move a muscle. Snezhana sighed in feigned annoyance, yet continued to smile.

"Very well," she said. She pulled the trigger, shooting Yeremiy in the kneecap. He screamed and fell to his side, his hand pressing against the wound.

"You're crazy!" he said.

"I suppose you may have trouble walking now," Snezhana said, ignoring Yeremiy's cries. "That's fine, my men will escort you up." On cue, Adam and Igor entered the room. They opened the cell and pulled Yeremiy to his feet. Then they dragged him out of the room, closing the door behind them. Before they did, Snezhana smiled at her other captives and winked.

The captives sat in stunned silence, all sitting on the floor in their cells.

GRIGORY'S GADGET

"I can't believe she just shot him," Lilia said.

"In the leg," Alexi replied. "He'll be fine."

"Could you possibly be more of an arrogant idiot?" Nikolai shouted at Alexi. "Oh, it's alright, she just broke his kneecap with a bullet. That just happens. That's life."

"Calm down," Alexi replied. Nikolai climbed to his feet, clenching his fists, but Demyan grabbed him and pulled him back to the floor.

"We're all going to die," Lilia said.

"No we're not," Anya replied. "We're going to be alright."

"How can you say that?" Lilia asked. "You certainly can't be basing that on the rest of our lives up to this point. We've all lost everything we ever wanted and everyone we've ever loved. The cave-in at the mines, the airship crash, the plague, *murder*. We always lose! And now we're going to die!"

"No we're not," Zoya said. "Lodninsk was the source of all the pain we've endured. That's where we lost our families. But we're free. We make our own luck now."

"Our luck has landed us in iron cells," Nikolai said. "On the ship of a crazy person."

"My aunt is not crazy," Alexi said. "Or at least, she wasn't the last time I saw her…"

"Oh, that's comforting," Anya said with a snort. "Thank you."

"We need to get out of here," Demyan said, glancing around.

"How?" Nikolai asked. "We're locked in here. We don't have any weapons."

Zoya sat up with a jolt.

"I do!" she said, grinning. She glanced at the door, then reached down to her boot. A moment later, she produced a small dagger.

"Where did you get that from?" Demyan asked.

"I lifted it when we were on the *Ocean's Legend*, as extra protection," Zoya said. "I completely forgot I had it tucked away in my boot."

"No offense, Zoya," Nikolai said, "but that little dagger isn't going to do much against pistols."

"No, but it should be small enough to pick these locks."

Zoya stood and began working on the lock of her cell.

"But what happens once we're out? They'll just throw us back in again," Anya said.

"I doubt they're even guarding this room right now," Zoya replied. "We're supposed to be locked in. They're probably busy trying to get Yeremiy to cooperate. Plus, most of the crew is probably still in town."

"That's a lot of assumptions," Alexi said. He sat on the floor of his cell and made no move to get up.

"Do you have a better plan?" Zoya asked.

"Yes," Alexi replied. "Sit down."

Zoya opened her cell door. Demyan and Nikolai stood and walked to the front of their cell.

"We're with you," Demyan said.

GRIGORY'S GADGET

Zoya unlocked their cell door as well.

"If you want to get shot," Alexi said as the friends headed toward the door, "you're going about it exactly the right way."

Zoya placed her ear against the door. She nodded to her friends and opened it.

Outside the door, Gotfrid sat at a small table, reading a book by lamplight.

"Did you think we'd actually leave you unguarded?" Gotfrid asked without looking up. He licked his finger and turned a page in his book.

"You're outnumbered," Nikolai said boldly, raising his fists.

"And yet you are the ones who are outmatched," Gotfrid replied. He closed his book and stood. Zoya pointed her dagger at him, her hand unwavering.

"Put that toy down," Gotfrid said, pulling out his pistol. "Make note of this: we always have a gun. At least one gun. Now, get back in your cells right now, and I won't tell the captain about your pathetic escape attempt."

Zoya, unable to admit defeat, lunged at Gotfrid and grabbed his gun. Gotfrid yelped and fell toward the wall. The pistol went off, blowing a hole in the small table. Zoya's friends rushed to join the ambush.

Just as the friends turned to run up the stairs, Pyotr, Adam, and Igor appeared with guns drawn.

"What's going on?" Adam asked.

"We've got a feisty bunch here," Gotfrid replied, straightening the glasses on his face and wrenching his pistol back from Zoya. "Thought they'd try to escape."

"Oh really?" Igor said, smirking wickedly. "Captain won't be pleased about that."

"Get back in your cells right now!" Pyotr demanded, his voice cracking.

"Move it!" Gotfrid yelled. The friends shuffled back into their cells.

"Shake out your coats," Gotfrid demanded. "We need to make sure you're not hiding anything else in them."

"Here!" Anya shouted, removing her coat and shoving it into the cell bars. She spread the coat as wide as she could, shielding Zoya from the pirates' view. "See, nothing in my coat!"

Zoya took advantage of the distraction. She shoved the gadget between her back and the wall then held up her coat.

Gotfrid and the other pirates, satisfied, left the room. They closed the door behind them and locked it.

"That was close," Zoya said after a few moments. Alexi laughed.

"I told you," he said. "But hey, I guess you didn't get shot. Yet."

CHAPTER SIX

"Crew!" Captain Edmund Sokoll shouted as he approached the *Ocean's Legend* on the docks. "Come down and give us a hand, will you?" The men with him carried crates full of food, coal, and fresh clothes.

When there was no response, Edmund yelled, "Fyodr! Ira! Samuil!" With a grumble, the captain stormed up the ramp to board his ship.

"No!" Edmund froze as he spotted the bodies of his crew. "Who did this? What bastard son of a—"

"Oh Eddie, quiet down," Snezhana told him. "You're not very good at being inconspicuous, are you?" She sat on the edge of the starboard paddlebox.

"You!" Captain Sokoll said angrily. "What are you doing here?"

"Now, is that any way to greet your sister? It's been so long, Eddie."

"What have you done? What are you up to?"

"So accusatory," Snezhana said. "Why do you assume I'm up to something?"

"Give me a reason to believe otherwise," Captain Sokoll growled.

"I simply wanted a nice reunion with my nephew," Snezhana said. "He's grown so much! And he's made some lovely friends, too."

"What have you done to them?" Edmund shouted, drawing his sword. "Enough with your games. Get to the point!" Edmund's crew drew their swords as well.

"You're still so old-fashioned," Snezhana said, standing. "Always going for the sword instead of the gun. You know I'd best you at both. Well, no need to worry about your son or his friends. They're safe and sound, on my ship."

"You kidnapped part of my crew?" Edmund asked. "You kidnapped my Alexi?"

"I've simply borrowed them, dear brother," Snezhana replied. "You'll get them back when I get what I want."

Edmund charged toward Snezhana, followed by Oleg and Olya. With a laugh, Snezhana leapt off the ship. She landed in a dinghy below. The *Hell's Jewel* had already sailed away from the dock.

"Sorry, Eddie!" Snezhana shouted as she rowed. "You've lost this round!"

Edmund sheathed his sword and grabbed his pistol. He shot at Snezhana and missed.

GRIGORY'S GADGET

"Tonia! Get those engines moving! Pavel, get in the pilot house, now! All hands on deck! Let's move!"

Zoya sat on the floor of her cell, holding the gadget in her hands. Absentmindedly, she continuously rotated it, her gaze fixed beyond the object.

"You should keep that hidden," Alexi said. "I'm sure my aunt or one of her crew will be back in here at some point." Zoya nodded and shoved the gadget into the pocket of her coat.

"So we're stuck in here until we get to Mirgorod," she said. She heard the engines of the *Hell's Jewel* whirring nearby. The ship had left the port of Nanowrinsk hours ago.

"I guess so," Demyan said.

The group sat in uncomfortable silence, standing, sitting, and lying down in turn. Every surface was cold and hard, though the constant chugging of the ship's engines was almost soothing. Alexi feel asleep, snoring softly.

After a few more hours passed, Adam and Igor burst into the room, followed by Gotfrid and Pyotr.

"Where is it?" Gotfrid asked.

"Where is what?" Zoya replied.

"You know what," Adam said, moving to stand in front of the cell.

Zoya looked up at him. "No, I don't."

"Stand up," Igor commanded. "All of you!" The captives did as they were told.

"Alexi," Gotfrid said, walking over to his cell. "I know that you know why you're here. We already searched their luggage. Where is the device?"

"Sorry." Alexi shrugged. "I'm afraid I'm as confused as they are."

"You're a wiseacre and a terrible liar," Gotfrid said. Alexi didn't respond.

"We can do this the easy way or the hard way," Adam said. "Tell us where it is."

Zoya stepped to the front of her cell. "Tell us *what* it is. A gadget, you say?" Adam lunged toward her, his arm reaching into the cell to grab her neck. Zoya stepped back quickly, just out of reach.

"Hey, leave her alone!" Demyan shouted.

"Don't be like Yeremiy," Gotfrid suggested. "We don't need anything from any of you except information. So tell us: where is the gadget?"

"That's pretty vague," Anya told him. Pyotr pointed his pistol at her, his hand wavering.

"Give us what we want!" he demanded.

"Whatever this gadget is," Lilia said. "We don't have it. We don't have a clue what you're talking about." Adam reached into the cell and grabbed Lilia's arm, pulling and slamming her into the bars. She shrieked. Gotfrid and Igor pointed their guns at Zoya and Anya.

"Now you listen," Adam growled into Lilia's ear. "We're being nice. This is your last chance, before

GRIGORY'S GADGET

you and your friends start losing body parts." He grabbed her by the hair and looked into her face. "You and I could have a lot of fun," he told her with a wicked grin. He grabbed the keys to her cell and began to open it.

"What do you think you're doing?" Snezhana demanded as she entered. Adam froze.

"We're interrogating them, Captain," he said, his voice shaking.

"And what interrogation tactic were you about to use?" Snezhana asked. Adam's face turned white.

"I was…nothing. Nothing, Captain," he stuttered.

"Nothing is right," Snezhana replied. "Unlock Alexi's cell and bring him to my cabin. I need to talk privately with my nephew."

"Aye, Captain," her men replied in unison.

Igor unlocked Alexi's cell then pulled him by the arm toward the door. As Adam passed by Snezhana, she pulled out her pistol and whacked him in the back of the head. Adam fell to the floor with a yelp.

"Get up," Snezhana said. Adam scurried to his feet and hurried out the door. The rest of the pirates left after him, closing and locking the door behind them.

Zoya lay on the ground, willing herself to sleep. She had lost track of how long it had been since they last saw Snezhana or her crew. Without a clock or a window, she found herself trapped in an eternally dingy twilight. One of the sconces on the wall had run out of oil, further dimming the room.

Zoya removed her jacket, bundling it into a ball to serve as a pillow. She turned on her side, her back to the door, and held the gadget in her hands. The device gave her an odd sense of comfort, despite being the apparent source of their troubles. *It's interesting, for sure, but what exactly is so special about it?*

Zoya hugged the gadget to her chest, remembering her grandmother's words. *Keep it safe. If you protect it, it will protect you. But what did that mean? At the very least, it means I should protect it from these pirates.* She let her eyes close, still hugging the gadget, and slowly drifted into sleep.

Zoya crept through the snow, doing her best to keep her footsteps silent. Large, fluffy snowflakes drifted down around her, gently building upon the already thick white coating of the stone scenery. Lilia crouched behind a low wall, trying not to be seen.

As Zoya rounded the corner of the alley, she saw Nikolai attempting to grab the bottom of a retractable ladder. When he saw her, he put his finger to his lips. Just then, Demyan appeared in the alley, standing between them. He looked at Zoya first. She backed away then directed Demyan toward Nikolai with a glance. Demyan followed her gaze, spotted Nikolai, and with a burst of energy began sprinting toward him.

GRIGORY'S GADGET

"Dangit, Zoya!" Nikolai yelled with a laugh. Demyan chased Nikolai to the end of the alley before tackling him into a snowbank.

Standing and pumping both fists into the air, Demyan declared, "You're it!"

Zoya awoke with a smile on her face, comforted by the happy memory. The low hum of machinery brought her only half-way to consciousness. Then the ship shuddered.

Zoya sat up, puzzled. Her friends, one by one, woke up with similar confusion. They heard gun shots above, as well as screams and shouts. Zoya slipped her coat back on, shoving the gadget back into its pocket.

"I guess we should get used to this sort of thing," Demyan grumbled, rubbing his eyes sleepily.

"Snezhana must be attacking a ship," Anya said.

"At least we don't have to fight this time," Lilia added.

They heard heavy feet clomping above, which became louder as they neared.

"Nevermind," Lilia mumbled.

The door burst open, and three figures appeared.

"Pavel!" Lilia shouted gleefully. Pavel, Olya, and Tonia stood triumphant in the doorway.

"We've come to break you out!" Pavel announced. Olya and Tonia strode toward the cells and worked to unlock them. Pavel turned to face the door, sword drawn.

"Hold it!" Igor shouted as he entered, waving his pistol. Gotfrid, Adam, and Pyotr were close behind. Pavel attacked Igor with his sword, moving so quickly he caught his enemy off guard and knocked his pistol to the ground.

Tonia and Olya opened the cells. Anya and Nikolai escaped first. Nikolai grabbed Igor's pistol, pointing it toward the group of pirates blocking the door.

Three more members of Snezhana's crew hustled in then, pushing the cell doors closed. The force knocked Zoya, Lilia, and Demyan to the floor.

"Go!" Pavel urged Anya and Nikolai as he, Olya, and Tonia fought. Anya ran to the bars of the girls' cell.

"Go!" Zoya agreed, shoving her bundle of fabric toward Anya. Anya took it, her face twisted in confusion. "Go!" Zoya insisted. Lilia and Demyan urged their friends to flee. Anya and Nikolai nodded quickly and sprinted out of the room.

Zoya reached through the bars of her cell and wrapped her arms around a pirate's throat. Olya drove her sword through the man's stomach, nodding thankfully at Zoya.

Tonia yelled as an enemy pirate sliced her arm with his sword. She pushed toward him, knocking him to the ground. Another pirate blocked Tonia's path before she finished the other.

GRIGORY'S GADGET

As Tonia and Olya held off Snezhana's crew, Pavel rushed back to the cells to try to get the doors open again.

"Pavel!" Lilia screamed as a warning, but it was too late. Adam lunged toward Pavel and drove his sword into Pavel's back then ripped it out brutally. Pavel fell to the ground, gasping.

The three captives screamed incoherently. Tonia and Olya, seeing that the odds were against them, rushed out of the room and back above deck. Snezhana's crew followed them, leaving Pavel's limp body in the middle of the room.

"Pavel," Lilia gasped between sobs. She reached toward his face then stopped about an inch away.

"Don't worry about me," he whispered. He coughed, producing a spatter of blood. After a few moments of labored breathing, he turned his gaze toward Zoya.

"Is it safe?" he asked her. Zoya furrowed her brow, the action forcing tears to stream down her face.

"Please," Pavel insisted. "Is it safe?"

"Why?" Zoya asked as a wave of confused anger washed over her. "That gadget? Why is it so important?"

"Your blessing and your curse," Pavel said. "Keep it safe. If you protect it, it will protect you." Zoya gasped, moving as close to Pavel as she could.

"What does that mean?" she asked. "Pavel, what is the gadget? What does it mean?"

Pavel drew a deep breath, his body shuddering. More blood spilled from his mouth, dripping down to join the pool forming on the floor. Lilia moved past Zoya, reaching toward Pavel through the bars of their cell. She put a hand on his shoulder, her eyes clouded by tears.

"It's alright, Pavel," she cooed. "I'm sure this is nothing compared to your battle with the Gibel crab." Pavel smiled, closing his eyes. He reached for his necklace then pulled it off and handed it to Lilia. For the first time, Lilia was able to properly see the shape of the pendant. The brass was formed into a sprig of heather.

"No," she said, "you need this." Pavel dropped the pendant, giving Lilia another smile. His breathing slowed, and a moment later his face went limp.

"Pavel," Lilia sobbed. Her hand tightened on his shoulder. "Pavel!"

Zoya pulled Lilia into a tight hug.

"Why him?" Lilia whispered, blinking away tears. "He was the only pirate who was truly kind to us. And he was murdered by that scum Adam."

"I know," Zoya said. "He deserved better."

Anya and Nikolai found that the main deck of Snezhana's ship was slick with rain. Wind howled and the sails billowed violently above. The crews of the *Ocean's Legend* and *Hell's Jewel* battled all around

GRIGORY'S GADGET

them. Some fought with bare hands, others with swords. A few pirates perched themselves above the main deck, shooting bullets into the fray.

"Run!" Alexi shouted to them from across the deck. He ran toward his father's ship, which had been tethered alongside Snezhana's. Anya and Nikolai rushed after him, slipping on the deck as they ran. One of Snezhana's crew shouted after them, but was intercepted by Oleg.

"Quick, below deck!" Alexi yelled when they were back on the *Ocean's Legend*. Anya and Nikolai did as they were told and ran down to their cabin.

"They'll be fine, right?" Anya asked as the two of them crouched by the door. Her body shook all over.

"Of course," Nikolai replied. "They'll be here any moment."

The two sat in silence and listened to the shouts and screams from above, partially drowned out by the pouring rain. After what felt like an eternity, the shouts and screams began to quiet until only the rain could be heard.

"Is it over?" Nikolai asked, peeking up the stairs. Anya followed him into the hall. "There, see? The others will probably come any second now." They waited silently by the stairs as the ship jerked into motion. Through the porthole, they could see that they were moving away from the *Hell's Jewel*. A moment later, Alexi came down the stairs. His face was sullen, his eyes distant.

"You can come back up," he said quietly.

"What's wrong?" Anya asked.

"Where are the others?" Nikolai added. Alexi said nothing and simply turned to go above deck. Anya and Nikolai looked at each other with worried expressions then followed Alexi upstairs.

Captain Sokoll's remaining crew stood on the main deck of the *Ocean's Legend*. Their numbers had decreased significantly; Anya wondered if there were enough pirates left to sail the ship. On top of that, each member of the crew seemed to be injured, from superficial cuts to bullet wounds. It was a sad sight to behold.

"Anya, Nikolai." Edmund greeted them solemnly as they appeared. "We are all very glad you've returned safely to us." The two of them glanced around, looking for their friends.

"We were not able to rescue Zoya, Lilia, or Demyan," Edmund continued. "Despite our best efforts."

"What does that mean?" Anya asked, stepping forward. "Are they alright? Are we going back for them?"

"Where's Pavel?" Nikolai asked, glancing around the deck. "He, Tonia, and Olya rescued us. They were going to rescue the others, too. I see Tonia and Olya, but where is Pavel?"

"Our dear Pavel gave his life, trying to save our crew," Edmund said. "He was a good man, brave and dutiful. May he rest in peace."

GRIGORY'S GADGET

Anya brought her hand to her mouth, tears beginning to well in her eyes. Nikolai looked at her, his mouth agape, then pulled her into a hug.

"And the others?" Anya said. "What about our friends?"

"Alive," Tonia said, standing near the captain. "But still locked in their cells on that foul woman's ship."

Anya let out a forceful sigh, leaning into Nikolai's hug.

"Oh, they're still alive," she said. "We'll get them back."

"Pavel would not want us to give up!" Edmund said, his voice bellowing through the falling rain. "Let him not die in vain! We must push forward, and finish our rescue mission to save our crew! For Pavel!"

"For Pavel!" the crew shouted back in unison.

The *Ocean's Legend* moved at top speed, chasing the *Hell's Jewel*. The crew worked as hard as they could, given their injuries. Captain Edmund told the crew to rest and recover, the better to battle Snezhana once more. They didn't seem to listen.

Anya worked up in the rigging, slick with the rain, helping the sails to best catch the heavy wind. Nikolai was below deck helping Tonia shovel coal in the boiler room.

As Anya tightened a rope above, she saw Alexi trudging across the main deck and into the captain's cabin. Curious, she climbed down the shrouds.

Before she could get near the cabin to eavesdrop, Captain Sokoll burst out with a wide grin on his face. Anya side-stepped, pretending she had been heading toward the bow.

"Good work, boy!" the captain was saying happily. Alexi followed him out of the cabin, looking notably less pleased than his father.

"Oleg!" Edmund shouted as he walked toward the pilot house. "Reduce our speed! Crew, take a breath. We can take a break from this foolish chase for now. Snezhana won't evade us for long."

Anya's face went red.

"What?" she said, crossing the deck toward the captain. "Why aren't we chasing them? She still has Zoya and Lilia and Demyan!"

"Aye, but she's got the faster ship," Edmund said. "It's a fool's errand to try to catch up to her now." He clasped Anya's shoulder. "Don't worry, we will get your friends back. We need to bide our time and come up with a plan." The captain then sauntered toward the saloon where he demanded a cup of ale.

Anya turned, confused, with tears in her eyes. She strode over to Alexi, who was still standing by the captain's cabin.

Before Anya could say anything, he grabbed her by the arm and led her across the deck. They climbed down the stairs, to Alexi's cabin. Alexi glanced up and down the empty hallway then closed the door.

"What's going on?" Anya demanded. "What did you say to your father? Why did he stop the chase?"

"I told him I have the gadget," Alexi said.

"You what?" Anya stared at Alexi for a moment, processing. "Why would that…"

"Now you see what kind of person my father really is," Alexi said. "He doesn't care about your friends, and he doesn't care about you. He hardly cares about me! All he cares about is that gadget."

"So you told him you have it," Anya said, processing. "Knowing full-well that he would abandon my friends and let them *die* on Snezhana's ship?"

"They won't die," Alexi said. "How long do you think it will take for my father to demand proof that the gadget is on this ship? As soon as he knows it's not in his possession, he'll resume the chase."

"Did you think through this plan at all?" Anya asked. "You lied to your father to make a point, and now what? He'll probably kill you, and your aunt will probably kill my friends!"

"I can't let him get the gadget. I need my aunt to get away, to keep the gadget away from him. She won't hurt your friends."

"Did she tell you that when you had your private chat?"

Alexi folded his arms. "Yes."

Anya groaned and brought her hands to her face. "Here's one of many holes in your plan you may not have considered: the gadget *is* on this ship." Anya reached into the hidden pocket in her coat and pulled out the gadget. Alexi grabbed it and shoved it back into Anya's coat, pushing Anya against the wall.

"Why do you have it?" Alexi asked, his face hardly an inch from Anya's.

"Zoya sneaked it to me when the crew rushed in to rescue us," Anya said. "We thought it would be safer away from your aunt, so Zoya wouldn't have to lie about not having it."

Alexi pushed Anya away, bringing his hands to his face and groaning.

"Oh, Anya, if Zoya doesn't have it, I don't know what my aunt will do." He turned to face her again.

"You said she wouldn't hurt them."

"If they had they gadget, if they cooperated. That was the deal." Alexi placed his hands on Anya's shoulders. "You do not have the gadget. You don't have it. You keep it hidden. You do not mention it, not to anyone!" Anya nodded. Alexi turned to open the door.

"What will your father do to you?" Anya asked. "When he finds out you don't have it?" Alexi closed the door again and sighed.

"All you need to worry about is that he *will* continue chasing Snezhana. Don't worry about me."

GRIGORY'S GADGET

It didn't take long after the battle between Edmund's and Snezhana's crews for Pavel's body to be removed from the brig. His blood still soaked the floor in the center of the room. Zoya, Lilia, and Demyan sat as far from it as they could, their backs against the back walls. For hours, they sat in mourning. Aside from the pirates who took Pavel's body, none of Snezhana's crew disturbed them.

Zoya sat, almost catatonic, as Lilia sobbed beside her. In time, Lilia's sobbing turned to silent weeping and eventually to silence as she passed out from exhaustion. *I hope she's dreaming of something more pleasant.*

"Zoya," Demyan said, breaking the silence with his hoarse voice. Zoya looked over at him. "Why did you take sword lessons?" Zoya inched toward the front of her cell, eying the blood-stained floor.

"What do you mean, why?" she asked.

"I mean, what compelled you to do that? What made you think you'd need to learn to fight with a sword?"

"You know what Lodninsk was like," Zoya replied. "After what happened to my mother, especially."

"So you were just going to start carrying a sword around?" Demyan asked. "How quickly do you think you'd be arrested for something like that?"

"We didn't just learn how to fight with a sword," Zoya said, feeling somewhat annoyed. "Isaak taught us how to fight in general, how to defend ourselves."

"That's still dangerous," Demyan said.

"Don't you think I know that? The soldiers murdered Isaak and his family. I know that, I was there." Zoya could feel her face flush with anger.

"And it easily could have been you," Demyan said. He blinked back the moisture building in his eyes. "You need to think these things through, Zoya. You need to be careful. Bravery sounds noble, but it isn't a good thing. Look what it did to Pavel."

Zoya sat back, staring at Demyan, and let out a small laugh.

"Bravery isn't a good thing?" she asked. "What is a good thing? Silently shuffling through the day, being pushed around by soldiers, watching our families killed off one by one while we sit powerless? That's what we're trying to escape, Demyan. What exactly do you think we're looking for?"

"Safety," Demyan said. "Safety and stability and comfort."

"Well, sometimes it takes bravery to get there." Zoya inched her way back toward the wall. "Don't be naive." Zoya folded her arms and turned away from Demyan. Her head was pounding, her stomach fluttering uneasily.

They sat in silence once more. Time crawled by, or sped by. There was no way of knowing. Lilia awoke from the refuge of sleep and sat quietly staring at the drying blood on the floor. Finally, the door opened. Gotfrid and Pyotr entered, their pistols already drawn.

"Haven't we had enough excitement for now?" Demyan said.

"I'm afraid we need a favor," Gotfrid replied.

"We don't owe you any favors," Zoya said.

"Let me rephrase: we've got a job for you, and you can either comply or lose the use of your left leg." Gotfrid pointed his pistol at Zoya's kneecap.

"What do you want?" Demyan asked.

"Our newest crew member isn't being cooperative," Gotfrid said. "Shooting him didn't seem to work, and we simply don't have time to torture cooperation out of him. So, the captain thinks the three of you will find a way, since you're so crafty." Gotfrid's last few words were riddled with sarcasm.

"Stand up," Pyotr said, waving his gun from Demyan to Lilia to Zoya. Zoya and Demyan obeyed, but Lilia stayed seated on the ground, staring blankly into the distance.

"I said stand up," Pyotr repeated. Zoya crouched down beside Lilia.

"Lilia," she whispered. "Come on, get up." She lightly touched Lilia's shoulder. Her eyes seemed to come back into focus, then peered up at Zoya. Without a word, Lilia allowed Zoya to pull her to her feet.

Gotfrid and Pyotr unlocked their cells.

"Don't try anything," Pyotr said. "Like you said, you've had enough excitement."

The pirates led their captives up to the main deck. The wind howled through the sails, blowing sheets of driving rain. Zoya turned toward the stern of the ship and spotted the *Ocean's Legend* off in the distance. She stopped dead in her tracks.

"They aren't following us," she said. "They're going the other way." Demyan and Lilia followed Zoya's gaze.

"Edmund may not be the brightest," Gotfrid said, "but he knows when he's been defeated." He looked at the captives with false condolence. "Sorry, no one's coming to rescue you. Now move."

Gotfrid and Pyotr shoved the three of them forward, toward the pilot house.

The interior of the *Hell's Jewel*'s pilot house was much more elaborate than that of the *Ocean's Legend*. The walls were all dark wood, with spiraling, gilded crown molding. A large desk dominated the back of the room, opposite the wheel. There Yeremiy sat, hunched over with his head laying on a stack of maps and charts. Where he had been shot by Snezhana, his pant leg had been cut off. Bandages had been wrapped tightly around his knee.

"Just take me back to Nanowrinsk," he groaned as the group entered the room. "Take me back or kill me. I will not work for pirates." He lifted his head and, when he saw the other captives, sat straight in his chair.

GRIGORY'S GADGET

"Now what?" he asked.

"I thought you might like some company," Gotfrid said, pushing Zoya, Lilia, and Demyan farther into the room. Pyotr left, closing the door of the pilot house behind him. Gotfrid crossed the room to take up the wheel.

"Where are the others?" Yeremiy asked.

"They were rescued," Demyan replied. "That's why the other ship attacked, to rescue us."

"Some of us," Lilia added, watching the rain out the window.

"Is that what all the commotion was?" Yeremiy asked. "I suppose I was a bit preoccupied, having a bullet removed from my kneecap."

"Did you fix that up yourself?" Zoya asked him.

"No," Yeremiy replied, glancing down at his wounded leg. "Apparently there's a quite good doctor on this pirate ship. They probably kidnapped him too."

"Not everyone is on a pirate ship because they've been kidnapped," Lilia said. She held Pavel's charm in her hand, playing idly with its chain.

"No," Yeremiy agreed. "Some people are just immoral." Lilia took a step toward Yeremiy, but stopped as Zoya grabbed her wrist. Zoya pulled her back, mouthing the word *no*. Gotfrid chuckled from where he stood.

"So, what's your plan?" Zoya asked after an awkward silence. "Are you just going to sit here until the pirates get frustrated and kill you?"

"If that's how it has to be," Yeremiy replied. "As I said when you walked in, I am either returned home or killed. I will not lead these pirates to Mirgorod, or anywhere else."

"We told you, navigator," Gotfrid said, "we can find Mirgorod. The problem is that we'd be arrested as soon as we entered its port. If you don't find a covert way into the city, you'll be arrested as well."

Yeremiy folded his arms.

"Do it for us," Demyan said. He walked over to the desk and sat on its edge. "We're not pirates. We're captives just like you. We were on our way to Mirgorod when we were kidnapped."

"I'm sorry to hear that, but I'm afraid that's not my problem. Mirgorod is thousands of miles away from my home. I'm not going to travel that far, against my will, just because some kids had some rotten luck."

"Now who's immoral?" Lilia asked. She walked toward him, standing next to Demyan. "You're just selfish and a coward. We just lost a friend who was ten times the man you are. And he was a pirate. So get off your high horse and stop ignoring reality. You're on this pirate ship whether you like it or not. So, you can waste your time, waste your life, and wither and die in here. Or, you can do something good. You can do something useful. Help us." Lilia's friends all exchanged surprised glances. Yeremiy was stunned silent.

"Our best chance of surviving this," Zoya said after a moment, "is if we work together. We need to help each other. If you help us get to Mirgorod, we'll escape this ship, and we'll help you get back home."

"That's really your only way," Demyan said. Yeremiy leaned back, wincing as he moved his injured leg. He cast his eyes briefly toward Gotfrid then let out a sigh.

"Fine," he said. He looked at the three friends. "You make a good point. But I will hold you to your word."

"We keep our word," Zoya told him. "We'll make sure you get back home, somehow."

"Somehow," Yeremiy replied. He looked once again toward Gotfrid, who was smiling back at him. Yeremiy clenched and unclenched his fists. "Right."

Snezhana stood at her desk in her cabin, a cup of rum in her hand. It shook in her hand. She took a deep breath then took a sip.

"Captain," Gotfrid said as he entered the room. "The navigator has decided to cooperate." Snezhana smiled at him and took another sip.

"Excellent," she said. "That was good thinking on your part." Gotfrid stared at Snezhana for a moment then gazed out the window. Lightning streaked across the sky, briefly illuminating the ocean speckled by heavy rain.

"It was a shot in the dark. I'm happy you trusted me enough to try, Captain." he said.

"Some people are moved more by compassion than by threats," Snezhana said. "With all his self-righteous accusations and whining about his fiancée, I thought I might give compassion a try."

"It hardly seems to be your usual style," Gotfrid said.

"My usual style almost got me killed in Lodninsk," she replied. "I've told you that story. Sometimes you need to try something different."

"Very good, Captain."

"Go," Snezhana said. "Get a heading from our newly-cooperative navigator. Time is of the essence."

Gotfrid nodded and left the room.

Snezhana put her cup on the desk and sighed contentedly. She reached for the wireless telegraph perched in the corner and turned the dial. At first, the only sounds were crackling and fizzing.

Damn this storm. Just as she was about to turn the volume back down, a series of beeps came through. Snezhana scribbled dots and dashes onto a piece of parchment and decoded them.

Three major battles between Morozhia and Starzapad. Morozhia claimed victory in two battles but lost more soldiers. Will Vernulaia join the war?

Snezhana growled in spite of herself. That was the last thing she needed.

"Don't worry, Boris," she said. "I'm on my way."

Snezhana turned the device off, stood, and walked out of her cabin into the pouring rain. She trudged below deck where Adam scrubbed vigorously at the floor.

"Am I dismissed, Captain?" he asked shyly. Snezhana tilted her head then poured her rum onto the floor next to him.

"You missed a spot," she said. The man resumed scrubbing, shaking his head.

"Captain, forgive me," he said. "I know the one with purple hair is special, but—"

"We need her alive, and we need her to cooperate," Snezhana said. "If you hurt her friends, she won't cooperate. And she seems rash. She'd probably do something stupid that would get her killed."

Snezhana kicked Adam in the gut. He collapsed on the ground and gasped.

"I do not tolerate insubordination. I will blame this incident on your pure ignorance. Do not disappoint me again."

CHAPTER SEVEN

The next morning Anya lay in her hammock, hugging her coat. She kept it on, with the gadget tucked within, even though it was far too warm for such a heavy coat. They had to be pretty far south now, and Anya wondered how far they were from Mirgorod.

She hadn't noticed when Nikolai got up to get breakfast, but as she lay there, Nikolai rushed in.

"Why aren't we chasing them anymore?" he demanded, out of breath. Anya didn't respond.

"Anya," Nikolai pressed. "The captain stopped the chase. We're slowing down. Snezhana is getting away!"

"I know," Anya replied softly. She looked up and out of the doorway, checking that no one was nearby. Then she looked at Nikolai.

"He thinks Alexi has the gadget," Anya whispered.

GRIGORY'S GADGET

"Why would he—" Nikolai started, sitting on his cot. "So he just—"

"He doesn't care about us," Anya said. "He doesn't care about our friends. He just wants the gadget."

"When did Alexi even get the gadget?" Nikolai asked. "Why would Zoya give it to him?"

"She didn't," Anya replied. "He lied. He doesn't have it." Nikolai punched one of the crates in the room.

"I knew it! I knew he was working with his aunt! Now she has Zoya and the gadget, and they're getting away!"

Nikolai rose to his feet and stomped out of the cabin, heading above deck.

"Nikolai!" Anya stood. "Where are you going?" She glanced around the room, removing her coat and bundling it into a ball. She lifted the lid of one of the crates and buried the coat inside. Then she followed Nikolai to the main deck.

When she got there, she saw Edmund with his hands wrapped around Alexi's throat, shoving him into the smokestack.

"You treacherous brat!" he snarled. Alexi's face turned bright red. His hands clawed at his father's.

Edmund threw his son to the rain-drenched deck. Alexi inhaled with a loud, raspy breath as his face began to return to its normal color. He stayed down, coughing, staring only at the wood beneath him.

"Crew!" Edmund announced. "Alexi is not to eat a single piece of food nor drink a drop of ale or anything else until I give further notice!" He used his foot to turn Alexi over on to his back then pressed into Alexi's chest with his heel.

"If any one of you tries to sneak him a morsel," Edmund continued, "I'll dump you into the ocean!"

Edmund stormed into the pilot house, slamming the door behind him.

"That's what he gets for lying," Nikolai muttered as he began to head below deck. Anya grabbed him by the arm.

"I'm getting really sick of this attitude," she said. "Alexi is on our side. What does he have to do to prove that?" Nikolai ripped his arm out of her grip.

"Get your head out of the clouds, Anya," he spat. "I don't know why you've grown so fond of him, but he's using you." In a huff, Nikolai continued below deck.

The *Ocean's Legend* had turned around, and the crew brought her back up to full speed to resume their pursuit of the *Hell's Jewel*. Nikolai and Anya, in Pavel's absence, prepared breakfast. They ate their meals in silence, each overcome by how much, and yet how little, they wanted to say. After they finished cleaning up the saloon, Nikolai went to help in the boiler room.

GRIGORY'S GADGET

The monotonous work of shoveling coal into the furnace helped to keep Nikolai calm. *Scoop and toss. Scoop and toss. Scoop and toss.* He lost track of time and became lost in the repetitive motion. Eventually, Tonia clapped him on the shoulder and told him his shift was over. He nodded, breathing heavily, his lungs raw from soot. Then he left the boiler room.

He sat alone in the cabin, lying on the cot and staring at the ceiling. Briefly, he pondered where Anya was. In frustration, he pushed the thought from his mind. His stomach growled.

Nikolai sat up. He hadn't eaten since breakfast, and the sun was already setting. Did the crew already have dinner? Had he missed it? Or had dinner not happened yet? He climbed the stairs to the saloon.

When he got there, the room was empty. Nikolai searched through the cabinets and cupboards. They were filled with new, yet still stale, loaves of bread and salted meats.

At least in Lodninsk we had eggs and potatoes.

As Nikolai was about to close one cupboard, he noticed another door within it. Pushing aside a few packages of meat, he opened the door and gasped. Hidden in the secret space were lemons and limes, rice, rum, and seasoned jerky. Nikolai glanced around the room and, after seeing that no one was around, grabbed a lime. It had been too long since he'd had any fruit. Lodninsk usually received only one shipment of fruit in the entire year, and most citizens' rations did not include any of it. It was generally brought to the heads of government and, if there was enough, to the high-ranking military officers. Every once in a while, a handful of fruit would be delivered to the orphanage as a display of the government's charity and empathy.

Nikolai grabbed a knife and cut the lime into quarters. With a satisfied sigh, he sank down the floor, sucking on the tart morsels. After he finished, he grabbed another one, as well as some jerky.

"What are you doing?" Startled, Nikolai turned to see Alexi standing behind him with crossed arms.

"I was hungry," Nikolai said.

"That's the captain's food," Alexi said. "And this isn't the best time to make him mad." Nikolai felt his face flush.

"I didn't know!" he said. "Why should the captain get all this good food, when we're stuck with stale, bland crap?"

"Because he's the captain," Alexi replied.

"What's going on?" Edmund's voice boomed. "Alexi, didn't I make myself clear?" When he saw Nikolai, his face turned bright red. "Are you sneaking food to Alexi? My food, no less?" Nikolai was stunned speechless, staring desperately between Alexi and Edmund. He dropped the knife and food.

"No," Alexi said, turning to face his father. "He wasn't stealing the food, he was putting it back. I stole it." Edmund grabbed Alexi's shirt collar and thrust him into the nearest table.

"Do you have a death wish, boy? I told you you're not to eat until I say so!"

"It was a moment of weakness, Captain," Alexi said. "I was angry and hungry. It won't happen again."

"You're damn right it won't," Edmund said. He grabbed his son by the hair and pulled him close. "I have a mind to maroon you, boy. You better hope my anger subsides by the time we take back—" Edmund stopped, glancing at Nikolai.

"By the time we rescue my crew," he finished. He slammed Alexi's head into the table, then walked out of the saloon.

Alexi stood still at the table for a moment, hunched over and breathing heavily. Nikolai stared at him, eyes wide.

"Why did you lie?" he asked.

Alexi pulled out a chair and sat, holding his head in his hands. "Because he would have killed you."

"He didn't kill you," Nikolai said.

Alexi gave a forced laugh. "He will have me whipped. He will deny me food. He will overwork me, beat me. But he won't kill me. I'm his son."

Nikolai thought for a moment. "If I were allowed to I'd pour you a tall glass of ale right now." Alexi chuckled. Nikolai smiled slightly then nodded and returned to his cabin.

When Nikolai trudged into the cabin, Anya lay on her hammock, mending a hole in one of her shirts.

"What did you do?" Nikolai asked. "Did that happen when you were up in the rigging?" Anya didn't respond and kept sewing her shirt. Nikolai sat down on his cot and stared at her.

"What, you're not talking to me?" he asked.

"I don't have anything to say," Anya replied. Nikolai groaned and leaned back on the cot.

"Don't make me say it," he whined.

Anya stopped her sewing and looked up. "Say what?"

Nikolai lay down on the cot and stared up at the ceiling. "You were right."

Anya smirked. "About what? You'll have to narrow it down."

Nikolai let out a sputtered laugh. Then he turned to face Anya.

"You were right about Alexi. I think, anyway. He's either on our side or he's crazy."

Anya put down her sewing project. "What made you change your mind?"

Nikolai grimaced. "I, sort of, maybe, inadvertently stole some of the captain's private stash of food."

Anya looked at Nikolai with a deadpan expression.

"You did what?"

"I didn't know!" Nikolai said. "It wasn't labeled! It *was* sort of hidden, I guess..." Anya sighed and shook her head.

GRIGORY'S GADGET

"So, what," Anya said. "Alexi saw you and didn't tell on you?" Nikolai bit his lip.

"That's sort of what happened," he said. "Not all of what happened." Anya stared silently at Nikolai, waiting for him to explain.

"Alexi caught me, and then a second later, the captain walked in," Nikolai said. "And Alexi took the blame. He said I was putting the food back, that he was the one who stole it." Anya punched Nikolai in the arm.

"Ow!" he yelped. Anya punched him again then started smacking him frantically.

"Why would you do that?" she demanded.

Nikolai stood and backed away, shielding himself with his arms. "Stop! Stop! What was I supposed to do?"

"What's the captain going to do to him now?" Anya asked, sitting back onto her hammock.

"Nothing, I guess," Nikolai replied. "Nothing more anyway. For now." Anya groaned and hung her head in her hands.

"Where is he?" she asked after a moment.

"He was still in the saloon when I left," Nikolai replied. Without another word, Anya ran above deck.

Sure enough, when Anya entered the saloon, Alexi was still there. He was slumped over with his head resting on the table, staring out the windows.

"Nikolai told me what you did," she said softly, pulling up a chair next to Alexi. "Thank you." Alexi sat up slowly and looked at her.

"I couldn't stand by and watch your friend get beaten or thrown into the sea," he said.

"Well, you've won him over," Anya said with a weak smile. Her smile quickly faded as she asked, "Are you going to be ok?" Alexi nodded.

"Once we get Zoya, Demyan, and Lilia back, he'll calm down," he replied.

"Because of the gadget."

Alexi's eyes glanced around the room before fixing on Anya's. "Which is not currently on this ship," he said.

Anya leaned back, staring out of the window. "But if having it on this ship would calm him down—"

"Absolutely not." He leaned in and lowered his voice to a whisper. "He will abandon your friends. Do not give him what he wants; it only makes him more dangerous."

Anya tilted her head. "So what's your plan?" she asked. "We're going to rescue them. Isn't that giving him what he wants, too?"

"That's what he thinks," Alexi replied. He clenched his fists. Anya gently placed her hands over his.

"There's a plan," he said. "I can't say more than that. Just know there's a plan."

"Ok." Anya sighed.

"Anyway," Alexi said after a moment. "I'm going to go relieve Oleg of his duties in the pilot house."

"I'll come with you," Anya said. "You need the company."

Alexi laughed. "Alright, I won't argue."

Lilia and Demyan had fallen asleep in the pilot house, propped against the wall as they sat on the floor. Demyan's head dropped to the side, resting on Zoya's shoulder. Zoya leaned her head on his, her gaze transfixed on the rear window. She eyed the lights of the *Ocean's Legend*, which was still visible through the sheets of rain. In the darkness, she couldn't discern if it was getting farther away or closer. Igor had relieved Gotfrid from the wheel, and Yeremiy was busy scribbling on a piece of parchment.

"Hello," Pyotr said cheerily as he entered with a metal tray. He paused once he entered, wiping away his polite smile and replacing it with an intentional frown.

"Captain wants you to eat," he said flatly. Zoya woke her friends, and the three of them rushed over to Pyotr. The food was the usual: stale bread and salted meat. But they were so hungry it tasted like a feast.

Pyotr placed a plate next to Yeremiy. The navigator hardly acknowledged it, other than to move it out of his way as he wrote.

"Writing a letter?" Pyotr asked. "We don't get postal service out here." He chuckled.

"Mr. Robertov," Snezhana said as she entered the pilot house. "Thank you very much for cooperating. Gotfrid tells me you're ready to give us a heading." Yeremiy turned around and nodded silently.

"Good," Snezhana said. "Igor will stay at the wheel for the next few hours, you're to direct him. As for you three ..." Snezhana turned to face Zoya, Lilia, and Demyan. "Follow me."

"Where are we going?" Lilia asked.

"Back to your cells," Snezhana replied.

"What?" Demyan asked. "Why?"

"We let you out to play, you did what you were supposed to do, and now it's back to your cages."

With no option but to obey, the friends sullenly followed Snezhana and Pyotr. Gotfrid waited for them when they returned. This time, the friends were directed to enter separate cells, with Zoya in the center.

"What exactly do you want from us?" Zoya asked as Gotfrid locked the cell doors. Snezhana smiled.

"You know exactly what I want," she replied. Zoya crossed her arms.

"Maybe I do," she said. "Maybe I don't. Either way, why keep us alive and locked up? Why not just take it?" Both Lilia and Demyan glared at her.

"You really know nothing about the device, do you?" Snezhana asked, leaning in toward Zoya's cell. "That's a shame. Regardless, I need you alive. Your

GRIGORY'S GADGET

friends, however, are certainly expendable. Consider their presence here a kindness, and one that can easily be revoked." With that, Snezhana left with Pyotr and Gotfrid.

Zoya paced her cell, running her fingers across its bars.

"It's because the gadget is protecting you, right?" Lilia said after a few minutes. Her face was streaked with tears. "That's what Pavel told you, protect it and it will protect you?"

"Maybe," Zoya replied, unconvinced.

"Well, maybe," Lilia went on, "if she tried to take it forcefully, it would hurt her in some way? Maybe it's magical?"

"Maybe," Zoya said again. She continued pacing. When she walked to the side of her cell adjoining Demyan's, he reached out and grabbed her arm.

"Stop," he said, holding her to prevent her from walking away. "What are you thinking?" Zoya took a deep breath and let it out in a huff.

"I'm thinking I don't have it," she said.

"You don't have it? The gadget?" Lilia asked. "What? Where is it?"

Zoya wrestled her arm away from Demyan and continued pacing.

"I gave it to Anya when she escaped. I thought it would be safer on our ship." Zoya stopped in her tracks, furrowing her brow. "On *Captain Sokoll's* ship." Lilia slid to the floor, her gaze distant.

"But now it's hopeless," she said. "If Snezhana or any of her crew finds out you don't have it, who knows what they'll do to us? Kill us, probably."

"Maybe," Zoya replied.

Zoya continued her pacing. Lilia and Demyan watched her silently and eventually were overcome with exhaustion. It wasn't until both of them were snoring that Zoya finally stopped to rest.

The next morning, Igor and Pyotr walked in with stale bread and ale. Zoya was barely awake, her eyelids heavy. Her bones and muscles ached all over from the days spent locked in the cells.

"I want to speak to your captain," Zoya croaked as Igor and Pyotr slid food into their cells. The pirates didn't acknowledge her, walking out of the room in silence.

Zoya grabbed her food and devoured it. She stood and resumed her pacing. As she did, she rolled her neck and stretched her arms.

"What are you doing?" Lilia asked.

"I can't stand it in here," Zoya replied. "I can't take this any longer."

"I don't think we have a choice," Demyan said.

Zoya grabbed the bars of her cell, using them as leverage to stretch her legs.

"Mirgorod is still hundreds, if not thousands, of miles away," Zoya groaned. "I can't stay locked up like this for that much longer!"

"Again," Demyan said. "We don't have a choice."

GRIGORY'S GADGET

"Of course we do," Zoya said. She began to pace again. Demyan shot a worried glance at Lilia.

For dinner, Adam walked down with more stale bread and ale, along with some salted meat.

"I want to speak to your captain," Zoya demanded again. Adam, just like Igor and Pyotr, ignored her and left without a word.

Zoya tossed and turned on the floor all night, dozing in and out of a sleep filled with nightmares. She awoke to the sound of Gotfrid bringing them breakfast. As he placed the food in front of her cell, Zoya grabbed his arm tight.

"I need to speak with your captain," Zoya growled at him. Gotfrid rolled his eyes.

"And why is that?" he asked.

"Because I don't have the gadget anymore," Zoya replied. "Her brother has it now." Gotfrid's eyes went wide as he wrestled his arm away.

"How and when did that happen?" he demanded.

"When our friends escaped, I gave it to them," Zoya said. She smiled in spite of herself. This should get her out of this cell.

Gotfrid covered his mouth and looked away. Then, without a word, he left.

"Hey!" Zoya shouted after him.

"What are you thinking?" Demyan asked. "They'll kill us now! What's wrong with you?"

"Zoya," Lilia said. "Please tell us you have some sort of plan."

"She'll have to turn around now," Zoya said. "She'll have to battle the captain again, to try to get the gadget. And they'll come down and rescue us like they tried to last time."

"Pavel died last time," Lilia said. "And we weren't rescued last time!"

"And you're assuming they won't kill us before this supposed battle," Demyan said.

"No," Zoya said. "Because we could be a trade, right? Or maybe not a trade, but hostages? As long as we're prisoners on this ship, the captain won't blow it to pieces."

"We're dead," Lilia sighed.

Hours passed after Gotfrid left, and Zoya began to worry that he didn't believe she was telling the truth. Then, just as she was beginning to lose hope, Snezhana burst into the room.

"Unlock them all," she said to her men. Zoya and her friends were pulled from their cells and dragged up above deck.

The sky was dark, and a heavy rain still fell, soaking the deck of the ship. Lightning flashed in the distance.

Snezhana grabbed Zoya by the back of her neck and shoved her toward the stern of the ship. The *Ocean's Legend* was following them, and appeared to be gaining.

"If my brother has the device," Snezhana said, "why is he still chasing us?"

GRIGORY'S GADGET

"Because we're his crew," Zoya replied, a smile forming on her lips.

"You don't know my brother very well," Snezhana told her. "Or you're lying."

Zoya ripped off her coat, which had become too warm as it was, and threw it onto the wet deck.

"Search it," Zoya said, spreading her arms. "It's not in my coat, and I don't have any pockets big enough for it."

"Well, here's an idea," Snezhana said, grabbing Zoya by the arm. "As a fun game, I'll tie you and your friends to my masts. And for every bit of damage done to my ship or my crew, we'll take something from you. Fingers, toes? Hands, arms? I suppose it depends on the tide of battle." Zoya twisted out of Snezhana's grip and ran.

"Just where do you think you'll run to?" Snezhana mocked, making no move to stop her.

Zoya ran to the starboard side of the ship, skidding on the wet deck. The *Ocean's Legend* was closer, much closer, than before. She glanced down at the water, her mind working in a furious blur.

No, she thought, *that's a horrible idea.*

In an instant, Zoya was surrounded by Snezhana's crew. She could see Lilia and Demyan had been cornered as well, also against the side of the ship.

"Nowhere to run," Adam said, moving toward her. Zoya jumped onto the railing of the ship, then leapt to the paddlebox. Her feet slid on the wet surface, but she managed to keep her balance. She turned back to the pirates, who were laughing.

"Somewhere to swim!" she shouted. Before she could stop herself, Zoya propelled off the paddlebox and into the dark ocean below.

"Zoya!" Demyan cried out.

Before Zoya hit the water, she heard Lilia cry, "Demyan, no!"

Zoya hit the cold water hard. She flailed underwater for a moment, weighed down by and twisted in her clothing. Then she bobbed to the surface, sputtering for air. She heard a splash far to her right as the *Hell's Jewel* moved past her. A moment later, there was another splash.

Demyan and Lilia struggled to the surface of the choppy ocean, gasping for breath. Zoya began swimming toward them, and they swam toward her.

"This was a stupid idea," Lilia shouted to Zoya once she was within earshot.

"I know," Zoya replied.

Members of Snezhana's crew were shouting angrily above, and the captain herself gave orders to bring the boat around and intercept the escapees.

"Just swim," Demyan shouted. The friends turned toward the *Ocean's Legend* and swam as hard as they could. Zoya thought back to their physical education classes. Swimming had been Zoya's favorite session, if for no other reason but that the pool and room were always kept warm. Swimming in the freezing, turbulent ocean was a much less pleasant experience.

"Zoya," Lilia said. "What if they don't see us?" For a moment, Zoya didn't reply.

"They will," she said at last. "They will."

Anya yawned as she sat by the window of the pilot house.

"You know you can go to bed," Alexi said as he steered the *Ocean's Legend*.

"No," she replied. "I'm ok." She glanced at Alexi, her eyelids drooping. "Don't *you* need some sleep?"

"I like being awake at night," Alexi said. "It's quiet, solitary."

"Oh." Anya stood to leave.

"Oh, I didn't mean it like that," Alexi said, grabbing Anya by the arm. "I just mean it's calmer. No one hurrying about, no captain shouting." Alexi pulled Anya closer to him, moving a lock of hair behind her ear.

"I do appreciate the company," he told her.

"You think you're so smooth," Anya said, teasing. She smiled at him then blushed and looked out the window.

Anya's smile dropped.

"Why is your aunt turning around?" she asked. Alexi followed her gaze.

"I don't know," he said, grabbing the wheel. "Is she attacking us?" He began to turn the ship to face off against the *Hell's Jewel*.

"Wait," Anya said, pointing. "Look. What's that in the water?" Amid the rain-speckled ocean surface, three pale figures moved toward the *Ocean's Legend*.

"Just some fish, probably," Alexi said, focused on the other ship.

"No!" Anya exclaimed. "It's people! It's three people!" She ran out of the pilot house and toward the bow.

"Everyone wake up!" she shouted as she ran. "Wake up! They're in the water!"

A moment later, Captain Edmund stomped grumpily out of his cabin.

"What are you going on about?" he demanded.

"It's Zoya and Lilia and Demyan," Anya yelled urgently, pointing to the water.

"What?" The captain came to stand beside her, and gave out a hearty laugh when he spotted the three figures.

"Well, I'll be damned!" The captain immediately shouted orders to the crew that were awake, sending Olya to find those who were sleeping.

"What's going on?" Nikolai asked as he appeared above deck. Anya dragged him to the side of the ship and pointed to their friends in the water. Nikolai laughed and hugged Anya.

"Those idiots!" he cried gleefully. "How are we going to get them out?"

"Follow me," Oleg said, brushing past them toward the starboard dinghy. He got in and gestured for Nikolai and Anya to do the same. Then Olya

GRIGORY'S GADGET

lowered the dinghy down into the ocean. Oleg picked up the oars and began to row toward Zoya, Lilia, and Demyan.

Anya glanced at Oleg's prosthetic hand which gripped the top of the oar.

"You and your sister both have those metal hands," she said. "I don't mean to be rude, but how do they work? I mean, how do you move them?"

"Didn't ask for an explanation," Oleg replied. "I just asked for a hand." Anya frowned.

"Well I think it's fantastic," Nikolai said. "I would feel so formidable if I had a prosthetic like that. A mechanical, indestructible limb!"

Oleg stared at Nikolai coolly.

"There they are," Anya said, pointing to the water.

She and Nikolai extended their arms and hoisted their friends into the small boat. Zoya, Lilia, and Demyan were all gasping for breath.

"I'm so tired," Zoya mumbled, her words choppy, as the dinghy returned to the *Ocean's Legend*. She shivered.

"This bed is really uncomfortable," Lilia said drowsily. Anya exchanged a concerned look with Nikolai.

"You're not in a bed, you're on a boat," Anya said.

"Oh, good," Lilia replied. "Then the eggplants are almost ready."

When the dinghy was lifted back up alongside the ship, Anya, Nikolai, and Oleg carefully and slowly lifted the others onto the deck. Demyan stumbled and fell, his arms and legs weakened by the swim. Zoya clung to the railing and watched as Olya and Oleg gently placed Lilia on the deck.

Tonia rushed over with heavy blankets, wrapping them around the three friends.

"You need to get out of your wet clothes," Anya said, offering her hand to help Zoya to her feet.

"You need to help Lilia," Zoya told her. "She's not looking too good. I don't know what's wrong." Lilia was lying on the ground, chuckling softly.

Anya and Nikolai gently lifted Lilia to a sitting position, each draping one of her arms over their shoulders. Slowly, they carried her toward the saloon.

"Someone boil water for tea!" Anya called out at the crew. Zoya and Demyan followed their friends toward the saloon, helped by Tonia and Olya. Once they were inside, they collapsed into chairs and huddled in their blankets.

"I'll get dry clothes," Anya told them and rushed below deck.

"From where?" Zoya asked. "Snezhana took all our suitcases."

"I'm sure there are spare clothes somewhere," Anya replied, determined.

Lilia threw off her blanket, nearly falling off her chair in the process. Then she started to remove her shoes, and her socks.

"Lilia, what are you doing?" Demyan asked.

"No shoes in the house," Lilia replied, waving her socks in the air. Nikolai turned to Zoya and Demyan.

"Did she eat something weird?" he asked.

"No, it was all the same food," Demyan replied. "Bread and meat and ale."

"But did she eat it?" Zoya asked, watching Lilia. "Did she actually eat any of her food? I don't remember."

"I'll get some food for her, then," Nikolai said, hurrying to the pantry.

As he cut up bread and salted meat, Anya returned with a pile of clothes, gloating.

"Everybody out!" she ordered the crew that had gathered in the saloon. "Just for two minutes, so they can change." They obliged and filed outside or down below.

Zoya and Demyan, using their blankets for additional privacy, swapped their drenched clothes for the dry ones. Nikolai poured them some tea. They grabbed for it eagerly, relishing the warmth of the cup.

Anya struggled to help Lilia into her dry clothes. She continued to whine and throw her blanket on the ground.

"I don't want it," she mumbled. Nikolai grabbed the blanket, wrapped it around Lilia, and then hugged her tightly to prevent her from throwing it off again.

"I've got her," he told Anya.

CHAPTER EIGHT

Anya and Nikolai helped their friends down to the cabin after making sure they were all fed Zoya, Demyan, and Lilia fell into their hammocks with hardly the strength to shift into a comfortable position. Zoya forced her eyes to stay open, watching Lilia, who was still acting delirious.

"You should get some sleep," Anya said.

"I'll keep an eye on Lilia," Zoya replied, trying to sit up on her hammock.

"That's not sleeping," Anya argued. "Nikolai and I will keep an eye on Lilia, and you two. You just escaped a pirate ship by swimming through stormy, choppy water. Go to sleep."

"Yes ma'am," Demyan mumbled. Zoya obliged as well, hugging her blanket.

It wasn't long before both Anya and Nikolai fell asleep too.

GRIGORY'S GADGET

The next morning, the rain continued pounding the wooden ship. A crash of thunder jolted Zoya awake. She felt the ship sway from the violent waves outside. Lilia stirred in her hammock then looked at Zoya.

"How long is this storm going to last?" she asked drowsily. Nikolai roused at the question, slowly waking up. He turned to look at Lilia and smiled.

"Feeling better?" he asked. She yawned and nodded. The others slowly began to wake.

Zoya stretched her arms, groaning at the soreness of her entire body. "Do you think the captain would give me a break from shoveling coal today? I'm not sure I could even lift the empty shovel."

"Whose fault is that?" Demyan grumbled as he sat up. He winced and rubbed his shoulder.

"What?" Zoya asked.

"Maybe if you actually used your brain for once…"

"Excuse me?" Anya said, standing between Demyan and Zoya. "How rude. What's wrong with you?"

"What's wrong with me is I'm tired, and sore, hungry, and trapped on a pirate ship that's feuding with another pirate ship—all because of Zoya!"

"You're blaming this all on me?" Zoya asked.

"Guys, let's just take a moment to breath," Lilia said. Demyan ignored her.

"You never think before you act!" Demyan said. "You just do the first thing that comes to mind, and it gets us in trouble, Zoya! It's going to get us killed!"

"Well at least I do *something*!" Zoya replied. "Better than being a useless loser like you!" Her breath caught in her throat as her eyes went wide.

"I...I didn't mean that," Zoya said. "I'm sorry." Demyan stood and stumbled out of the room, clumsily climbing the steps to the saloon.

"Demyan!" Zoya stood to follow him. Nikolai put up his hand.

"I'll handle it," he said. "You all just need to rest."

Zoya sat back in her hammock, tears clouding her vision. Anya hugged her.

"We'll get through this," Anya said.

As the girls sat in their hammocks, Oleg walked by on his way above deck.

"Oh, good," he said. "The captain will be happy to know you're awake. He wants to see you in the saloon." Oleg continued on his way upstairs.

"I wonder what he wants," Anya muttered sarcastically. Zoya looked at her in confusion, wiping tears out of her eyes. Anya simply mouthed the word *gadget* then headed out of the cabin. Zoya and Lilia followed.

Many of the crew were in the saloon. When Anya, Zoya, and Lilia entered, everyone cheered and raised

GRIGORY'S GADGET

a cup of ale. Demyan sat at a table next to Nikolai. He didn't look up.

Anya looked out the windows, searching for the *Hell's Jewel*. It was nowhere in sight. She wondered if it was really gone, or simply obscured by the driving rain. *She should be chasing us, shouldn't she?*

"There they are!" Captain Sokoll boasted. He held a bottle of rum in his hand. "Our brave heroes! Returned to us through the storm!" The crew cheered again. Tonia handed Anya, Zoya, and Lilia cups of ale and led them to the same table as their friends. For an hour, the crew cheered and laughed and asked the apparent heroes about their escape. Finishing a cup of ale, Anya patted Zoya on the shoulder then stood and walked to where Alexi sat.

"Is your aunt still chasing us? I don't see her ship."

Alexi shook his head. "Looks like she's doing the smart thing and getting out of this storm. It's getting really rough out there, and there's no sign of it letting up."

"Why aren't we doing the same?" she asked.

Alexi gave her an incredulous look. "Oleg tried to convince the captain that we should find land. He's struggling to steer the ship with all these waves. But the captain just scoffed. He said we're too busy celebrating." Anya glanced toward Captain Sokoll, who was laughing heartily as he smacked Demyan on the back.

"I think he's drunk," Anya commented.

A few moments later, Edmund ambled toward Alexi.

"Anya, I need a moment with Alexi," he said. Anya nodded and moved to another table close by.

"You want to redeem yourself, boy?" the captain asked Alexi. Anya could hear him clearly. In his drunken state, he must have lost the ability to whisper. "You get me that gadget, right now." Alexi stared out of the window at the rain, then back at his father.

"No," he said.

Captain Sokoll stared back. "What do you mean, no? Is that a joke?"

"No, sir," Alexi replied.

"You really do have a death wish, don't you?" Captain Sokoll growled. He stood and reached for Alexi's collar.

"A toast!" Anya yelled, standing. "To Zoya and Lilia and Demyan!" The crew cheered and raised their cups. Captain Sokoll, glaring at his son, raised his bottle of rum. He drank the last bit of it and slammed it onto the table. Then he stepped away. Anya, sighing with relief, returned to her friends.

A loud clap of thunder startled everyone in the room.

"That sounded close," Zoya noted. "Captain, should we head for land? Would that be safer?"

"We're fine!" the captain insisted. "Don't you worry about a thing. We're celebrating!"

"He's drunk," Lilia said. "Very drunk."

GRIGORY'S GADGET

"Nikolai," Anya whispered. "Go talk to Oleg. He already tried to convince to captain to find land. Tell him the captain's too drunk to notice a change in course."

"That sounds a little like mutiny," Nikolai said.

"I'm sure the captain will pass out any minute now," Zoya replied. "Someone has to be in charge while he's asleep, right?" Nikolai grumbled. Zoya could feel Demyan's glare, but ignored it.

"If I get in trouble," he said, "I'm getting you guys in trouble, too."

"Fair enough," Zoya and Anya replied in unison.

A moment later, a loud *thud* sounded on the main deck. Zoya looked out to see a large piece of one of the main sails ripped and blowing about in the storm.

"No one fastened the sails?" Anya asked.

"Don't you dare go out there," Lilia replied. "I know that look in your eye. It's too dangerous."

"It's dangerous to let our sails fly in a storm like this," Anya replied. She crossed her arms and sighed. "But you're right. I guess we'll just hope for the best at this point."

"Looks like we're relying on the wheels," Zoya said. "I'm going to the boiler room. I should be able to help, at least a little."

Nikolai returned to the room and shouted for everyone's attention.

"We need to get to land!" he yelled. "Celebration's over!" The crew put down their ale and looked toward the captain.

"Where are you doing?" Captain Sokoll slurred. "I'm the captain! I didn't say the party is over!"

"Captain, it's too dangerous," Nikolai said.

"Are you trying to undermine me?" Captain Sokoll asked, grabbing at Nikolai. Nikolai backed away as the captain stumbled forward.

"Fine!" Captain Sokoll shouted, throwing his hands in the air. "Fair enough, get to work, get my ship safely to land. Alexi! Go fix that sail!"

Alexi laughed.

"Do I look like I'm joking?"

"Damn the sail," Alexi replied. "The sails aren't doing anything for us in this wind and it's too risky to fasten them now. We need to rely on the paddle wheels."

Captain Sokoll grabbed Alexi by the shoulder and threw him against the door of the saloon. He moved toward him, pushing him out into the rain.

"You do as you're told, boy!" Captain Sokoll said, knocking Alexi to the ground.

"Sir," Anya shouted, following them. "I think he's right. It's too dangerous. We should go back inside."

Captain Sokoll looked at her and laughed. "You and Alexi have gotten close." Anya didn't respond. "Perhaps you can enlighten me. Why has he been so disrespectful lately? So insubordinate?"

"I don't know, Captain," Anya replied hesitantly.

GRIGORY'S GADGET

"Well, you'd be wise not to follow his example," Captain Sokoll said. "So, tell me. Where is my gadget?"

"I'm not sure what you're talking about," Anya said. Captain Sokoll slapped Anya across the face, knocking her to the ground. Her hands slipped on the slick deck as she tried to get back up.

"Anya!" Alexi cried out, climbing to his feet. He turned and tackled his father. The two men fell to the ground, shouting over the rain. They struggled for a moment but, despite his drunkenness, Captain Sokoll was stronger and threw Alexi off.

"You think you can get the best of me?" Captain Sokoll laughed. "I am your captain! I am your father! I own you!"

"Go to hell!" Alexi yelled. Lightning arced through the sky, followed quickly by a clap of thunder. The crew had gathered on the main deck, unsure how to react to the scene before them. Captain Sokoll pulled out his sword and pointed it at Alexi. Then, he pointed it at Anya.

"Climb up there," he demanded, "and collapse the sails. Now."

"Alexi, don't," Anya pleaded. Captain Sokoll slashed at Anya, ripping through the sleeve of her shirt and drawing blood. Anya stumbled back, covering the small wound.

"Anya," Alexi said flatly. "Go inside." Anya looked to Captain Sokoll, who smiled.

"Start climbing," he said, "and she can go." Alexi edged toward the side of the ship, grabbing on to the shrouds. Anya backed away reluctantly, glancing between Alexi and Captain Sokoll.

Nikolai and Lilia stepped forward and grabbed Anya's shoulders, pulling her back toward the saloon. Once inside, Anya wrestled out of their grip and ran to watch from the doorway. Demyan stepped outside and approached the captain. Anya followed him.

"Damnit, Anya, stop!" Nikolai ran after her, followed by Lilia.

"Captain," Demyan shouted. "I think we can forget about the sails. We should focus on keeping the crew safe. All of the crew." Captain Sokoll growled and moved quickly toward Demyan. He pinned him against the metal smokestack, pressing his blade on Demyan's neck.

"Do not tell me what I should or shouldn't do!" Captain Sokoll shouted in his face. "I am the captain! And I grow tired of all this insubordination!"

"I'm sorry, sir," Demyan said quickly. "I was just...I'm frightened, sir. I didn't mean to speak out of turn." Captain Sokoll backed away and lowered his sword.

"Aye," he said. "You haven't been through a little storm before. But you can trust your captain." Demyan nodded, keeping his back against the smokestack. As he stood there, the hairs on the back of his neck stood up. Before Demyan could react, a

GRIGORY'S GADGET

bolt of lightning struck the metal, and the force sent Demyan flying across the ship.

The boiler room was frantic with activity. Tonia and Olya were fueling the engine, trying to keep the speed up. Zoya darted around, checking gauges. She stumbled as the ship rocked from the violent waves outside.

"Tonia!" she shouted. "How's the water level?"

Tonia ran over to a small glass window and peered through it.

"Looking good," Tonia replied.

A moment later, a loud clap of thunder startled the crew. Olya, who was nearest the boilers, was thrown across the room. She groaned on the floor, her hair standing on end. Sparks crackled on her metal hand, the fingers twitching.

"What the hell was that?" Tonia asked.

"Did lightning just strike the ship?" Zoya asked, baffled. She glanced down at the floor, which was covered in water.

"We're losing water," she said. Her mind went blank, trying to remember what to do. She backed toward the doorway, digging through her brain, trying to find the answer.

"I got it," Tonia said, running to the water valve. "Find the hole and plug it up, I'll send more water in." Zoya hesitated, glancing around the room.

"Wait, Tonia don't!" she shouted. It was too late. As Tonia let cold water rush into the boiler system, it created a huge influx of steam, and the boiler exploded.

Zoya cried out as the heat and force of the explosion knocked her backward. She flew through the doorway and crashed into a pile of crates. The skin on her arms and face stung. She coughed and scrambled to her hands and knees, wincing as she realized she was covered in burns and splinters.

The room was filled with smoke and steam, too thick to see through. Zoya felt around and pulled herself toward the stairs as she heard water rushing into the ship. When she found the stairs, she stood and stumbled up toward the saloon. As she did, she could feel the ship tipping.

When Zoya reached the saloon, she saw her friends crowded in the corner. Demyan lay unconscious between them.

"Zoya!" Lilia shouted. "You're ok!"

"The boilers exploded," she croaked, coughing. "What happened? What happened to Demyan?"

"He was standing by the smokestack," Nikolai said, his voice frantic. "When the lightning hit, he flew across the deck."

"He has a pulse," Anya added. "And he's breathing." Zoya crawled over to them, grabbing Demyan's hand.

GRIGORY'S GADGET

"Zoya," Lilia said. "What do we do? If the boilers exploded, and the ship…"

"I don't know," Zoya replied, tears in her eyes. "I heard water rushing in below deck, and the ship is tipping." Zoya's friends fell silent, glancing around the saloon. The ship creaked, and the chairs and tables began to inch along the floor as the ship tilted further.

Alexi stumbled into the saloon carrying Oleg. Oleg appeared unconscious and his head was covered in blood. Anya stood clumsily and staggered over to them.

"Are you alright?" she asked.

"I am, he's not," Alexi replied. He gently placed Oleg on the floor. "We're capsizing." He climbed around the room, knocking over tables and chairs and shoving them down the sloping floor. "We can make a barricade to protect ourselves."

"From what?" Nikolai asked.

"Broken wood, shards of glass. I'm guessing that's what hit Oleg. I found him like this in the pilot house, bleeding from a gash in his head."

"Will it matter?" Lilia asked. "If we're capsizing? It sounds like that would be a quicker death than…" Lilia was shaking.

"We're not sinking yet," Alexi replied. "If you want to jump back into the water, be my guest." Lilia helped grab the chairs and tables, building a wooden fort. Nikolai and Zoya followed suit, placing the tables and chairs so that the legs faced the wall, which was tilting more and more with each passing minute. Anya tried to help Oleg. She ripped off his shirt and used it to apply pressure to his wound.

"Where is everyone else?" Zoya asked, her gaze still fixed on Demyan.

"Some were flung into the sea when the lightning struck," Alexi said as he piled chairs. "Others were lost in the explosion. The few that survived stole one of the dinghies when they realized the ship was capsizing. I doubt they'll make it far. Where are Tonia and Olya?"

"I didn't see them," Zoya said. "I don't think they made it out of the boiler room. I think they might be—"

"Then I think we're all that's left of my father's crew."

"Where is your father?" Anya asked.

"In his cabin, last I saw," Alexi replied.

The ship shuddered violently. Everyone grabbed at the walls and tables and chairs, breathing quick shallow breaths. The tables and chairs shifted, settling onto the wall which was now almost completely horizontal.

Demyan stirred suddenly, drawing a deep, raspy breath.

"What happened?" he asked. "What's happening?" He looked around at the mess of wooden legs surrounding him. Zoya put a hand on his shoulder.

"You were almost struck by lightning," she said. "And, now the ship is capsizing."

"What?" he exclaimed. He sat up quickly, bumping his head on a chair and falling back down. "Ow."

"Just relax," Zoya told him. "We'll be ok, you just need to rest."

"But the ship—"

"We'll be fine," Zoya insisted.

The group resigned themselves to silence for what felt like an eternity, each hyper-aware of every sound, every movement. The ocean's waves roared as thunder rumbled, accompanied by the loud creaking of the sideways ship. Zoya took Demyan's hand, and Lilia's. Lilia in turn grabbed Nikolai's. Nikolai offered his hand to Anya. She grasped it, and seized Alexi's hand as well. The friends held onto each other tight, as if the effort would keep the ship afloat.

Alexi pulled himself up so that he was sitting on the wall of the saloon with his back against the ceiling. "I think we've stopped tipping."

"Well that's good, right?" Nikolai said, sitting up as well. He leaned over to nearest window. "We're still above water too, it doesn't look like we're sinking."

"Maybe we'll just float to land," Lilia suggested. "Or another ship will see us, and rescue us."

"Yeah, maybe," Zoya replied, not really believing it. The group was silent for a while longer, listening to the rain pounding on the walls and windows.

"How's Oleg?" Alexi asked.

Anya reached over and touched Oleg's neck. She grimaced. "I'm sorry, Alexi. He's dead."

A loud thud sounded above them, followed by a series of softer thuds. The friends looked around, trying to see through the maze of wooden legs. Then, in the doorway to the saloon, Alexi saw a silhouette tumble inside. As it fell to the corner, he realized it was Captain Sokoll.

"Alexi," the captain groaned weakly. "Is that you?" Alexi's face turned red when he saw his father.

"Yes, sir."

"Oh, good," Captain Sokoll said, smiling. "You're alive."

Alexi scowled. "You're happy about that, Captain?"

Captain Sokoll coughed and eased himself more comfortably onto his side. "Of course. I'm your father."

"Of all people to survive," Nikolai grumbled. Lilia shushed him.

"Alexi, come here," Captain Sokoll said, his voice hardly above a whisper. Alexi hesitated, but then did as he was told. As he neared his father, he noticed a large red stain on his shirt.

"Are you bleeding, Captain?" Alexi asked.

"Son," Captain Sokoll said. "Don't worry, I'll be fine. It's nothing."

Alexi furrowed his brow. "We need to get you stitched up. What happened?" Without waiting for an answer, Alexi unbuttoned his father's shirt. A large yet shallow laceration stretched down his abdomen. Alexi looked around for anything he could use to tend to the wound.

"Someone try to get some kraken ink or rum," he said. He took Captain Sokoll's shirt and began wrapping the injury. Anya climbed her way up to the cupboards, grabbing a bottle of rum that hadn't shattered. A tense silence fell over the room as Alexi tended to his father.

"Just let him die," Nikolai said.

Lilia glared at him. "What's wrong with you? I mean, he's a jerk, but you're actually wishing him dead?"

"He would have let *you* die," Nikolai replied. "When Alexi, Anya, and I were rescued from Snezhana's ship, he thought we had the gadget. And he was going to let you die." Lilia stared at him, unsure how to respond.

"But you did have the gadget," Zoya said. "I gave it to Anya." Her face turned pale as she glanced around. "Where is it?" She stood and walked toward Anya.

"Wait, what?" Nikolai said. "She had it?" He held his head and leaned back.

Zoya grabbed Anya and pulled her away from Captain Sokoll and Alexi.

"Where is it?" she whispered.

Anya's eyes went wide. "It was in our cabin. I hid it in one of the boxes."

Without hesitation, Zoya climbed over to the stairs and started easing her way below deck.

"Zoya! Be careful!" Demyan called. Zoya couldn't tell if he said that out of concern or annoyance. She pushed the thought from her head.

Zoya inched herself along the wall, following the stairs. Water was seeping in below deck, and as Zoya neared the cabin she found herself knee-deep in the cold water. The salt stung the cuts on her legs, but she continued toward the room. The crates had all toppled over, most of them spilling their contents. Zoya pulled herself up into the cabin, perching on the doorway, and began digging.

"Come on, where is it?" She grabbed frantically at everything in front of her, starting with the crates that were still dry. Then, she jumped back down into the hall to dig through the crates and contents that were floating in the water.

Finally, Zoya saw a faint glint of metal shining through the water. She grabbed for it, pulling up the gadget with a sigh of relief. She grabbed one of the hammocks that was still dry, and used it to wipe as much water as she could off of the gadget. As Zoya

GRIGORY'S GADGET

left the cabin, she looked for some way to hide it. She waded down the hall, scanning each of the cabins. Toward the end, she found a small leather satchel. She grabbed the bag, stuffed the gadget inside and slung it across her shoulder before heading back above deck.

Captain Sokoll was barely conscious when she returned, for which she was thankful.

"I found it," she whispered to her friends. "But I don't know how well this will hide it." She held her bag close to herself.

"You mean if we survive?" Lilia asked.

Zoya sighed. "There's water up to our cabin. I don't know how well the ship will continue to float like this."

"The rain's lightening up, at least," Nikolai said. Zoya listened and realized he was right. It was merely drizzling outside.

"Let's see what our situation is," she said, standing again. She climbed over the tables and chairs then out of the saloon door.

The deck was a charred mess of broken wood, soaked by the still-falling rain. The port-side paddle wheel was completely gone, and the wheel on the starboard side was almost entirely under water. Waves lapped up on the deck, though they appeared odd to Zoya.

She sat on the doorframe then eased herself onto a capstan to get a better look.

"Land!" she shouted ecstatically. Off in the distance, through the rain, Zoya could barely make out a sandy beach and green trees beyond it.

"Land!" she called again. Anya popped her head out of the saloon door to look then gestured for the others to look as well.

"Oh thank goodness," Lilia sighed.

Zoya glanced down at the ocean and smiled. She hopped down from her perch on the capstan, landing in about two feet of water. The saltiness of it stung at the lesions on her legs. She grimaced.

"We hit a sand bar," she told her friends. "We're not sinking."

Zoya and her friends explored the wreckage of the *Ocean's Legend* the next day, after the rain slowed to a light drizzle. Alexi stayed behind in the saloon, tending to his father, who was now completely unconscious. Anya found swords as they explored, and distributed them to her friends.

"Just in case," she said. The friends nodded and gladly armed themselves.

"This dinghy is still intact," Zoya said, pointing to the tiny boat. It was still roped to the main ship, bobbing in the shallow water. "Let's take it to land and see what's around."

Anya eagerly climbed into the boat, followed by Zoya and a more hesitant Demyan.

GRIGORY'S GADGET

"I kind of want to stay here," Nikolai said, scratching his head. "Explore the ship a little more. You can go check out the land, and come back to let us know if there's anything good."

"You want to snoop in the captain's cabin," Demyan said with a knowing look. Nikolai didn't deny it.

"I'll stay too, make sure he doesn't hurt himself," Lilia said. Demyan took the oars of the dinghy and started to row. Anya grabbed his arm.

"Let me row," she said. "You've been through enough physical trauma." Demyan released the oars, scooting himself to the front of the dinghy as Anya rowed the three of them to shore.

Nikolai scrambled eagerly up to the door of the captain's cabin. Lilia followed, eying the door of the saloon. She didn't see Alexi looking out, and so she followed Nikolai into the cabin.

The room was in complete disarray. A large four-poster bed had toppled onto an oaken desk, which itself was leaning against the wall. Papers and parchment were scattered everywhere.

"Are you looking for anything in particular?" Lilia asked as Nikolai rummaged through the cabin.

"He must have information on Zoya's gadget," Nikolai replied. "He's so obsessed with it."

"Was he really going to abandon us?"

Nikolai stopped rummaging and looked up at Lilia.

"Yes," he replied. "When he thought Alexi had the gadget, he stopped chasing Snezhana's ship. Without any hesitation."

"But Anya had the gadget," Lilia stated.

"Well, he didn't know that," Nikolai said, continuing to sort through the papers. "Neither did I."

"So he was just chasing the gadget," Lilia said. She sat down, tears welling up in her eyes.

"Is that what Pavel died for?" she asked. "For that *stupid* gadget?" She thought for a moment. "Would he have abandoned us, too?" Nikolai crawled over to her and grabbed her by the shoulders, looking her in the eyes.

"Absolutely not," he said. "Pavel was one of the good guys. Even if he did know about the gadget, Pavel would never have abandoned us. He was our friend."

"But he did know about it," Lilia replied. "When he…when he was dying, he told Zoya to protect it."

Nikolai was silent for a moment, thinking. "He was our friend," he said at last. "Gadget or no gadget." Lilia nodded as tears rolled down her cheeks. Nikolai pulled her into a tight hug.

"It'll be ok," he whispered. He stepped back and looked at Lilia's face. Brushing some hair behind her ear, he leaned in toward her.

"What are you doing?" Lilia asked, pushing him away. "Were you…were you about to kiss me?" Nikolai's face turned beet red.

GRIGORY'S GADGET

"I was," he started, "I thought...No, of course not." He stood back up and turned away from her.

"I'm sorry," Lilia said after a moment. "I didn't mean to react like that. It was just unexpected."

"It's fine," Nikolai mumbled. He climbed up toward the door.

"Nikolai!" Lilia called, but he had already exited the room.

Alexi propped his back against the floor, shutting his eyes in an attempt to get some rest. After tending to his father, he had thrown Oleg's body into the stairwell. He had felt a pang of guilt as he did so, but he didn't want his father to see the body.

Captain Sokoll's wound had stopped bleeding, but the man was still pale and weak. He stirred, looking up at his son. "Alexi." He coughed.

"Yes, Captain?" Alexi replied, not bothering to open his eyes.

"Please, Alexi," Captain Sokoll said. "Not captain. Father." Alexi peered at Captain Sokoll.

"You've always told me differently, Captain," he stated. Captain Sokoll struggled to pull himself up, leaning against the wall. Alexi noticed that the captain's prosthetic leg, which would normally bend at the knee and ankle, was completely rigid. *It must have been damaged by the lightning or the explosion.*

"Son," Captain Sokoll said, "what am I captain of now? My ship is destroyed, my crew is dead. All I have left is you, son. You are all I care about."

"That's a lie," Alexi replied. "All you care about is that gadget."

"I care about that gadget because I care about you," Captain Sokoll said. "Alexi, that gadget could get us everything we've ever wanted."

Alexi considered his father for a moment.

"So it can bring back the dead?" Alexi asked.

Captain Sokoll's expression turned to one of deep sadness. "No. The gadget would not be able to bring your mother back. But it could—"

"Then it can't give me everything I've ever wanted," Alexi said. "I know what you want. Fame, money, power. You want that gadget to feed your pride."

"No, Alexi," Captain Sokoll said. "The gadget would protect you."

"Protect me? Since when do you care about protecting me? Are you protecting me when you beat me? Have me whipped? Have me starved? You sent me up into the shrouds in the middle of one of the worst storms we've ever seen."

"Disciplining you is protecting you," Captain Sokoll said. Alexi shook his head and turned away from his father.

"And I sent you up into the rigging because I knew I could trust you to do it," Captain Sokoll said. "I know you're brave enough and skilled enough."

GRIGORY'S GADGET

"And easy to manipulate," Alexi said. "As soon as I try to care about something else...someone else...you find a way to use that against me. To hurt me or to hurt her."

"She needed to be put in her place," Captain Sokoll said. Alexi felt his face turn red as he stood and faced his father.

"Put in her place? She isn't some—" He stopped himself short, anger making his thoughts race. He took a deep breath and stared his father in the eye. "Is that how you thought of mom?"

Captain Sokoll eyed his son.

"Your mother never spoke out of turn like your little lady friend does," he said.

"Because you threatened her, right?" Alexi said. "You beat her, like you beat me. Oh, no, I'm sorry. You disciplined her. Is that right?"

"Everyone needs to be disciplined," Captain Sokoll told his son. "It's a fact of life."

"What about you?" Alexi crouched down next to his father. "Who disciplines you?"

Captain Sokoll laughed. "I've done my time, boy," he said. "And I'm coming out on top."

Alexi pulled his dagger from its sheath and held it against his father's throat. "I could kill you right now, and it would be completely justified. After everything you did to me, after everything you did to mom...She killed herself because of you."

Captain Sokoll stared up at his son, his expression calm. "You won't kill me, though," he challenged. "You won't kill your own father."

Alexi stood there, tense, with the knife still pressed against his father's throat. As much as he wanted to slice the captain's arteries open, his hand was paralyzed.

He heard a series of thuds above him, and looked up to see Nikolai climbing back into the saloon. Nikolai paused when he saw the scene before him then turned to leave the saloon again.

"Nikolai," Alexi called. "It's alright. Come on in." He stood, holding the dagger by his side.

Nikolai hesitantly climbed back inside, easing down onto the stacked tables. "Sorry to interrupt."

"No," Alexi said "Your timing is perfect." He held out the dagger, hilt first, to Nikolai. Nikolai stared back at him, confused.

"I know you want my father dead," Alexi said. "You saw how quickly he'd betray you and your friends. So, here's your chance. Kill him." Nikolai stepped away.

"I don't—" he started. "No. I'm not a killer. As much as I hate your father, I can't. I can't kill someone."

Alexi pulled out his pistol and pointed it at Nikolai's head.

"Yes, you can."

CHAPTER NINE

"You two are worrying me," Anya said as she rowed. "Are you really refusing to talk to each other?"

Zoya and Demyan glanced at each other, their faces red.

"I was hit by lightning."

"I was in a boiler explosion." Zoya's and Demyan's mouths twitched into smiles for a moment.

"We're understandably tired," Zoya said. "We don't want to talk about it right now."

"Fine," Anya said. "Your relationship is your business, I guess."

"Speaking of relationships, what's going on between you and Alexi?" Zoya smirked. "You seem especially chummy lately.

Anya grinned. "It's complicated. I don't want to talk about it right now."

As they neared the beach, Zoya and Demyan hopped out of the boat to pull it up on the beach. About a hundred feet from the ocean, the sand gave way to dense trees. Unlike the pine trees in Koravsk, these trees had broad leaves. They were a rich green and were still drenched from the rain.

"Look how green they are," Anya said. "They're beautiful." The three of them walked to the edge of the tree line, peering into the forest.

"The color is really intense," Demyan said. "They look a lot different from the pine trees in Koravsk."

"And we thought those were colorful," Zoya said.

"Oh no." Anya groaned, looking down the beach. Zoya and Demyan followed her gaze.

The *Hell's Jewel* was careened less than a mile down, significantly less damaged than Captain Sokoll's ship. Her crew was readying dinghies in the water.

Zoya, Demyan, and Anya stepped into the trees to hide, watching the pirates.

"What do we do?" Demyan asked. "They're going to find the others."

"Maybe they'll see the wreck and assume everyone is dead," Zoya said. "And then they'll just leave." As Anya watched, she saw Nikolai climb out of the captain's cabin and trudge toward the saloon.

"Nik—" Demyan started to shout. Zoya clamped her hand over his mouth and pulled him farther into the trees.

GRIGORY'S GADGET

"He can't hear you," she whispered. "But Snezhana's crew might." Demyan nodded.

Anya heard the sound of snapping branches and rustling leaves behind them. They turned, pulling out their swords.

"I thought I told you to remember," Gotfrid told them, "that we always have guns." He stepped into view, aiming his pistol at Zoya. Adam and Pyotr appeared as well, both with guns drawn.

"You're alive?" Pyotr asked Zoya and Demyan in sincere wonder.

"And I'm sure you'd like to stay that way," Adam added. "So I suggest you move, back to your boat." Zoya, Anya, and Demyan began backing toward the beach, sheathing their swords. Zoya grabbed the strap of her bag, hugging it close to her body.

"How many are left alive on your ship?" Gotfrid asked as they walked. He did not receive an answer.

"Fine," he sighed. "Doesn't matter. If anyone else is alive, they're probably too injured to be useful. So, we'll just have to put them out of their misery."

Adam rowed the dinghy back toward the wrecked *Ocean's Legend*. Anya, Zoya, and Demyan sat silently, glaring at their captors.

"Don't look so angry," Gotfrid said to them. "Think of it like this: we're rescuing you. If we hadn't come along, all you'd have is a wrecked ship and an empty beach. We'll at least feed you." Still, the captives were silent.

As they neared the *Ocean's Legend*, they could hear Alexi and Nikolai shouting.

"What's going on?" Anya asked.

As Adam tethered the dinghy to the ship, Anya sprinted through the water. Gotfrid reached to stop her but she was too fast. When she reached the *Ocean's Legend*, she climbed the deck to the door of the saloon.

She peered in to see Nikolai and Alexi wrestling with a dagger. Captain Sokoll lay on the floor, laughing weakly.

"What's going on?" Anya demanded. Alexi shoved Nikolai away, breathing heavily. There was a large red mark on his cheek, presumably where Nikolai had punched him.

"He tried to make me kill the captain," Nikolai yelled. He leaned back onto one of the chairs. Anya looked between the two of them, stunned.

"Well," she said slowly. "There's some people here now that may do just that." Alexi looked up at her as he sheathed his dagger.

"She's here?" he asked.

"Her crew is, anyway," Anya said. She glanced behind her. Snezhana's men were standing guard over Zoya and Demyan by the dinghy, watching Anya with interest. Anya slid back down to the ground. A moment later, Alexi climbed out of the saloon, followed by Nikolai.

GRIGORY'S GADGET

"Is there anyone else?" Gotfrid asked them.

"My father is inside," Alexi said. "Injured. I don't think he has the strength to climb out."

"The Captain will be pleased to hear that," Adam said.

Zoya glanced around. She leaned in toward Anya.

"Where's Lilia?" she whispered. Anya looked around, then shrugged, her eyes wide with concern.

"Oh, good," Pyotr said, looking down past the wrecked ship. "Here comes the captain now." The others followed his gaze to see Snezhana on another dinghy rowed by Igor.

"Well, look who's alive," she said as she stepped out of her small boat. "That was quite the stunt you pulled. Where's the third one?"

"Nikolai!" Lilia's voice echoed out of the ship. "I found something! Nikolai!" She appeared in the doorway of the captain's cabin and clumsily crawled out. She held a bundle of parchment. As she landed in the water, she noticed the company she was in.

"What did you find, dear?" Snezhana asked in a sing-song voice. She nodded to Adam, who marched toward Lilia. Nikolai ran and tackled him.

"Stay away from her!" he shouted as they went down. Gotfrid and Pyotr grabbed Nikolai and dragged him off of Adam, slamming him into the ship's deck. Pyotr pointed his pistol at Nikolai, while Gotfrid pointed his at Lilia.

"Hand over those papers," Gotfrid told Lilia. Lilia backed away, hugging the papers to her chest.

"You can give them to me," Snezhana said, "or we can pull them from your dead hands." Reluctantly, Lilia obliged and offered the papers to Gotfrid. Gotfrid shuffled through them then brought them to Snezhana.

Snezhana examined the papers, looking disappointed.

"I should have known," she said. "Eddie was always one step behind. This isn't anything I didn't already know." She tossed the papers into the air, and they floated down to the water. Zoya lunged at them, snatching them out of the ocean as quickly as she could. Snezhana observed her and laughed. Adam and Igor charged toward Zoya, but stopped as Snezhana put up her hand.

"Let her keep them," Snezhana said. Then she turned to Alexi.

"Where is my brother?" she asked.

"Inside the saloon," Alexi replied. "He's injured."

"Oh." Snezhana pouted. "That is a shame." She strutted to the ship and climbed up to the saloon.

Snezhana peered into the room and chuckled at the mess of tables and chairs. Then she spotted her brother lying on the floor. He was still leaning against the wall, his abdomen wrapped in a blood-soaked shirt.

GRIGORY'S GADGET

"Your moment has come at last," he said. "You can finally kill me." Snezhana climbed down to sit beside him.

"Oh Eddie," she said. "I could have killed you a thousand times."

Captain Sokoll laughed, wincing at the pain of his wound. "So, what, you just didn't want to do the deed yourself? Well, now it looks like you can sit back and watch as nature takes its course."

"No," Snezhana said. "I don't think I will."

Captain Sokoll frowned. "So you are going to kill me?"

Snezhana smiled. "Of course not. I'm going to bring you on to my ship, and have my doctor tend to your wounds." Captain Sokoll furrowed his brow.

"And why would you do that?" he asked.

"Because I'll also ask him to make new ones," Snezhana said, her tone cheery. "And then he'll tend to those, too. And then he'll make some more…"

Captain Sokoll spat at his sister. "Where's the dignity in that?"

"Oh, is it dignity you want?" Snezhana replied. "Do you want me to treat you with the respect you deserve?"

"Yes," Captain Sokoll growled. Snezhana pounced at him, her fingers wrapping around his throat.

"I will treat you with the same level of respect you showed me," Snezhana snarled, "when you framed me for murder and left me to rot in that frozen prison."

"Snezhana, I—" Captain Sokoll gasped.

Snezhana slammed his head onto the floor, keeping her grip on his throat. "Do you know how they treat inmates in Lodninsk? No, I doubt you do. But I'll be happy to show you."

Snezhana stood then, calling for Adam and Igor to fetch Captain Sokoll and bring him to the *Hell's Jewel*.

Zoya leaned against the deck of the *Ocean's Legend*, hugging her bag as Demyan wrapped an arm around her shoulders. The papers Snezhana had thrown into the water had smudged and smeared to the point that the words were nearly illegible. All Zoya could make out was a drawn image of the gadget, the blurred figure of a human, and the name *G. Orlov* scribbled in the corner.

"Did you read any of it before you climbed out of the cabin?" Zoya asked Lilia. Lilia shook her head, her eyes cast to the ground.

"I was so excited to find something," she said, "I rushed right out." Zoya nodded, staring at the name on the paper. *G. Orlov? A long lost relative, maybe? But what does that mean? Someone alive or dead? How old is this gadget, anyway?*

Igor and Adam headed into the saloon to fetch Captain Sokoll. A moment later, Snezhana climbed out and leapt back down to the water.

GRIGORY'S GADGET

"Zoya," she said flatly. "We're finished with the games. Where is the gadget?" Zoya glanced at her then at Demyan. Demyan shook his head.

"Wrong answer," Snezhana stated. "Gotfrid, grab her bag." Gotfrid moved toward Zoya, who pulled out her sword.

"I told you—" Gotfrid said.

"You have a gun," Zoya replied. "I don't care. You'll have to kill me if you want this gadget, and I get the sense that you don't want to do that." Gotfrid smirked and put away his pistol. Then he unsheathed his sword.

"Let's see if you can even fight."

Zoya readied her stance and watched Gotfrid. He lunged at her, and she parried easily, moving away from the ship.

Snezhana unsheathed her own blade.

"I said I am finished with these games." She and Gotfrid both stalked Zoya, forcing her toward the edge of the sandbar. Pyotr had both his pistol and his sword out, ready to attack the others if they tried to help Zoya. Demyan rushed at him, knocking the pistol from his hand. Pyotr fell into the water, holding up his sword defensively. When Demyan didn't continue attacking him, he clambered back to his feet.

Gotfrid turned to confront Demyan as Snezhana continued driving Zoya deeper into the water. Zoya stumbled, falling into water up to her shoulders. Her bag floated next to her. Snezhana plunged her sword into the water between its straps and pulled the bag toward her. Zoya jumped at the bag, scraping her arm on the edge of Snezhana's blade. She pulled the gadget out then pulled herself back toward the sandbar, raising her sword. Blood dripped down her arm, falling into the water.

"You're stubborn," Snezhana said. "And you do have some skill with a blade. But this is not a fight you'll win."

"I disagree," Zoya replied. Snezhana lunged forward, swinging her blade almost too fast for Zoya to see. Zoya felt the burn of the cut on her arm, making her grip on the sword weaker. Snezhana took advantage and knocked the sword out of Zoya's hand. She grabbed the gadget, but Zoya still refused to let it go. Zoya held the gadget with both hands, struggling against Snezhana's grasp. Then the gadget shifted, as if it were about to break. Snezhana let go and Zoya flew backwards into the shallow water.

Zoya tried to let go of the gadget as well, but it clung to her right hand. As she stared, the gadget enveloped it, unfolding and revealing layer upon layer of metal, wires, and gears. It continued to unfold, moving up her arm.

"What's happening?" Zoya asked, frantically climbing to her feet. Her hand and forearm were covered in what looked like armor, and still the gadget continued up her arm. The others backed away with horrified looks.

GRIGORY'S GADGET

Adrenaline pumped furiously through Zoya's veins. She clenched the fist that was armored by the gadget, feeling a surge of strength and energy. Then she looked up at Snezhana, raised her hand, and opened it. Out of her palm shot a bright light of sparks and flames. It sailed just past Snezhana's head, traveled another fifty feet, and then exploded.

Snezhana pulled out her pistol, her eyes full of fear.

"Stop whatever it is you're doing," she demanded. "Right now."

"I don't know how," Zoya shouted back. The gadget had progressed over her shoulder and began to armor her chest. Zoya grabbed at the gadget with her left hand, trying to pry it off. It wouldn't budge. Zoya fell into the water as the armor spread across her chest and around her neck. Pyotr sprinted toward her.

"Pyotr, what are you doing?" Gotfrid shouted. The boy pulled out his pistol and held it by the barrel. He whacked Zoya in the back of the head. She passed out.

Zoya groaned as she awoke, lying on the beach. She grabbed her right arm with her left. The gadget was gone.

Zoya sat up and looked around. Her friends sat on the beach beside her, guarded by Gotfrid and Adam. Several members of Snezhana's crew were boarding the *Hell's Jewel* carrying boxes and crates. The crew members that were already on the ship were unfurling the sails.

"Alexi has it," Lilia said when she noticed Zoya was awake. "When you passed out, the gadget turned back into a ball. And then he took it."

"We took your weapons as well," Gotfrid said. "Lest you get any ideas."

"Where's the captain?" Zoya asked her friends.

"She's on her ship," Adam replied. Zoya glared at him.

"Not that captain," she said.

"She's the only captain there is," Adam stated. "Oh, do you mean Edmund? What exactly is he captain of?"

"He's sitting on the beach, over there," Demyan said, ignoring Adam and pointing down the shore.

"Alexi is there as well," Anya added. Zoya peered up at Gotfrid and Adam.

"Aren't you tired of being Snezhana's watchdogs?" she asked.

"We do whatever our captain asks of us," Gotfrid replied.

Zoya smirked. "Of course you do." She looked directly at Gotfrid. "Too bad that won't make her return your affection."

Gotfrid laughed and pulled out his gun, pointing it at Zoya.

"Oh, touchy subject," Zoya said.

GRIGORY'S GADGET

"Well I'll be damned." Yeremiy leaned on a wooden crutch as he limped up the beach. "You survived your swim?"

"Your leg seems to be healing nicely," Lilia said. Yeremiy had clean bandages around his knee.

"Yes," Yeremiy agreed, patting his wounded leg. "They're actually taking rather good care of me on that ship." Yeremiy watched Gotfrid and Adam out of the corners of his eyes as he spoke.

Alexi stood and approached the group, leaving his father behind. He had Zoya's bag slung around his shoulder.

"My aunt needs your help," he told Gotfrid.

Gotfrid peered at Alexi and crossed his arms. "So go help her," he replied.

Alexi sighed. "She specifically requested you, both of you. She said she needs someone she trusts." Gotfrid's face turned red.

"I'll keep watch on this bunch," Yeremiy told Gotfrid. "Go ahead."

"Wait, what?" Lilia asked, looking at Yeremiy with narrowed eyes.

"As will I," Alexi added, ignoring Lilia's confusion. Adam stepped toward him, uncomfortably close.

"Relax, Adam," Alexi told him. "My aunt and I have come to an understanding. I'm part of your crew now."

"We'll see about that," Adam said. Gotfrid gave Adam a pat on the back then strode toward the *Hell's Jewel*. With a grunt, Adam followed.

Nikolai clenched his fists. Zoya looked at him and touched his arm lightly.

"That was easier than expected," Anya said, standing up. Alexi tilted his head as he regarded her.

"What are you talking about?" he asked.

"Now we can escape," Anya said. "Come on, you and Yeremiy don't actually intend to keep us prisoner, right?"

"Actually," Yeremiy replied. "I do. Do you have any idea what they'd do to me if I let you escape? My only way home is doing as I'm told."

"I thought you were trying to help us," Lilia said. "You said you'd rather die than help pirates. What changed?"

Yeremiy wrung his hands, glancing back toward the *Hell's Jewel*, then at Alexi.

"I'd rather not discuss it in mixed company." His gaze stayed fix on Alexi, who shrugged and waved a hand.

"Well like I said," Alexi said. "My aunt and I have reached an understanding. I know you haven't had a good experience with her—"

"A good experience?" Zoya said, standing. Her friends all stood behind her. "She's been horrible to us, and we've seen her treat other people even worse. I know you have issues with your father, and

GRIGORY'S GADGET

maybe your aunt is better than he is. But I don't want anything to do with either of them."

Alexi pulled out his pistol and aimed it at Zoya. Anya stepped forward, blocking his aim.

"Anya, move," Alexi told her.

"You're not going to shoot me," Anya said. "And you're not going to shoot Zoya. You're not going to shoot anyone, and you're going to let us go."

"I can't do that, Anya," Alexi said. "I will shoot you if I have to." Anya stepped forward until the pistol was touching her chest.

"What happened to sticking together?" Yeremiy asked, inching forward. "You're the ones who told me that our best chance of surviving is to work together. Now, this ship is headed to Mirgorod, which is where you said you want to go. And whatever this gadget thing is, they have it."

"He has it," Zoya corrected, looking at Alexi. She sighed, feeling defeated. "You make a good point. I can't just leave without that gadget, especially after seeing what it can do…"

Nikolai rushed Alexi.

"Give her the gadget," he demanded. "I don't care what your motives are or who you're working for. But I can see that you care about Anya, and guess what, Anya cares about Zoya. And the rest of us. So give us the gadget and let us go, unless you really want to see Anya suffering. Which, I don't know, maybe you do. Maybe you're just that sick—"

Alexi punched Nikolai in the face.

"I don't have the gadget," Alexi said quietly. "I sneaked it to Anya when no one was looking." Anya nodded and patted a small bag slung around her shoulders. Nikolai glanced between them, holding his hand on his face.

"Ok then," he said. "Well, good."

Zoya peered down the beach.

"No one is paying attention to us," she told her friends. "We can run into the trees—"

"Excuse me," Yeremiy interrupted. "I haven't changed my mind. You said we'd work together. You deserted me once already, now you're scheming to do so again. I promise you, if you stay with the *Hell's Jewel*, we'll all get what we want."

"How's that?" Alexi asked, crossing his arms. "What are you up to?" Yeremiy's face flushed bright red.

"Come with us," Lilia urged, ignoring Alexi. Her eyes lit up. "You're a navigator, right? We don't need the pirates. Do you know where we are? Do you know where the nearest town is?"

Yeremiy glanced around, sticking his hands into his pockets. He bobbed his head back and forth then nodded.

"The storm had me all sorts of turned-around," he admitted. "But, we're definitely somewhere in Chereplazh."

"Chereplazh?" Zoya said. "Really?"

GRIGORY'S GADGET

"Chereplazh is so densely populated," Nikolai thought aloud, "if we go in any direction we're bound to run into a town before long."

"No! You're not running anywhere! More to the point, I *can't* run anywhere!" Yeremiy gestured to his wounded leg.

"I'm sorry," Demyan told him. "You can come with us or not, but we're done being prisoners, and we're going." Demyan grabbed Zoya by the hand and sprinted into the woods.

"We can't just leave him!" Lilia called to her friends, glancing at Yeremiy.

"I'll make sure he gets home safe," Alexi said. "I promise."

With a hesitant nod, Lilia ran after Demyan and Zoya. Nikolai stared at Alexi for a moment then turned and followed his friends.

Anya glanced around, grabbed Alexi, and kissed him full on the lips.

"Thank you," she told him. Then she ran as well.

"Stop!" Yeremiy shouted, trying to chase the group into the woods. "Please!" He stumbled on his crutch, hobbling as fast as he could manage.

The forest was dense with foliage. As they ran, the friends climbed and leapt over tree roots and fallen branches, pushing heavy fronds out of their way. Behind them, they could hear the voices of the pirates giving chase. Then, the forest gave way to a cobblestone road. A few hundred feet away, the road was bordered by brick buildings.

"Come on!" Zoya urged her friends, running toward the town. She and her friends ran between the buildings, turning off the main street and through side streets. They charged through a bazaar packed with people. Turning down another side street and then into an alley, the friends collapsed on the ground, gasping for breath. They listened for the pirates' shouts, but heard nothing other than the bustle of the town.

"Now what?" Lilia asked, glancing around at her friends.

"Let's find somewhere to lay low for a while," Zoya suggested. After she and her friends finished catching their breath, they slowly headed out of the alley.

The sun peeked through the clouds, its light reflecting on the large windows of the town's buildings. The town had a warm feel to it, its bricks all reds, oranges, and browns. Shop fronts lined the street, colorful awnings sheltering fresh meats, clothing, and pottery. As Zoya and her friends roamed the street, a tram whizzed by on steel tracks, carrying two dozen passengers.

At the corner, the friends spotted a small shop labeled *Agnessa's Creperie and Tea Shop*.

"What's a creperie?" Demyan asked as they walked toward the shop.

GRIGORY'S GADGET

"It's food," Lilia replied, placing her hand on her stomach. "Delicious food, and with tea, too!"

"Doesn't look like a place pirates would frequent," Nikolai said.

"Then in we go," Zoya told her friends.

As they entered, they were met with a blast of warm, sweet-smelling air. The scent of teas, fruits, and batter made the friends salivate.

"Only problem," Zoya said, "is we don't have money."

"On the contrary," Anya said, pulling a small satchel out of the one that held the gadget. "Alexi dropped this in the bag as well." She jingled the satchel and smiled.

"Seems like he's really on our side," Lilia said.

"I don't think he's on anyone's side," Nikolai replied, "other than his own."

"I thought you were starting to like him," Anya said.

"That was before he tried to make me commit murder," Nikolai said, folding his arms.

"Well," Zoya said, "all that matters is we have money, so we can eat!"

A stout woman with tan skin and curly, bright-red hair worked the counter. The name *Nessa* was scribbled on a nametag pinned to her ruffled blouse. She smiled as the friends approached.

"Welcome to Agnessa's," she greeted. "What can I get for you?" Her voice was melodious and cheerful. Lilia stepped forward.

"A cup of tea, please," she said, "with sugar. And one creper." Nessa chuckled softly.

"You mean a crepe?" she asked. Lilia's face flushed.

"Um, yes," she said. "Sorry. I've only ever read about them; we don't have creperies where we're from."

"Well, you're in for a treat," Nessa said. "What would you like on the crepe?" Lilia blushed again, glancing around the counter. Nessa gestured to a hand-written sign beside her.

"We have all these fruits," she said, pointing, "as well as chocolate sauce, peanut butter, honey, confectioner's sugar. There are also meats and cheeses if you prefer."

Lilia's mouth hung open as she studied the list. "You have all of this? Here?"

"Yes," Nessa replied. "We get all of our fruits fresh from the bazaar every week."

"Fresh?" Lilia repeated. Her head was spinning. She placed her hands over her mouth and studied the list of choices some more.

"Oh, strawberries, please," she said after a moment. "And apples. And honey." Nessa nodded and smiled, scribbling on a note pad.

The others huddled by the list of toppings, studying it intently. Zoya ordered next, a crepe with strawberries, bananas, and peanut butter with a cup of tea.

GRIGORY'S GADGET

"I need some meat," Anya said as she stepped forward to order. "Is it salted meat?"

"Also fresh," Nessa replied. "We also get our meat fresh from the bazaar." Anya's mouth watered at the thought.

"Oh, chicken with Gouda, please," Anya said, smiling. "And tea, of course." Nikolai and Demyan followed Anya's lead, each getting a crepe with chicken and cheese.

After placing their orders, the friends sat at a table in the back of the creperie, as far from the windows and door as possible.

"I can't wait," Zoya said. "Fresh fruit! I've never had fresh fruit before."

"Only the half-rotted-then-frozen stuff," Demyan agreed.

Nessa brought them their cups of tea, and a few minutes later their crepes.

"So where are you all from that you've never had the pleasure of eating crepes before?" she asked.

"Lodninsk, Morozhia" Lilia replied.

"You don't say," Nessa said. "Don't see many people from Morozhia here. I figured I'd see even less since the war started. Unless, are you refugees?" Nessa's face turned as red as her hair as she realized the rude directness of her question.

"No, not refugees," Anya answered, unperturbed. "We're moving to Mirgorod." Nessa bit her lip and thought for a moment.

"I see," she said. "Anyway, I hope you enjoy your crepes."

Zoya ravaged her crepe, which was filled with more flavor than anything she had ever eaten before. For the first time she could remember, she actually enjoyed food. This was not bland salted meat, or stale bread, or watered-down stew. This was tart, sweet, tender, and juicy. Once the friends finished eating, they leaned back with a satisfied sigh.

The bell above the door chimed as the door open. Zoya sat up straight and glanced nervously at the door, expecting to see one of the pirates. Instead, she saw a short, bearded man. His skin was rough and appeared to be covered in ash. Or was the skin itself gray?

"Good day, Czibor," Nessa said to the man with a smile. Czibor nodded in greeting and sat at a table by the windows. Nessa poured him a cup of tea and walked behind the counter to prepare his order.

Lilia, despite herself, stared at Czibor as he sipped his tea.

"No," she muttered slowly. "It can't be."

"What?" Zoya asked, doing her best not to look directly at the stranger. "Why are you staring?"

Lilia gestured for Demyan and Nikolai to look. Red-faced, they followed her gaze.

"That isn't..." Lilia started. "Is it?"

"I don't think so," Demyan said, turning back to his cup of tea.

GRIGORY'S GADGET

"No way," Nikolai uttered. He stared, slack-jawed, at the man.

"What?" Zoya asked again.

"Do we have a problem?" Czibor asked, glaring at Lilia. Lilia glanced down, her face turning red.

"No, sir," she said. "Sorry."

Nessa walked over to Czibor and whispered something in his ear. The man huffed and glared at the friends more intensely.

"Morozhian pigs!" he spat. "Figures." Nessa glanced warily between her customers, wringing her hands.

"Hey," Nikolai objected. "Who are you calling pigs?"

"Now, let's all be civil," Nessa said. "We all are here for a bit of peace and quiet, a cup of tea, a nice crepe." Czibor shook his head and turned back to his table.

"You're all the same," he grumbled, sipping his tea. "I'm sure me and my folk are so *amusing* to you."

"Not amusing," Lilia defended. "Just...well, I thought you were mythical." Czibor guffawed then shook his head.

"What do they teach you people in Morozhia?" he asked. "Maybe you're too young to remember anything before the Segregation Mandate. But did they truly erase us from your history books?"

"I don't understand," Anya interrupted.

"So you *are* a Skarbnik," Nikolai said to Czibor. The man nodded.

"Yes," he said. "As real as any of you, and just as deserving of rights and freedom and dignity! Chereplazh is a good, modern nation, best get used to it! We don't need backward-thinking imbeciles mucking it all up!"

"Czibor," Nessa said, raising a hand. "They aren't trying to start any trouble."

"Vestnik give me strength," Czibor mumbled, glancing up.

"The Segregation Mandate," Nikolai said to his friends. "It sounds familiar. I think they must have glossed over it in school."

Zoya lowered her voice. "So he's a Skarbnik? Like, one of those cave-dwelling fairies or whatever?" Her voice wasn't lowered enough.

"Fairies!" Czibor protested, standing. "Bah! We're people, same as anyone else! A little shorter, but a lot tougher." Czibor flexed his arms in demonstration. The friends assumed he had impressive muscles, but his loose jacket hid them. "You don't remember what the Segregation Mandate was? I'll tell you. I had a cousin who lived in Morozhia all those years ago. Good, hardworking miner. Had a wife and three kids. That Segregation Mandate? It drove them all underground, into the caves. They weren't allowed on the surface under any circumstances or else they'd be arrested, given some sorry excuse of a trial, and executed. So, he and his family lived underground, feeding off scraps they could find in the tunnels under cities. Few years later, they all

GRIGORY'S GADGET

died in the Great Skarbnik Riot in the mines near Lodninsk."

"When was that?" Anya asked.

"About seven years ago," Czibor replied. "Now, you must remember that?"

"That was the year of the cave-in," Demyan said, his eyes wide. He and Anya stared at the Skarbnik, moisture building in their eyes.

"They caused the cave-in?" Anya asked through clenched teeth. "Do you have any idea how many people were killed in that cave-in?"

"Do you?" Czibor asked coolly. Anya's face turned red as she stood, slamming her fist on the table.

"My father and brother were killed in your so-called riot!" she shouted. "And both of Demyan's parents!"

Nessa scurried behind her counter, making up more cups of tea.

"And my cousin and his family," Czibor said to Anya. "Reports here said hundreds of humans died in that riot. And *thousands* of Skarbniki. The Skarbniki didn't cause that cave-in; your military did. That was how they quelled the riot."

Anya sunk back into her seat, her gaze a thousand yards away.

"Tea," Nessa insisted, placing fresh cups in front of all her customers. "Please, no need to relive those awful times."

"You know," Czibor said, "I've always heard Morozhians had restrictions on what they were allowed to know, allowed to learn. But this is ridiculous. I feel sorry for you kids. At least you're out of there now. Maybe there's hope for you." He turned back to his table and took the new cup of tea with a nod to Nessa. Nessa breathed a sigh of relief as the conversation calmed down.

The friends looked thoughtfully into their own cups of tea.

"Where do we even begin?" Zoya wondered. "If they told us such blatant lies about things happening right in our city, who knows how much we have wrong?"

"I have a great idea!" Nessa declared. "Valoselo has a fantastic public library just a few blocks from here. It's the biggest in the country. Not just books, though it has plenty of those. It also has newspapers going back at least two decades, probably more. I hear they can save them using tiny photographs."

"Microfilm," Czibor said

"Anyway, they're closed by now, but they'll be open all day tomorrow."

After finishing his tea, Czibor stood and walked toward the exit. He nodded a goodnight to Nessa and somewhat begrudgingly to the five friends. Nessa busied herself cleaning up his dishes.

"That sounds great!" Lilia said. "A library is much more my speed, especially compared to a pir—" She cut herself short, her face turning red.

GRIGORY'S GADGET

"We don't have a place to stay," Zoya said. She looked at Anya. "You don't happen to have enough money for a hotel room, do you?"

"You need a place to stay?" Nessa asked, setting Czibor's dishes behind the counter. "I've got a back room to this place I keep for guests, visiting family, and such. You help me clean and close for the night, you can stay free of charge. Assuming you'll have breakfast here in the morning." Nessa winked and smiled.

"That's very kind of you," Anya agreed. "Thank you very much!"

CHAPTER TEN

Yeremiy stumbled out onto the cobblestone path, glancing hopelessly at the edge of the town of Valoselo. He bent over, trying to catch his breath as he straightened his glasses, leaning heavily on his crutch. Gotfrid, Igor, Adam, and Pyotr emerged from the trees, red-faced and out of breath. Adam grabbed Yeremiy by the collar and swung him against a tree.

"You had one job!" he yelled. "How could you let them escape?"

"The other one, Alexi," Yeremiy stammered. "He said he would help watch, but he let them go. I couldn't run fast enough to catch them."

"Snezhana is dealing with that little brat," Gotfrid stated. He walked up to Yeremiy, grabbing his arm and pulling him close.

"You can fix this," Gotfrid told him. "If you ever want to get home to your fiancée, you need to help

GRIGORY'S GADGET

us find them." Gotfrid turned to the other men. "We'll split up, comb this town. The highest priority is that we find Zoya. Start with the port. They'll be looking for a way to Mirgorod, I'm sure."

As the men headed into the town, Gotfrid pulled Yeremiy aside again. He pulled a sack of coins out of his pocket, then unfastened one of his holsters and handed it and the pistol within it to Yeremiy.

"Don't make me regret this," Gotfrid told him. Yeremiy nodded and strapped the holster to his hip.

Lilia scrubbed down a table in Agnessa's Creperie and Tea Shop, eying Nikolai, who was mopping the floor across the room. She looked down at the table, scrunched her eyebrows, and looked back up. Fidgeting with Pavel's necklace with one hand, she walked toward Nikolai.

"Nikolai," Lilia said softly. "Can we talk?"

Nikolai stopped sweeping and looked up then glanced toward their friends. Zoya was washing dishes as Demyan and Anya cleaned the counter top and griddles.

"Um, sure," he said.

Lilia kept her voice low. "I just wanted to talk about when you tried to kiss me." Nikolai sniffed and began to sweep again.

"It's not a big deal," he said. "Forget about it. It's fine."

"No, it's not fine," Lilia said, grabbing the handle of the broom. Nikolai looked at her with hurt in his eyes.

"I didn't mean," he started, "I, I'm sorry. I didn't mean to offend you."

"That's not what I mean," Lilia replied. "I wasn't offended. I mean, what isn't fine is that you're upset."

"I'm not upset."

Lilia tilted her head.

"You tried to kiss me, I pushed you away, and you ran away to the other side of the ship," Lilia recalled. "It's safe to assume you're upset."

"It doesn't matter." Nikolai pulled the broom from Lilia's grasp and walked toward the dustpan, which hung on the wall.

"Of course it matters," Lilia said, following him and lowering her whisper even more. "You're my friend. Just because I don't have *other types* of feelings for you, that hasn't changed. I care about you. There's too much going on right now, Nikolai, for either of us to lose a friend."

Nikolai grabbed the dustpan and stood silently, his back to Lilia. He took a deep breath and turned back around.

"You're right," he said. "I am upset. But you're also right that neither of us wants to lose a friend." He walked over to the small pile of dust and dirt he'd swept and began pushing it into the dustpan.

GRIGORY'S GADGET

"How can I help?" Lilia asked. Nikolai gave a weak smile.

"Just be my friend," he said. Lilia nodded, deciding not to push the issue any further.

The Valoselo Library was a grand building, surrounded on all sides by stone steps that gave it the semblance of a pyramid. The building itself was stone as well, with two large columns bordering its main entrance. Each of the library's windows was made of stained glass, depicting scenes from history and fiction alike.

"Let's hide in the single most conspicuous building in town," Nikolai said with disdain.

"No one will be looking for us in a library," Anya replied, matching his tone.

"Plus, I bet it's *huge* inside," Lilia added, her eyes wide with wonder. She'd never seen a library so magnificent.

"Let's hurry," Zoya insisted. "This sunlight makes my hair even brighter than usual. If any of the pirates are around, they'll spot me in an instant."

"I told you, you should have stolen Nessa's hat," Anya said. "If you pinned up your hair, it would have hidden it almost completely."

"And I told you I'm not stealing from a perfectly nice woman who gave us food and shelter!" Zoya replied. "We've been spending way too much time with pirates."

"Alright, alright," Nikolai interrupted. "Let's go!"

The friends scurried up the steps to the library, surrounding Zoya, who kept her head low.

"It took me so long to get over being self-conscious about my hair," Zoya grumbled as they climbed. "Back to square one."

The friends opened the library's massive door with a collective huff, then froze in awe.

The library was four stories tall, and the entryway was open to all four levels. The floors were shining marble and had swirls of gold and silver spiraling down rows of bookshelves. The shelves themselves were dark, polished wood and extended from floor to ceiling on each level of the building. Gaslights dotted the shelves every six feet, adding to the natural light cast by the building's stained glass windows. A pale statue marked the end of each row of shelves, each one the image of a notable scientist or poet.

"Forget Mirgorod," Lilia said with a wide smile. "This is my paradise."

"Mine, too," Demyan and Nikolai agreed.

"Where do we even start?" Anya asked, turning in a half-circle, taking it all in.

"Well, Nessa suggested reading newspapers on microfilm," Zoya said. "I guess we can look for that first?"

Lilia turned to the left and walked toward a large desk by the entrance. A young dandy sporting a purple brocade vest slouched miserably in his chair,

GRIGORY'S GADGET

"How can I help?" Lilia asked. Nikolai gave a weak smile.

"Just be my friend," he said. Lilia nodded, deciding not to push the issue any further.

The Valoselo Library was a grand building, surrounded on all sides by stone steps that gave it the semblance of a pyramid. The building itself was stone as well, with two large columns bordering its main entrance. Each of the library's windows was made of stained glass, depicting scenes from history and fiction alike.

"Let's hide in the single most conspicuous building in town," Nikolai said with disdain.

"No one will be looking for us in a library," Anya replied, matching his tone.

"Plus, I bet it's *huge* inside," Lilia added, her eyes wide with wonder. She'd never seen a library so magnificent.

"Let's hurry," Zoya insisted. "This sunlight makes my hair even brighter than usual. If any of the pirates are around, they'll spot me in an instant."

"I told you, you should have stolen Nessa's hat," Anya said. "If you pinned up your hair, it would have hidden it almost completely."

"And I told you I'm not stealing from a perfectly nice woman who gave us food and shelter!" Zoya replied. "We've been spending way too much time with pirates."

"Alright, alright," Nikolai interrupted. "Let's go!"

The friends scurried up the steps to the library, surrounding Zoya, who kept her head low.

"It took me so long to get over being self-conscious about my hair," Zoya grumbled as they climbed. "Back to square one."

The friends opened the library's massive door with a collective huff, then froze in awe.

The library was four stories tall, and the entryway was open to all four levels. The floors were shining marble and had swirls of gold and silver spiraling down rows of bookshelves. The shelves themselves were dark, polished wood and extended from floor to ceiling on each level of the building. Gaslights dotted the shelves every six feet, adding to the natural light cast by the building's stained glass windows. A pale statue marked the end of each row of shelves, each one the image of a notable scientist or poet.

"Forget Mirgorod," Lilia said with a wide smile. "This is my paradise."

"Mine, too," Demyan and Nikolai agreed.

"Where do we even start?" Anya asked, turning in a half-circle, taking it all in.

"Well, Nessa suggested reading newspapers on microfilm," Zoya said. "I guess we can look for that first?"

Lilia turned to the left and walked toward a large desk by the entrance. A young dandy sporting a purple brocade vest slouched miserably in his chair,

GRIGORY'S GADGET

obviously bored. His dark hair was short and neat, and he had a well-manicured moustache. He perked up slightly as the friends approached.

"How may I assist you?" he asked in a practiced tone.

"We're hoping to read some newspapers on microfilm," Lilia said.

"Really?" the dandy asked. "Alright, I'll go fetch my mother. She's the librarian." The dandy stood and walked, with a complete lack of urgency, down one of the rows of shelves.

"Ooh, mythology," Nikolai said, reading the label of a nearby bookshelf. He walked over to it and began perusing its contents.

"There are so many *different* books." Nikolai ran his fingers along the spines of the books, eyes wide with excitement. "All different stories from all different times and places. And it just keeps going!" Lilia and Demyan joined him.

"They've found their element," Anya said to Zoya, who smiled.

A few moments later, an older woman emerged from another row of shelves. Her gray hair was tucked back in a neat bun, and she wore a simple but elegant dress of brown and gold. She smiled at the friends.

"We don't get many folks in the library on a Sunday," she said. "Especially on such a lovely Sunday." The woman nodded and turned, gesturing for the friends to follow her to the other side of the library. The gold in her dress shone as they passed by the stained glass windows.

"Oh, how rude, my apologies," the librarian said abruptly, turning to face the friends. "My name is Miss Pasternack. It's lovely to meet you." The friends introduced themselves in turn.

"Miss?" Anya questioned with a glance back toward her dandy son.

"Divorced," Miss Pasternack responded. "Had I waited on that another year, I'd be widowed. Oh well."

Lilia glanced at her friends, equal parts concerned and amused. Miss Pasternack led them to a winding iron staircase that descended below the main floor. As they walked down the stairs, Lilia was once again overcome with awe at the size of the library. The basement level was as tall as the main level, but ranged farther, mimicking the footprint of the exterior stairs.

Once they reached the bottom, Miss Pasternack opened a door to the right, revealing a dark room with more shelves. Instead of books, these shelves contained folders of files. In the center of the room was a device that, at a glance, looked to be an open suitcase. Upon closer inspection, it was much more complex than that.

"We have one of the first *electric* microfilm readers," Miss Pasternack explained. "All of our microfilms are filed in this room geographically then chronologically then alphabetically. When you find

GRIGORY'S GADGET

what you're looking for, insert the sheet here." She gestured to the back of the device in the center of the room. "Flip this switch here. You can zoom in and out with this lever, move up and down with this dial, and side to side with that dial."

When Miss Pasternack flipped the machine on, it projected light onto the back of the reader. She slid in a sample sheet to demonstrate how the machine worked.

"It's electric?" Demyan asked.

"Yes," Miss Pasternack replied. "Much safer than using a gas lamp. We've lost precious documents due to fires in the past. Electricity is quite the novel invention."

"Fascinating," Demyan said, taking a closer look at the device.

"I'll leave you to your research," Miss Pasternack told the friends. "If you require any assistance, I'll be on the main floor." She nodded politely and left the room.

With a grin, Nikolai pulled out a leather-bound book and placed it on the table. The hefty tome released a plume of dust as it landed with a *thud*.

"Did you have that the whole time?" Zoya asked.

"Yes," Nikolai said with pride. "I took it from the mythology section. Thought it might be useful. Look at the title."

The title was stamped into the cover of the book: *Powerful Items of Myths and Legends*. Zoya frowned, skeptical.

"I don't know," she said. "Doesn't the fact that it exists automatically make it *not* a myth?"

"Not necessarily," Nikolai said. "Most myths are based on *something* real, just exaggerated or misinterpreted over time."

"You look through that," Anya suggested, "and we'll start looking through newspapers."

Nodding in agreement, Nikolai and Demyan opened the leather book and began reading. Lilia, Anya, and Zoya began to sift through the files on the shelf labeled *Morozhia*. The task was even more daunting than they initially realized. The better part of a day passed before Nikolai called to his friends.

"Ah-ha!" he announced. "I told you! Look at this." Nikolai turned the book around so the girls could see. Before Lilia could read very far, Nikolai began to explain with great enthusiasm.

"A ball of metal in its inert form," he said, "but actually disguised armor. When it's triggered, it becomes magical armor that defends against any weapon, as well as giving the wearer magical powers." Nikolai shrugged and gave a slight laugh. "I don't know about magic, but that sounds a lot like your gadget."

"The Bronnerush," Zoya read aloud. She continued reading down the page. "Invented and forged over three hundred years ago by..." Zoya trailed off, furrowing her brow. She looked up at her friends. "Grigory Orlov. Do you think he's a distant relative?" Zoya kept reading.

GRIGORY'S GADGET

"Wait," she said a moment later. "He was from Vernulaia! Er, I mean, it wasn't Vernulaia back then. It says he eventually fled to a remote location in the frozen tundra of the north because he was afraid of the Bronnerush's power."

"Lodninsk, I'm guessing?" Demyan asked. Zoya nodded.

"Well, did I tell you, or did I tell you?" Nikolai gloated. "I knew that book would have some useful information!"

"Purple hair," Zoya gasped. "It even explains the purple hair. After the forging of the Bronnerush, Grigory Orlov's hair began to grow bright purple, a result of his exposure to the device's power."

"So I guess that would make you a direct descendant," Anya said. Zoya collapsed into a nearby chair. Demyan rushed over to her and started massaging her shoulders.

"My head hurts," she said. She sat silently for a moment, letting the flood of information sink in. Lilia and Anya returned to examining microfilm.

"Hey, look at this," Lilia told her friends, pointing to the article projected on the reader. The article she gestured to was titled "Pirates Invading Lodninsk" and had an engraving of Snezhana.

"What?" Zoya gasped as she walked toward the device. She leaned over and started to read the article.

"What was Snezhana doing in Lodninsk?" Lilia wondered.

"What's the date of the paper?" Demyan asked. Zoya looked up at the corner of the page.

"It's from ten years ago," she said. She continued reading.

"Do you think she was looking for the gadget back then?" Anya whispered. "Do you think she knew it was in Lodninsk?"

Zoya's hands tightened into fists, pushing into the surface of the table. She began breathing heavily as tears welled up in her eyes.

"Zoya, what is it?" Demyan asked gently. He placed a hand on her shoulder. Zoya slammed her fists on the table and backed toward the wall, covering her face with her hands. Lilia glanced at her friends with concern.

"She—" Zoya started, her voice cracking. "She's the one. She's the one that killed my mother."

Anya leaned over to read the article.

"Pirates ran amok in the mining city of Lodninsk," Anya read aloud. "Leading a series of assaults and muggings, which have resulted in several injuries and murders."

"It doesn't say anything about your mother," Lilia noted.

"The timing works out," Zoya replied. "And I remember that her murder was not an isolated incident."

"Why didn't our newspaper say it was pirates?" Nikolai asked. "I don't remember hearing anything about pirates."

"They probably buried that detail," Anya suggested. "Seems like they bury a lot of details."

"It's a good thing we escaped," Demyan said. Lilia wondered if he meant escaping from Lodninsk or the pirates. *Both*, she decided.

Zoya stared blankly into the distance.

"We need to go," she stated after a moment. "We should get out of Valoselo." Without waiting for her friends to reply, Zoya exited the room and climbed the spiral stairs.

As the group ran through the buildings toward the edge of town, Nikolai could see spotlights shining up into the evening sky. A large crowd had gathered around a huge zeppelin sitting by the beach. Nikolai and his friends stood behind them.

Two magnificently dressed people stood on a platform in front of the crowd. The man had bright blue hair shaped such that it resembled an ocean wave, while the woman beside him sported short pastel pink hair poking out around her aviator goggles. Both wore brocade suits of red, orange, and gold.

"And the view is just spectacular, folks, I'll tell ya!" the man declared. "Yes sir, the airship is by far the best mode of transportation! Whether you want to go over land or sea, you can rely on our airships!"

In front of the couple, people were signing a piece of paper and handing money up to the woman.

"Thank you very much," she said as each customer paid.

"We'll be making stops in all the major cities in Chereplazh then we'll set off to Mirgorod, Vernulaia!"

"Scammers. I've heard of these two. They take all of the money then claim the weather isn't cooperating." Nikolai spun around to see Yeremiy walking out from the shadows between the buildings. Startled, Nikolai and his friends backed away from Yeremiy while searching for a way out.

"Sorry," Gotfrid said, stepping out of the crowd. "There's no escaping now. Let's not make a scene. You don't want any of these innocent people killed, do you?"

"You can't do anything here," Zoya said. "If you harm anyone, you'll be arrested!"

"Sounds like a risk I'm willing to take," Gotfrid said, looking at the other members of Snezhana's crew as they appeared and surrounded the captives. "Are you willing to bet your friends' lives on that?"

The pirates drew their pistols and pointed them at Zoya's friends.

"Fine," Zoya said. "Let's not make a scene, though, like you said. We'll go without any trouble." Already the pirates' pistols had drawn the attention of some people in the crowd. They glanced about nervously.

"I have a quick draw," Gotfrid stated as he put his pistol in its holster. "In case you're thinking of trying anything."

GRIGORY'S GADGET

As soon as the pirates' put their guns away, Anya charged forward and knocked Gotfrid on to his back. The group of friends sprinted away, into the crowd. Nikolai heard a gunshot and turned to see an old man fall to the ground with blood spreading across his abdomen. The crowd began to scream and yell, dispersing in every direction.

"No, wait!" the airship man shouted. "It's alright! Don't go!" The woman grabbed his arm, and their bag of cash, and pulled him with her as she ran into the airship.

Members of the panicking crowd pushed Lilia to the ground as they ran by. Nikolai stopped to help her up and came face to face with Adam. Adam grabbed Lilia, only to be promptly punched in the face by Nikolai. The pirate let out a yelp of pain then reached for his pistol. Lilia wrestled out of his grip as he lifted the pistol and shot Nikolai. Nikolai stumbled backward as sharp pain spread through his shoulder. He squeezed the wound. With a growl of pain, he charged toward Adam.

"I don't think so," Igor said. Nikolai turned to see that he had grabbed Lilia and held a pistol to her head. "That's enough of that." Zoya, Demyan, and Anya had been apprehended by the other pirates.

"Give up," Gotfrid said. "You can't get away from us, we'll just find you again. Besides, I thought you all wanted to go to Mirgorod? See, we all have the same goal in mind."

"How are you going to get to Mirgorod without your navigator?" Nikolai growled. Yeremiy was nowhere to be seen.

"We'll make due," Gotfrid replied. "Mr. Robertov took notes on his maps, which we still have."

The pirates pushed their captives toward the edge of the city as the last remnants of the panicked crowd fled. Nikolai heard the distant shouts of police he and his friends disappeared into the trees.

Zoya's gaze was fixed intensely on the lights of the *Hell's Jewel* as they approached it on the dinghy. The thought of Snezhana murdering her mother pushed all other thoughts out of her mind.

"Are you ok?" Demyan asked her.

"Absolutely," she replied, still looking at the ship before them.

Nikolai let out a painful cry, still gripping his shoulder. Lilia helped him to apply pressure to his wound.

"He needs your doctor," she told Gotfrid. "As soon as we get on the ship, he needs his wound cleaned."

"You're not in any position to make demands," Gotfrid replied coolly. Tears welled in Lilia's eyes as she glared at the pirates.

Snezhana stood by the edge of the ship as the dinghy was lifted. Zoya sprang out of the little boat and ran toward Snezhana. Before the pirates could

GRIGORY'S GADGET

stop Zoya, she had slapped the pirate captain across the face. Igor and Adam rushed to restrain her, grabbing her by the arms and dragging her back. Snezhana laughed.

"You know who I am," Zoya accused.

"Of course," Snezhana replied. "We have met before, dear. You're Zoya." Snezhana turned to her crew. "Did she hit her head or something?" The crew laughed.

"No," Zoya went on. "I mean you know *exactly* who I am. I'm the daughter of the woman you slaughtered mercilessly in the streets of Lodninsk!"

Snezhana's expression turned dark. "Do not presume to accuse me of crimes I did not commit, especially not on my own ship."

"You're a liar and a thief," Zoya told her. "And you are a murderer. You should still be rotting in prison. Or better yet, you should be hanged."

Snezhana grabbed Zoya her by the chin and peering into her eyes.

"I did not kill your mother," she stated. "But I did rot in that prison in Lodninsk for nine years nonetheless. You want to know who killed your mother? Who framed me and sent me to that prison? My weaselly little brother. Your Captain Edmund Sokoll." Snezhana stepped back and regarded her other prisoners.

"Send them all down to the brig," she commanded. "And make sure Zoya is not in the same cell as my brother. I don't want him dead just yet."

Before the group disappeared below deck, Snezhana shouted, "Wait." She walked over to the prisoners with a smirk.

"Take their bags," she told her crew. "I know Alexi gave the gadget to one of you. I think it should be kept safe with me now."

In the brig of the ship, Captain Sokoll was fast asleep on the floor of his own cell. Fresh bandages covered the wound on his abdomen. Alexi, in a separate cell, smiled as the other captives were brought in.

"Well this is much better company," he said. Anya, Lilia, and Zoya were thrown into the empty cell, Demyan and Nikolai in with Alexi.

"Don't I get to see your doctor?" Nikolai asked, still holding his shoulder. Ignoring him, the pirates left the room.

Zoya walked over to the side of the cell and glared at Alexi.

"You knew, didn't you?" she said. "You knew your aunt killed my mother?" Alexi tilted his head, glancing at his father.

"Did she tell you that?" he asked. Zoya shook her head.

"She denied it," Zoya said. "But—"

"She didn't do it," Alexi said.

GRIGORY'S GADGET

"But I saw the old newspaper article," Zoya replied. "She went to prison for it."

Alexi pointed to Captain Sokoll.

"My father shows affection in strange ways. He framed her to get rid of the competition."

"Competition?" Zoya asked.

"For the gadget," Alexi replied. "For years they searched for it together, but as they got close to finding it, my father decided he didn't like the idea of sharing power."

Zoya collapsed onto the floor and leaned against the wall.

"So he killed my mother because…"

"Because she shared your purple hair," Alexi said. "So he knew she had the gadget, or at least knew where it was."

Zoya looked Alexi over for a moment. "Were you there?"

Alexi shook his head. "I hadn't joined my father's crew yet. I was too young. I still lived with my mother." He cleared his throat and turned away. Captain Sokoll started to stir from his sleep.

"Oh, good," he mumbled when he saw the others in the room. "They brought me my crew."

"We're not your crew," Anya told him. Captain Sokoll chuckled as he lifted himself to a sitting position propped against the wall.

"Well, we are between ships at the moment," Captain Sokoll said. "I'll admit that's not ideal. But don't worry, your captain is resourceful."

"We're not your crew, and you're not our captain, *Edmund*," Lilia said.

Captain Sokoll bristled when Lilia said his name. "Alexi, what's gotten into them?"

"They don't like the taste of betrayal." Alexi shrugged.

"Well neither do I," Captain Sokoll said. His face turned red. "This seems like betrayal alright, betrayal of your captain."

"You killed my mother," Zoya said, rising again to her feet. Captain Sokoll looked at her, expressionless and silent. Zoya laughed sadly.

"You won't even deny it," she said. "You don't even have the decency to deny it."

"I have the decency not to lie to my crew," Captain Sokoll replied.

"That's a load of crap," Anya said. "You had plenty of opportunities to tell us the truth."

"I didn't say I told you the truth," Captain Sokoll replied. "I said I don't lie. Sometimes omissions must be made for the good of the crew."

"Don't try to argue with him," Alexi said. "He's got an answer for everything."

"Nikolai?" Demyan said suddenly. He leaned over Nikolai, who had collapsed onto the floor. Nikolai was breathing heavily, his skin soaked in sweat.

"Nikolai?" Lilia called.

"Come on Nikolai," Demyan said. "Stay with us." He patted Nikolai's face then shook his unwounded shoulder. Nikolai didn't respond.

GRIGORY'S GADGET

"Snezhana!" Lilia yelled. "Snezhana! We need a doctor!" The friends listened for a moment, but heard no one coming.

"They're all busy preparing this god-awful ship," Captain Sokoll said. "I told her this ship is too big. On my ship, you'd be able to hear yelling from down here."

"That's because your ship has no walls left," Alexi mocked.

"You've got a brave tongue, boy, when there're bars between us," Captain Sokoll replied, his tone dark. "We'll see how brave you are when we get out of here."

A moment later, the engines of the ship grew louder, and the *Hell's Jewel* jerked into motion.

"Something doesn't sound right," Zoya said. She put her ear to the wall and listened to the sounds of the boiler room. Then she backed away until her back pressed into the bars of her cell.

"Snezhana!" She yelled as loudly as she could. "Snezhana!"

"Zoya, what's wrong?" Lilia asked.

"I've already been in one boiler explosion too many," Zoya replied. "Snezhana!"

"She can't hear you," Captain Sokoll told her. Zoya felt inside her pockets and glanced around the room.

"We need to get out of here," she said. "Right now. Do we have anything to pick the locks?"

"My aunt and her crew were extra cautious this time," Alexi told her.

Zoya smiled. "Give me your belt."

"Excuse me?" he asked.

"Not the one keeping your pants up," Zoya said, rolling her eyes. "The one over your shoulder, with the big buckle." Still puzzled, Alexi obliged and handed over his belt. Zoya lifted the prong of the buckle and stuck it into the lock on her cell.

"You can't just jam something into a lock and expect it to open," Alexi told her. "You got lucky with that knife before, but lock picking is a skill."

The lock on Zoya's cell clicked open.

"A skill I thought everyone had," Zoya said, swinging her door open. "Or is that just a Lodninski thing?"

She quickly unlocked Demyan, Nikolai' and Alexi's cell then stared at Captain Sokoll. Zoya stood motionless, the belt still in her hand, as Demyan and Alexi carried Nikolai out.

"Zoya," Alexi said, glancing between her and his father.

Zoya turned to Alexi then dropped his belt on the floor. Without a word, she turned and ran out of the room.

Before they reached the main deck, Pyotr and Igor intercepted them.

"Can't you just sit still for a little bit?" Pyotr asked.

"You just love being a pain, don't you?" Igor asked, moving toward them.

GRIGORY'S GADGET

"There's something wrong with the boilers," Zoya explained. "You need to warn your captain that there's too much pressure—"

"Enough with these tricks," Igor interrupted. "Now get back to your cells."

Before Igor and Pyotr could pull out their pistols, Zoya and her friends rushed past them, heading to the main deck.

Just as they reached the top of the stairs, the *Hell's Jewel's* boilers exploded.

CHAPTER ELEVEN

Zoya gasped for air as she reached the surface of the water. The force of the explosion had knocked her over the ship's railing. She looked around for her friends. One by one, Lilia, Anya, and Demyan surfaced. Demyan hoisted Nikolai up to keep him above water as well.

"Are you ok?" Zoya shouted to her friends.

"Nikolai isn't looking good," Demyan replied.

"We need to get to land!" Anya shouted.

They swam away from the sinking ship as Snezhana's crew dove into the water. Before long, they were clambering up the beach. Demyan brought Nikolai out of the water and laid him down on dry sand. Nikolai was still barely conscious. The wound on his shoulder was swollen and red.

"We need that doctor," Lilia cried.

GRIGORY'S GADGET

"Hopefully he survived the explosion," Demyan replied, glancing back at the wreckage. Smoke and fire engulfed the majority of the ship, which was sinking quickly. Demyan removed his belt and wrapped it tightly around Nikolai's wounded arm.

Gotfrid, Pyotr, and Igor scrambled up the beach, coughing violently. Pyotr and Igor were covered in minor burns. Gotfrid appeared relatively unharmed.

"Where's your doctor?" Zoya asked them. "Did he survive?"

"How the hell should we know?" Igor spat. The pirates fell onto their backs, breathing heavily.

"Where's the other one?" Lilia asked. "Adam?"

Igor frowned. He cleared his throat and replied, "Dead." Lilia's lips twitched into a smile.

A few moments later, Snezhana appeared.

"Doesn't a captain go down with her ship?" Zoya asked.

"We're pirates, dear," Snezhana replied, taking a seat in the sand. "Those types of honor codes don't really apply to us."

"You don't say."

"Oh good," Anya gasped, standing. "Alexi is ok!" He swam toward the beach, but appeared to be weighed down by something. As he reached the shore, he pulled an unconscious Captain Sokoll out of the water and dragged him to dry sand.

"You saved him," Zoya said. "I wish I could say I don't blame you. But I do."

"Zoya," Anya said. "He's his father."

"He's a murderer," Zoya said. She stood and walked away, looking for the doctor.

As she walked down the beach Zoya heard the whirring of engines from above. Over the trees a colorful airship appeared, its spotlights illuminating the shipwreck and the beach.

Slowly, the airship floated down to the ground, landing a few hundred feet from the survivors. The door to its gondola opened, and Yeremiy Robertov stepped out.

"Well," he said, putting his hands on his hips. "Looks like this was the perfect time to hijack an airship."

"I didn't know you had it in you, Mr. Robertov," Snezhana said as she approached the airship. "I'm impressed."

"Yes, good work, navigator," Gotfrid said, winking at Yeremiy. The survivors all gathered around the airship.

"How did you manage this?" Alexi asked. Yeremiy looked inside the airship gondola and gestured for someone to come over. A moment later, the bright-haired man and woman from Valoselo stepped forward. They smiled hesitantly at the pirates.

"I've made us some new friends," Yeremiy said. He gestured to the man and woman. "This is Vlad,

GRIGORY'S GADGET

and this is Svetlana. They're going to kindly fly us to Mirgorod in their airship."

Lilia stepped back. "No."

Zoya moved toward her, placing a hand on her shoulder. "Lilia, it will be alright. With our recent luck on marine ships, maybe we'll fare better on this." She nodded toward the airship.

Lilia shook her head. "Absolutely not. Those ships may not have survived, but *we* did. If something happens on the airship…"

"Come now, Lilia, this man got us a new ship." Captain Sokoll sat up and pointed toward the vessel. His voice was weak. "Now, I've never captained an airship before, but there's a first time for everything. I'll enjoy the challenge."

"This airship isn't for you," Yeremiy said. "This airship isn't for any of you pirate bastards. I'll be taking myself and my friends to Mirgorod, and then I'll get myself back home to Nanowrinsk. I made a promise."

"As nice as that is," Lilia said, "I'm not setting foot on that airship."

"Yeremiy," Demyan said. "Are there any first aid supplies on this airship?" Yeremiy looked to Vlad and Svetlana.

"Yes," Svetlana said. "We always make sure to keep the basics in stock." Demyan turned to Lilia.

"We need to worry about Nikolai right now," he said. "If we get him on that airship, he'll be off of this dirt and into somewhere more hygienic. We'll be able to clean out his wound and properly bandage it."

"We could bring him into the town," Lilia said.

"Not likely," Yeremiy replied. "We made quite the commotion in town. I suppose I should have mentioned: we really must be off soon. The authorities are hunting for us."

"For god's sake," Captain Sokoll said as he slowly climbed to his feet. "Just hit the girl over the head and knock her out." Lilia stumbled backwards, glaring at Captain Sokoll. Zoya, Anya, and Demyan stood in front of her, blocking his way.

"Fine!" Lilia shouted, waving her hands. "Fine, I'll go! Get me on the airship now before I change my mind."

As Zoya helped, Lilia boarded the airship, followed by their friends, Gotfrid pulled out his gun.

"We'll be coming too," he told Yeremiy. The other pirates pulled out their guns as well. Vlad and Svetlana ran behind the walls inside the gondola. Yeremiy laughed.

"Don't be foolish," he said. "I know all your guns are waterlogged. You couldn't shoot me if you tried."

Gotfrid threw his gun to the ground and clenched his fists.

"We had a deal, Yeremiy," he said.

"What?" Zoya asked, turning back around. "What are you talking about?"

GRIGORY'S GADGET

"Yes, I'm interested to know as well," Snezhana said, dropping her pistol. "What deal?" Yeremiy ignored them.

"Yes, we did." Yeremiy ran his fingers through his hair, muttering under his breath. "Fine. No weapons on the airship," he stated. "Waterlogged or not, it's too dangerous. I don't think any of us wants to be in another explosion."

"Absolutely not," Snezhana said. "You're not in any position to set such conditions." She unsheathed her sword and pointed it at Yeremiy.

"Captain," Gotfrid said, placing his hand on her arm. "If I may, I think he may be right. About guns, at least. We'll keep our swords."

"Absolutely not," Yeremiy replied. Gotfrid glared at him.

"Your friends, then," Gotfrid said. "They can have our weapons."

"What kind of foolhardy plan is that?" Igor shouted.

"Fine," Yeremiy replied. "Distribute any swords and daggers you have to my friends. Leave your guns on the beach."

Gotfrid nodded and turned to Snezhana, who eyed Yeremiy and Gotfrid warily. She removed her swords and daggers nonetheless. Once Snezhana was disarmed, Anya sprinted over to her. Without a word, she snatched the bag that held the gadget and returned to stand by her friends. Snezhana rolled her eyes.

"Why is he letting them on board?" Zoya asked Demyan. "What deal do they have?"

"Same one we heard, I'm betting," he replied. "He helps them get to Mirgorod, and they let him go home."

"But he refused that deal, remember?"

Demyan shrugged. "So he changed his mind. At least we'll get their weapons."

Zoya sighed and continued into the gondola.

By the entrance of the gondola was a full-size kitchen, stocked full of fresh fruits, vegetables, breads, and more. Beyond that was a dining and sitting area, decorated with green and blue striped wallpaper, mahogany furniture, and gilded trinkets. At the front of the gondola were the control and navigation rooms. Toward the back was a long corridor of cabins and two bathrooms. Lilia crouched in the corridor, away from any windows.

As the pirates boarded the airship, Zoya strode over to Yeremiy. "Could I ask a favor, since you decided to bring the pirates along?" She made no effort to hide her displeasure.

Yeremiy's face flushed. "Of course," he replied. "What can I do?"

"Tie Edmund up," Zoya said, "and put him in a different room. One of the cabins in the back."

Yeremiy smiled. "Gladly."

"You will address me as Captain!" Edmund said, limping toward Zoya.

"You're no captain," Zoya replied.

GRIGORY'S GADGET

Demyan stepped between Edmund and Zoya and folded his arms.

"I refuse to be tied up like an animal!" Edmund said.

"Have you not noticed you're woefully outnumbered?" Snezhana laughed. She looked to the other pirates. "I'm sure we can find some rope."

"Aye, Captain," Igor grinned. "I'll make sure he's nice and snug." He and the other surviving members of Snezhana's crew circled Edmund and shoved him toward the back of the gondola.

"Get your hands off me!" Edmund yelled, pushing back. He grunted as Igor jabbed him in his wounded side. Edmund doubled over. Snezhana and her crew took advantage of his pain, and dragged Edmund to the back of the ship.

After everyone had boarded the ship, Yeremiy distributed the pirates' swords and daggers to Zoya, Anya, and Demyan. Lilia, who sat on the floor, refused a weapon. She shook her head violently, closed her eyes, and tucked her head between her arms. Sighing, Yeremiy headed into the control room, followed by Vlad and Svetlana. Igor and Pyotr paced up and down the corridor, while Gotfrid stood silently by the cabin in which Edmund was stowed. Alexi and Snezhana leaned against a wall near the control room, watching everyone else.

Demyan and Zoya placed Nikolai comfortably on a couch in the gondola's parlor as Anya searched for the first aid supplies.

"Here," Anya said, stepping out of the kitchen with a small white kit. She pulled out some clean rags and began working on Nikolai's wound. The skin all around his shoulder was swollen and red, and he was still bleeding.

"Turn him over a bit," Anya told Demyan. Demyan obliged, moving Nikolai so that Anya could see the back of his shoulder.

"There's no exit wound," she said. "The bullet is still in there."

"So we need to get it out, right?" Zoya said.

"Yes, but I'm not a doctor," Anya replied. "Let's just clean it up for now. A doctor in Mirgorod can fix whatever we don't."

"His wound doesn't look good," Demyan said. "What if…"

"We don't have time for what ifs," Zoya interrupted. "We'll clean his wound, and he'll be fine."

"Yes, exactly," Anya agreed. "Of course, he'll be fine."

"You're not a doctor," Demyan said, staring at Anya. Anya ignored him, picking up a cloth and a bottle of clear liquid from the medical kit. She sniffed the liquid, wrinkled her nose, and soaked the cloth with it. Then she applied it to Nikolai's shoulder.

GRIGORY'S GADGET

Lilia still sat in the corridor, watching her friends tend to Nikolai.

Once Anya had finished bandaging Nikolai, Zoya walked toward the control room.

"Yeremiy," she called. "I noticed there are some speakers in the walls of the sitting area. Can this ship get telegrams or play music? It might help Lilia calm down."

Yeremiy turned to Vlad and Svetlana.

"Yes, sir," Vlad said. "I can turn on the telegraph. We also have a gramophone on board, and a large library of discs to play on it." Vlad grinned widely, then sauntered into a small side room where he started flipping switches and turning dials. After a moment, a series of beeps echoed out of the speakers. Zoya listened and tried to decipher them.

New steel ships give Starzapad edge over Morozhia at sea...Morozhia's fleet much greater...many small towns in ruins...Vernulaia may join war...

"Change it," Zoya said, rushing to where Vlad fiddled with the telegraph. "Something more soothing, maybe? Yes, perhaps one of the gramophone discs." Vlad's head bobbed up and down as he adjusted another dial. He moved to another panel, above which sat the large gramophone. Its base was a dark wood, engraved with images of airships, and its horn was polished brass. The beeping telegram faded away and was replaced by the soft sound of piano and violins emanating from the gramophone.

"Will that play through the speakers as well?" Zoya asked.

Vlad tapped a cluster of wires by the base of the gramophone. "We've modified this one so that it transmits through these," he said, grinning again.

"Thank you," Zoya said, returning to the sitting room.

"You don't think they're right?" Anya asked.

"Who?" Zoya replied.

"Whoever sent the telegram. Vernulaia wouldn't go to war?"

"Of course not," Zoya replied. "It must be a slow news day."

Alexi tut-tutted on the other side of the room.

"What is that about?" Anya asked him.

"I'm just amazed by your naiveté," he replied. Anya rolled her eyes and turned her attention back to Nikolai.

Zoya turned to look down the corridor. "This song is nice, isn't it, Lilia?"

Lilia, in spite of herself, began swaying to the melody. "It's a good dance tune," she said. She glanced over at Nikolai, asleep on the couch. "If Nikolai were awake, he'd complain about it. He'd say it's not exciting enough."

Demyan chuckled. "Maybe he'd say that in front of everyone, but I've caught him listening to this type of music quite a bit." The friends laughed, and began to relax on the airship. Anya reached into her bag and pulled out the gadget.

GRIGORY'S GADGET

"Here," she said, handing it to Zoya. "I think this will be safest with you." Zoya smiled and took the gadget. She turned it over in her hands, trying to figure out what had activated it before. Nothing immediately stood out. Zoya glanced up at the members of Snezhana's crew.

Gotfrid now stood by a window, his arms crossed behind his back as he peered out. Igor and Pyotr were still pacing, now joined by Alexi.

"Will you sit down already?" Anya asked.

"We're restless," Alexi said. "We're not used to not working. Not to mention your friend is bringing us to our execution."

"What are you talking about?" Anya asked.

"As soon as we land in Mirgorod, he'll have us arrested," Alexi explained. "That is, assuming every single one of us isn't arrested immediately anyway."

"I don't understand," Anya replied. "You all wanted to come on the ship."

"My father wanted to come on the ship. And Gotfrid."

Anya looked over at Snezhana, who had been listening.

"Gotfrid was very keen to come on this airship," Snezhana said. "That one always seems to have a plan. But I'm wondering now where his loyalties lie." She peered at Gotfrid, who had resumed his post by Edmund's door.

"I say we take the ship," Igor suggested, his hands forming fists. Zoya put a hand on the hilt of her sword.

"And how's that?" she asked. "Your friend Gotfrid liked to remind us you always have a gun. Well, that's not the case anymore, is it?" Igor grumbled and resumed his pacing.

"We'll get away, won't we Igor?" Pyotr asked. He looked up at Igor with wide eyes.

"Of course we will, kid," Igor replied.

"Stop telling him lies," Alexi said. "Poor boy's green enough as it is. You're only making it worse by treating him like a child."

"He is a child!" Igor replied.

"I am not!" Pyotr said. "Igor, do you actually think we'll get away? Do you think we'll be fine?" Igor glared at Alexi then looked at Pyotr.

"I don't know," Igor said. "But I'll be damned if I admit defeat."

"Attention everyone," Yeremiy said in an authoritative voice as he emerged from the control room. "For our safety, we will be landing outside of Mirgorod. As pirates and hijackers, we'd likely not get permission to land in Mirgorod's port unless we surrender."

"A wise decision," Snezhana said.

Zoya stood, her hand still on the hilt of her sword.

"What is it exactly you want in Mirgorod?" she asked Snezhana. Based on what they'd found in the library, Zoya figured she knew the answer. Snezhana

GRIGORY'S GADGET

wanted to find Grigory's Lab to discover the key to unlocking the Bronnerush's full power. Zoya wanted to hear it from Snezhana.

"At this point, I imagine we both want the same thing," Snezhana said.

"And what is that?"

"I want to destroy the Bronnerush."

Zoya stared at Snezhana, wrinkling her brow. Snezhana, seeing Zoya's obvious confusion, pointed to the gadget.

"That," she explained, "is called the Bronnerush."

"I know that," Zoya replied. She hugged the gadget close to her body. "You want to destroy it?"

"Yes," Snezhana said. "Look at how much trouble it's caused you. That's a small fraction of the trouble it's caused *me*. Because of this device, I've lost friends, family. My own brother framed me for a murder he committed and sent me to prison."

Zoya, staring at the Bronnerush, sat back in her seat. Snezhana took a seat across from her and folded her hands.

"I am sorry for the part I played in your mother's death," she said. "Though I wasn't the one who killed her, I was the one who led our crew to Lodninsk in the first place. The Bronnerush is nothing but trouble, Zoya. We must destroy it."

Zoya regarded Snezhana for a moment.

"If you protect it, it will protect you," she said. "That's what my grandmother told me before she died. All the trouble we've gotten into? That wasn't this gadget; it was petty sibling rivalry between you and your brother. The Bronnerush is mine to protect, not yours to destroy!"

"Zoya, you saw how dangerous the gadget is," Alexi said. "If Pyotr hadn't knocked you out, it likely would have enveloped your entire body. And those blasts it was shooting out of your hands..."

"It was protecting me," Zoya said. She pointed to Snezhana. "From her! From all of you!"

"Yes," Snezhana said. "It was. And as long as the Bronnerush exists, you will continue to need protection, because you will continue to be a target. If not from my brother, than from others. If we destroy it, you can just live your life. You won't have to worry about people like my brother abducting you, manipulating you, trying to steal from you. And believe me, there are many more like my brother, and many worse."

"I think she's right," Anya said, placing a hand on Zoya's shoulder. "We left Lodninsk because we didn't want to live in constant fear anymore. Because we wanted to be free. As long as we know people are after this gadget, we'll still be in fear."

"I agree," Demyan said. He reached over to Zoya and clasped her hand. Zoya nodded.

"If you want to destroy it, why didn't you just take it and throw it into the ocean?" Zoya asked.

"I thought about it," Snezhana said. "But the research I've done suggests it floats. And if it floats,

GRIGORY'S GADGET

it can be found again. I can't take that risk. It needs to be destroyed outright."

"But why do you need me?" Zoya slammed a fist into the table, eyes fixed on Snezhana. "Why kidnap me and my friends when you could have just stolen the gadget?"

Snezhana closed her eyes and took a breath. When she opened her eyes again, they were fixed on the table.

"The Bronnerush is connected to you, to your family," Snezhana said. "I don't know how. But you are the one who activated the gadget. I think you're the only one who *can* activate it."

"So you think I'm the only one who can destroy it?"

"Perhaps." Snezhana rubbed her temples. "I won't know how to destroy it until we find Grigory Orlov's lab in Mirgorod. But I think destroying the Bronnerush might destroy you as well."

Zoya's knuckles turned white as she grasped the Bronnerush tighter. She grasped it so tightly she feared, or perhaps hoped, the gadget might activate again.

"We're not sacrificing Zoya," Demyan said, standing. "How can you suggest that? You say you're sorry for the pain Zoya's gone through, and in the next breath say you want to kill her? To destroy some metal ball? Zoya's right, she needs to protect the gadget from people like you."

"That's how I thought you'd react," Snezhana said. "That's why I didn't tell you before."

"Why tell us now?" Zoya asked.

"Because it probably doesn't matter now. Because it's likely my crew is right, and we'll be arrested when we get to Mirgorod. Now, if you'll excuse me, I need a drink." Snezhana strode toward the kitchen, nearly knocking Yeremiy over as he emerged from the control room.

"Alright, get comfortable," Yeremiy announced as he entered, ignorant to the tension in the room. "It will be about a day's travel before we land outside of Mirgorod. I think we could all use some rest."

Zoya stood, hugging the gadget tight, and marched down the corridor to a cabin. Silently, everyone else followed suit.

"I'd rather stay in the corridor," Lilia said, gesturing toward the windows in the rooms.

"Close the curtains," Anya said. "Just imagine you're on a normal ship." Lilia fidgeted with her hands for a moment before finally entering a cabin.

"Nikolai's wound really isn't looking good," Demyan said as he carried Nikolai into a cabin.

"We'll get him to a doctor," Anya told him. "Replace the bandages in the morning. He'll be fine."

Demyan placed Nikolai onto a bed then sat on the other bed in the cabin. Zoya stood in the doorway, glancing around.

"Goodnight," she said at last. Her face flushed as she looked away.

GRIGORY'S GADGET

"Goodnight," Demyan replied with a tired smile.

"I wanted to say I'm sorry," Zoya said. She picked at the wood of the doorframe.

"About what?"

"What I said to you, before the boiler explosion." Zoya chuckled in spite of herself. "Before the *first* boiler explosion."

"Oh. That."

"I was frustrated," Zoya said. "I was angry, tired, confused. I shouldn't have taken that out on you."

Demyan crossed the room and pulled Zoya into a tight embrace. Zoya buried her face into Demyan's neck.

"It's alright," Demyan said. "I forgive you, if you can forgive me. I love you."

"I forgive you," Zoya replied. "I love you too. We need to rely on each other. You, me, Lilia, Anya, and Nikolai. We're the only ones we can trust."

Demyan nodded. He kissed Zoya's forehead then stepped back and stared into her eyes.

"We'll stick together, and we'll be fine," he said. "Right now, the best thing we can do is rest."

Zoya smiled and kissed Demyan goodnight. Then she wandered down the corridor toward her cabin.

As Zoya entered, Snezhana appeared by the doorway.

"Zoya," she said. "I meant what I said. I am very sorry for the part I've played in making your life worse, more difficult. In causing you loss." Snezhana grabbed Zoya's hand and looked her in the eye. "The best I can do, as penance, is to destroy that gadget and see you set free from all of this."

"Set free?" Zoya replied, pulling her hand away. "Death isn't freedom. Get out of my cabin."

War escalates...Sunday battle on Morozhian soil...Vernulaia expected to break peace treaty...

Zoya listened to the telegram as she sat by a window in the parlor. She looked out over the gray ocean and overcast skies as she picked at a plate of sliced apples.

"Has Lilia been out of her cabin yet today?" Anya asked, sitting next to Zoya.

"I don't think so," Zoya replied.

"Has she eaten?"

Zoya shook her head then glanced between the kitchen and the corridor. "I'll bring some food to her," Zoya said, standing.

Zoya grabbed an apple and an orange, along with a piece of soft bread. She looked at the store of fresh meat and decided against preparing a piece. It was doubtful Lilia would be able to keep much food down. Best start light. Zoya took the food and headed down the corridor.

She found Lilia curled up on her bed, turning Pavel's necklace over in her hands.

"Did we land yet?" she asked as Zoya entered.

"No," Zoya replied. "But I brought you some food."

GRIGORY'S GADGET

Zoya put the plate down on a small table next to the bed. Lilia didn't move.

"Do you want company?" Zoya asked. "Or would you rather be alone?"

"Alone for now," Lilia said. "But maybe come back in an hour?"

Zoya smiled. "No problem."

Zoya stepped back into the hall, closing Lilia's door behind her. She turned to head to the parlor and stopped. Zoya bit her lip and glanced over her shoulder toward the end of the corridor. She glanced back at the parlor. No one was paying attention to her. Instead they seemed to be enjoying the views out of the windows.

Zoya put her hand on the hilt of her sword and walked to the end of the hall. She stopped at the last door, and switched her grip from her sword to her dagger. Unsheathing it, Zoya opened the door slowly and quietly.

Edmund lay on the bed asleep. His arms and legs were bound, and his mouth gagged. Zoya stepped into the room and closed the door behind her.

She shook Edmund awake, making no effort to be gentle. The man started, opening his eyes wide. When he spotted Zoya, his face relaxed into a relieved smile. Zoya removed his gag.

"I knew sooner or later my crew would come free me," he said. "We can take Snezhana and the others, no problem. No problem at all."

"I'm not one of your crew," Zoya told him, glaring. "And I'm not here to free you."

"Don't be silly," Edmund replied. "Don't tell me that Snezhana—"

Zoya pressed her dagger to Edmund's throat and leaned in.

"I'm tired of your lies, your manipulation," Zoya said. "I'm here for one purpose, and that is to hear you tell me why you killed my mother."

Edmund laughed, stopping as Zoya pressed harder on her dagger.

"I don't even know who your mother is," Edmund said.

Zoya pulled back her dagger, and then sliced at Edmund's arm. He grunted at the pain, a thin line of blood trickling down his sleeve.

"Wrong answer," Zoya said, returning the blade to Edmund's throat.

"So feisty," Edmund said, grinning. "I suppose you must get that from your mother. I hear your father was quite the coward."

Zoya sliced at Edmund's other arm, tears welling in her eyes.

"Don't you dare," she said, her hand trembling as she returned the blade to his throat. "I will slit your throat if you say another word against either of my parents."

"You ask me to explain why I killed your mother, and then stipulate I can't speak ill of her. One way or another, you won't be happy with what I have to say."

"What's going on here?" Gotfrid opened the door and, seeing Zoya with her dagger, rushed into the room. He grabbed Zoya and began pulling her away from Edmund.

"Stop! Let me go!" She shouted. "He killed my mother. This bastard owes me an explanation!"

"He'll do plenty of explaining in prison," Gotfrid told her, overpowering her struggles and moving her toward the door. "And then he'll be hanged. Your mother will get justice."

Zoya shook Gotfrid off as he pulled her out of the room and shut the door. Her friends had gathered in the corridor, sad expressions on their faces.

"Don't look at me like that," Zoya said. "We all want him dead, don't we? You should have let me do it!"

Zoya pushed past her friends, hurrying down the corridor until she came to her room. She entered and slammed the door behind her.

"Lilia," Anya whispered. "Lilia, wake up." Lilia groaned and shifted in her bed.

"Come on, Lilia," Anya urged.

"I don't want to fly," Lilia murmured. "I want to be on the ground. I'm not opening my eyes until we're on the ground."

"We are on the ground!" Anya said. Lilia's eyes popped open.

"Oh my god," she said, jerking upright. "We crashed, didn't we? Ok let's go. Let's run out before we burn up!" Lilia scrambled to her feet and started lacing up her boots.

"Lilia!" Anya laughed. "We didn't crash. We landed safely, and we're just outside of Mirgorod." Lilia sat up and stared her friend in the face.

"Don't lie to me," she said.

"I'm not lying, look out the window," Anya said. Hesitantly, Lilia stood and leaned toward the window. The airship sat in a grassy field surrounded by a dense forest. Along the edge of the forest was a cobblestone road.

"Where's Mirgorod?" she asked.

"It's about two miles from here," Anya replied. "I saw it when we landed." Lilia's face lit up.

"What did it look like?"

"Beautiful!" Anya said. "It had tall, shining buildings and a boardwalk along the ocean."

"Well what are we waiting for?" Lilia asked. "Let's go!"

Outside, Yeremiy was looking at a map with Vlad, Svetlana, and Gotfrid. Demyan and Alexi stood chatting nearby. Nikolai was lying next to them, visibly exhausted but awake, on a gurney. Zoya stood there as well, silent, her eyes cast down to the ground. Edmund was lying on the ground by the back of the airship, his legs and arms tied, and a gag

GRIGORY'S GADGET

in his mouth. Snezhana, Pyotr, and Igor leaned against the front of the airship in silence.

"We can pick up the road about a quarter mile that way," Yeremiy said, pointing. "We should be able to blend right in. That's where you come in, Gotfrid." Gotfrid nodded.

"Wait," Lilia said, confused, as they eaves dropped. "Since when do Yeremiy and Gotfrid get along and work together?"

"I'm not sure," Anya said with a shrug. "I wish we knew what sort of deal they made."

"It is suspicious," Lilia said. "Well, as long as we all get to Mirgorod."

The two of them joined their friends.

"So, are we heading out soon?" Anya asked them.

"Yeah, any minute now," Alexi said. "Excuse me." He walked away from the group, heading toward the airship.

"How are you doing, Lilia?" Demyan asked.

"Fine," Lilia replied. "Now that we're on solid ground, I can breathe again. Nikolai, how are you?"

"My shoulder hurts like hell," Nikolai replied. "But I'm fine." The skin around the bandage on his shoulder was still swollen and red. Nikolai's face was covered in beads of sweat, and his eyes were unfocused.

"Are you sure you're alright?" Zoya asked. "Let me feel your forehead."

Zoya reached down, but Nikolai swatted away her hand.

"I'm fine," he insisted.

"Fine," Zoya said. "But as soon as we get to Mirgorod, we're getting you to a doctor."

"Alright," Snezhana announced as she stepped away from the airship. "Everybody off the ship? Let's start heading toward the city."

"I guess they'll have to untie Edmund's legs," Zoya muttered. She glanced around. "Wait, where did he go?" He was nowhere to be seen.

"Where is my weasel of a brother?" Snezhana demanded. She drew her sword. As the company began searching the area around the airship, Alexi walked back outside.

"Where were you?" Demyan demanded.

"Just making sure nothing was left behind," Alexi replied. "Are we all set to go?" Zoya marched up to him.

"You let him go, didn't you?" she asked.

"Who?"

"Your father," Zoya said. "He's gone."

"What?" Alexi gasped. He glanced around. "How?"

"You," Zoya said. "Who else would want to let him go?"

Alexi glared at her.

"I want my father tied up as much as any of you."

"And yet you rescued him from the *Hell's Jewel*," Zoya said.

"We have a complicated relationship," Alexi replied.

"We can see that."

"Enough!" Anya said. "This isn't productive. We need to find Edmund."

"I think we should just try to get to Mirgorod," Demyan suggested. "Keep alert."

"I agree," Snezhana said, walking over. "Edmund is wounded, and weaponless. If we don't stumble upon him, he'll be bound to run into Vernulaian authorities at some point. He can run for a time, but he'll have to face his fate eventually."

CHAPTER TWELVE

The group walked down the road toward Mirgorod, Demyan pushing Nikolai along on the gurney. Nikolai made no effort to hide his displeasure, listing complaints and insisting he could walk on his own. The weakness in his voice betrayed that lie. Vlad and Svetlana glanced back at their airship then at Yeremiy.

"You really want us to just abandon our airship?" Svetlana asked at last.

"It's locked up, isn't it?" Yeremiy replied. "I told you, after I make sure my friends make it safely into Mirgorod, you and your brother are to take me to Nanowrinsk." Svetlana and Vlad both twisted their lips into frowns.

"That may require extra compensation," Svetlana said.

"Insurance, in case something happens to the airship," Vlad added.

GRIGORY'S GADGET

"Yes, of course," Yeremiy said, waving a hand.

"Who knew you had it in you?" Snezhana asked Yeremiy with a grin. "Bribery? I would have thought that below your moral high ground."

"It was necessary," Yeremiy replied. "Don't think this makes me anything like you. Like a pirate."

"No of course not," Snezhana said. "You're *far* too righteous for that."

"We're almost to the city," Demyan announced, pointing ahead to the gates appearing through the trees. Tall buildings rose above the canopy and glistened in the sunlight. A small airship flew overhead.

"This is it, guys," Zoya said. "We've reached our destination!"

"So now what?" Lilia wondered. "We have to figure out where Grigory's lab was?"

"All of the books say the gadget is indestructible," Snezhana said. "But they also say Grigory left most of his writings and data in his lab. He must have had a way to destroy it."

"So we're looking for a hidden lab in a city we've never visited before?" Anya asked.

"Don't underestimate us," Demyan said. "You've got two archaeologists on your side. If anyone can find hidden places, it's us!" Demyan patted Nikolai on his good shoulder.

"You read books and look at old drawings," Anya told him. "When was the last time you found any hidden places?"

"There's a secret passage in Nikolai's basement," Demyan said. "It leads out to the alley." Anya laughed.

As the group approached the gates to the city, a large unit of police officers appeared, led by Edmund.

"What is he doing?" Snezhana growled.

"There they are!" Edmund cried, pointing toward the group. "They're the ones who hijacked that airship and kidnapped me!" Edmund grabbed the side of his abdomen where he had been wounded.

"No," Zoya gasped.

Yeremiy ran forward with Vlad and Svetlana. Gotfrid joined them.

"Please help us," Yeremiy said. "Please, they're pirates! They're armed!"

Lilia gaped at Yeremiy. "What? What are you doing?"

Snezhana's focus was on Gotfrid.

"What exactly do you think you're doing?" she shouted.

"You really should keep better watch over your captives," Gotfrid replied, nodding toward Yeremiy. "And your own crew."

The police drew their guns and surrounded the group.

"You are all under arrest," one officer stated. "If you do not come peacefully, we will not hesitate to use force against you."

GRIGORY'S GADGET

"What about Nikolai?" Lilia asked. She pointed toward Nikolai, who was now unconscious on the gurney.

"We will take him," the officer replied. Two officers rushed toward Demyan, handcuffing him and taking control of the gurney.

"It's ok," Zoya whispered to her friends. "We were supposed to be on a ship to Mirgorod. We'll explain what happened. We'll be fine."

As the police handcuffed the pirates, Alexi glared at his father.

"What was that about protecting me?" he spat. One of the officers glanced between Alexi and Edmund.

"I have no idea what he's talking about," Edmund pleaded. "He's obviously trying some ploy."

The police proceeded with their arrests, leading their prisoners into the city of Mirgorod.

Zoya and her friends hardly saw any of the city. The police locked them into the back of a windowless cart and brought them straight to the station. They were briskly led into a mighty marble building, and into booking in the basement. Immediately upon entering the police station, Zoya's bag, and the gadget within, was taken.

"What is this?" an officer asked, holding up the gadget.

E. A. HENNESSY

"It's a family heirloom," Zoya replied. "Please, it's very delicate." The officer gave Zoya a sideways look and shoved the gadget into a large bag. Then she began filling out a form with Zoya's details: hair, eye, and skin color, height, weight, age, nationality.

"We're not pirates," Zoya said, gesturing to Demyan, Lilia, and Anya. *Where did they take Nikolai?* "We were kidnapped, we were on a ship-"

"Silence," the officer said. "We will ask you questions when it's time."

After each person was similarly processed then stripped of everything except their essential clothing, they were led deeper into the basement of the building to the jail cells. They were all locked in individual cells that were separated by solid brick walls.

As the officers began to leave the room, Zoya shouted, "Don't we get to explain? Please!" The door of the room closed.

Down the hall, Snezhana was having a fit of cursing and shaking the bars of her cell.

"I will kill them all!" she shrieked.

"Nikolai!" Lilia shouted. Her voice echoed through the hall. There was no answer.

"What did they do with Nikolai?" Demyan asked. "Did anyone see?"

"They took him into another room," Anya replied. "With any luck they'll get him to a doctor."

"Good," Lilia sighed.

GRIGORY'S GADGET

Zoya began pacing her cell, her pulse racing. *What are they going to do with the gadget? What are they going to do with us?*

"I don't suppose anyone researched the Vernulaian justice system before we decided to move here?" Anya asked after a few moments.

"I didn't know it would be such a priority," Demyan replied. "I think we were more concerned with the university and the beach."

"Why would you want to move to Vernulaia, anyway?" Pyotr asked. "I've never heard anything good about it."

"It's supposed to be a paradise," Lilia said. "All of the brochures, all of the stories we were told said so."

"All propaganda," Snezhana muttered. "You've never left Morozhia before, have you?"

"No," the friends admitted.

"So," Zoya started. "What sort of things do they say about Vernulaia?"

"The same sort of stuff they say about your dear old home of Morozhia," Snezhana replied. "A totalitarian dictatorship, ruled with an iron fist with no regard for the happiness or well-being of its people."

"Why didn't anyone mention that before?" Lilia demanded.

Snezhana laughed. "And ruin your unbridled optimism about the future?" she said. "Besides, if you had decided you didn't want to go to Mirgorod after all, where would that have left me?"

"So much for your penance," Zoya muttered.

"I stand by what I said," Snezhana said. "I need to see the gadget destroyed. You need to see the gadget destroyed, despite the risks. You may not see that now, but you will unless you're an idiot like my brother."

"You've broken out of jail before," Anya interjected. "Mind sharing any tips with us?"

"She better hurry," Alexi said. "It won't take long before they find out who Snezhana is and that she's wanted in Lodninsk. She'll be on the next airship out of here pretty soon."

The conversation was interrupted by a loud creak as the door opened. A moment later, Edmund, Gotfrid, Yeremiy, Vlad, and Svetlana all filed in. Zoya listened as each was locked into their own cells.

"Well," Snezhana laughed after the officers left the room. "Didn't take them long to find your criminal record, eh Eddie?" Edmund didn't respond. For a painful amount of time, the jail was silent.

"Yeremiy," Lilia said at last. She waited for his response.

"Yes, Lilia?" Yeremiy replied.

"The first chance I get," she said, "I'm going to kill you."

"Lilia, you have to understand," Yeremiy said. "I made a deal with Gotfrid to help get Snezhana

GRIGORY'S GADGET

arrested, I had no idea he was actually working for Edmund."

"I don't have to understand anything," Lilia replied. "I understand that you betrayed us after we promised that we'd help each other. That we'd work together. You broke that promise, so the next chance I get, I am going to kill you."

"On that note," Snezhana said. "Gotfrid, the next time I get the chance, I'm going to kill you. But I'm sure mine and Lilia's tactics will be quite different. You see, Lilia strikes me as the sort to kill violently and quickly, in a fit of passion. That's not my style, as you know Gotfrid. And it's not yours either. So I'll be sure to kill you nice and slow."

"All empty threats," Gotfrid sneered. "You'll be off to Lodninsk soon enough. They may even put you to death."

"We'll see," Snezhana replied. "I really shouldn't be surprised Edmund planted a mole on my ship. Edmund and I have always been, as much as we hate to admit it, quite similar."

"What exactly is that supposed to mean?" Edmund asked from his cell. "You didn't have a mole on my ship. All of my crew completely loyal to me!"

"Are you sure about that?" Snezhana asked.

"Who was it?" Lilia asked. "Who was the mole on Edmund's ship?"

"Captain," Edmund shouted. "You'll address me as Captain!"

"A good man," Snezhana said, her voice somber. "It was Pavel."

A violent cacophony rang out from Edmund's cell as he cursed and hit the bars.

"He was working for you?" Zoya asked.

"That doesn't make any sense," Lilia said. "He was murdered by your crew while trying to rescue us from you."

"He was murdered by Adam," Snezhana said. "Adam was a new addition to the crew, a hothead who never listened or learned his place. And Pavel had to try to rescue you, to keep his cover."

"But he was loyal to Edmund," Lilia insisted. "He even told me a story about how he was captured and Edmund and his crew saved him."

Edmund grunted in his cell. A tense moment of silence followed.

"Pavel was never captured while on my crew," Edmund said at last, his voice so low the other prisoners could barely hear.

"Did Pavel tell you Edmund was the one who saved him?" Snezhana asked. Lilia didn't respond. Edmund grumbled unintelligibly in his cell.

"So when he told me to protect the gadget," Zoya said after a moment, "he meant to protect it from Edmund?"

"Yes," Snezhana replied.

"He should have been a little more specific," Anya said. "It would have saved us a lot of trouble."

GRIGORY'S GADGET

No one gave a response to Anya's comment, but continued to sit in silence in their cells.

The next morning, two police officers entered the room of holding cells.

"Zoya Orlova, Lilia Alkaeva, Anya Filipova, Demyan Volkov," the first officer announced. "Stand still in the center of your cells as they are unlocked. Then follow us."

The friends did as they were told. The officers led them out of the room and up to the main floor of the building. Sunlight shined through the windows, splashing the wooden floors with a warm glow. Police officers sat at rows of desks that filled the large room. The friends were brought into the chief's office.

"So we've checked your records," the chief told the friends as they sat down. She was a thin woman with even thinner gray hair. Her voice was deep and gravelly. "It appears you don't have any citizenship."

"What?" Zoya gasped. "That can't be right."

"We're from Lodninsk, Morozhia," Demyan told the officer.

"Yes, I see that," she replied. "But your citizenship has been revoked." Zoya and Demyan stared at the chief in silence.

"Why?" Lilia asked at last.

"According to our records," the chief began, "you fled the nation during a time of war."

"Fled?" Anya asked. "We weren't fleeing. We had applied for our visas to move to Mirgorod. We were on an immigrant ship when those pirates attacked it!"

"That ship never made it to Mirgorod. It appears to have been a ship working for the Kingdom of Starzapad. Everyone on board is considered a traitor to the state of Morozhia, and therefore to its ally, the state of Vernulaia."

"I don't believe this," Zoya sighed, sitting back in her chair. Lilia leaned forward.

"What happened to Nikolai?" she asked the chief. "Our friend, with the wounded shoulder. Is he ok?"

"We sent him off for medical treatment," the chief replied.

"Oh, good," Lilia sighed. "When can we see him?" The officer raised an eyebrow.

"You are still in custody, Miss Alkaeva," the chief told her.

"So," Anya said, "what do we do? What happens now?"

"We had no idea the ship wasn't going to Mirgorod," Lilia said. "We wanted to come to Mirgorod. We were on our way to study at the university."

"Well," the chief replied, "You'll be sent to our refugee camp outside the city. Once you're there, you'll be able to work until you've proven your

GRIGORY'S GADGET

loyalty and usefulness to Vernulaia. At that point, we will address the other offenses you have been charged with: illegal entry and piracy. Officer Rybkin!"

"Wait!" Anya said. "You haven't listened to us, we were kidnapped by the pirates."

"You're other charges will be addressed after you've proven your loyalty and usefulness in the refugee camp," the chief replied. "Rybkin, they're ready for you!"

Officer Rybkin, a lean, dark-skinned man, walked in. Without a word, he began to lead the friends out of the office.

"Wait, Rybkin," the chief said. "Leave Zoya Orlova. I have a few more questions for her." Zoya watched as her friends were carted out of the room. Demyan grabbed her hand before Officer Rybkin pulled him away.

"Please sit down," the chief told Zoya, gesturing to her seat.

"What is this about?" Zoya asked.

The chief pulled out the gadget and set it on the desk.

"What can you tell me about this?" she asked her. Zoya thought for a moment.

"It's a family heirloom," she said. "A gift from my grandmother."

"I see," the chief said, scribbling on a piece of paper. "And what did your grandmother tell you about this heirloom?"

"Not much," Zoya replied. "She passed away recently. I found it in her room while I was packing for the trip to Mirgorod...the trip I *thought* was going to take me to Mirgorod." The chief continued writing on her piece of paper.

"Your hair color," she said, looking up. "Is it natural, or did you dye it that obscene color?" Zoya started fidgeting with the end of her braid, her heart racing.

"It's natural," she admitted.

"Very interesting," the chief said, writing some more.

"Will I be joining my friends soon?" Zoya asked. "At the refugee camp?" The chief smiled.

"We have different plans for you," she said.

Lilia, Demyan, and Anya were brought to another room, filled with shelves of clothing. They were each handed a pair of brown pants, a blue shirt, and brown boots. The officers instructed them to change quickly so they could be taken to the refugee camp.

"Where do we change?" Lilia asked one of the officers. The officer gave her a sideways glance and didn't answer.

"I guess right here," Anya muttered. The friends quickly stripped out of their own clothes, which was stained from smoke and mud, and pulled on their new clothing.

GRIGORY'S GADGET

"Tuck in your shirts," an officer instructed them. The three friends obeyed and were brought to another door.

They were led through dark, winding halls until they found themselves in the alley behind the police station. There, a horse-drawn cart waited for them. The back of the cart, which was essentially a mobile jail cell, already housed Gotfrid, Igor, Pyotr, Edmund, and Alexi. When the officers opened the door to the cart, Anya ran in and hugged Alexi.

"Hands to yourself!" an officer shouted. Anya stepped back and took her own seat. Lilia and Demyan took seats as well.

"They're sending you to the refugee camps?" Demyan asked the pirates.

"Surprised they aren't hanging us?" Gotfrid asked. His finely tailored clothes had been replaced by the same brown pants and blue shirt. Gotfrid slumped in the baggy clothes as he pulled idly at the oversized cuffs.

"I'd take death over the camps they're sending us to," Edmund grumbled.

"What do you mean?" Lilia asked. The pirates chuckled.

"They call them refugee camps," Igor grumbled. "Makes 'em sound nice. What's the word?"

"Euphemism," Gotfrid said. Igor glared at Gotfrid.

"They say it's to prove your worth to the state. They work their refugees hard until they can't work any more, and anyone who can't work is discarded."

Pyotr, his gaze transfixed on the floor of the cart, twitched and began rubbing his hands.

"Those are just stories," Alexi insisted. "Don't be so melodramatic."

"You'll see, boy," Igor told him.

Anya shifted in her seat, glancing around the alley.

"So where's your aunt?" she asked Alexi.

"On her way to the docks," Alexi replied. "She's boarding the first ship to Morozhia."

"And Yeremiy?" Lilia asked. "What are they going to do to him?"

"He and his airship pilots were set free," Gotfrid explained. "It seems the police believed they had been kidnapped. They'll be heading back to their homes soon, I suspect."

"So that's it?" Lilia asked. "Yeremiy just gets to go home, like nothing happened?"

"Don't be bitter," Gotfrid told Lilia. "Loyalty is a dangerous thing in this world."

"What a horrible thing to say," Anya said.

"Horrible but true," Gotfrid replied.

"And you're so proud to be a shining example," Igor said, spitting at Gotfrid's feet.

Lilia glanced back at the police station.

"Where is Zoya?" she asked.

"I don't know," Demyan replied, "and I don't like this one bit. I have a bad feeling."

"She'll be ok," Anya insisted. "I'm sure she'll be out any minute."

GRIGORY'S GADGET

As she said that, the cart jerked into motion, heading down the alley.

"Wait!" Lilia called to the guards. "You forgot Zoya! You're missing someone!" The cart rolled on.

Pyotr, suddenly overwhelmed, began sobbing.

"Oh, come now," Igor said, wrapping an arm around the boy. "None of that. We're strong, fierce pirates, remember?"

Pyotr nodded but continued to sob.

"We'll figure something out, kid," Alexi told him. "We're not just strong and fierce, we're cunning, too."

Snezhana stood on the docks of Mirgorod, handcuffed and surrounded by militia.

"Are these really necessary?" she asked, holding up her hands.

"You're wanted for murder and escape," a soldier told her. "Any more complaining out of you, and we'll gladly put you in a full body restraint." Snezhana put her hands back down and sighed.

A large sidewheel steamer pulled into the dock. Its metal hull gleamed in the sunlight, elaborately decorated with curls of color. A large Vernulaian flag waved from atop the main mast. Banners of peace flew from the other masts.

"Heading through dangerous waters, are we?" Snezhana commented. None of the soldiers replied.

She inched toward one of them, a young man with freckles and blond hair.

"Would you mind terribly, getting me a glass of water?" she cooed. "I haven't had a thing to drink all day." The soldier looked around at his comrades. As he did, Snezhana grabbed the pistol from his hip, then wrapped the chain of her handcuffs around his neck.

"No one move," she demanded of the other soldiers. "You know I'd have no qualms about killing your little comrade here. Or any of you, or any civilians that get in my way." One of the other soldiers reached for his own gun. Snezhana pushed the barrel of her stolen pistol against her hostage's head.

"I said no one move," she told the soldiers. Snezhana heard shuffling behind her. She pushed the young soldier into his comrades, turning and pistol-whipping the soldier that had moved to attack her. The man went down, unconscious. The other soldiers began to rush at her. Snezhana wove through them, then turned and shot three times. The three quickest soldiers fell down, all shot in the chest.

Snezhana darted down the dock as the other soldiers rushed after her. She saw police gathering at the end of the dock and grinned. Leaping onto a dock piling, then across two small boats, and finally onto solid ground, she bolted down an alley, knocking over carts and garbage cans. Snezhana

GRIGORY'S GADGET

weaved through the city, down side streets, and into narrow alleys until she reached a small basement-level door. She climbed down the steps to it and knocked frantically. As she waited, she crouched on the steps, keeping out of sight from the main street.

A slot opened in the door, revealing two dark, squinting eyes.

"Fancy seeing your ugly mug here," a man growled.

"Fill an ugly mug with grog, and it looks pretty fine to me," Snezhana replied. The man closed the slot, then opened the door.

"Getting in trouble again, are we Snezhana?" the man asked. His beer belly shook as he laughed.

"Always," Snezhana smiled, entering. "It's good to see you, Boris."

The refugee camp was several miles outside of Mirgorod near the ocean. Barbed wire fences marked its border, and the cart had to proceed through two security gates to get inside. The camp itself appeared as an industrial complex; every other building was topped with a large smoke stack. The people Anya saw in the camp were hard at work, and appeared ragged and emaciated.

Anya grabbed Alexi's hand. He held her hand tightly as they moved through the camp. The cart traveled through the dirt paths that served as roads, finally stopping in front of a decrepit warehouse.

The police officers opened the back of the cart and instructed the prisoners to step out one at a time.

"This is where you'll sleep," one officer said, gesturing to the warehouse. "Find an empty bed inside. Your supervisor will be here shortly with your assignments." The officers locked up the cart and rolled it away, leaving the prisoners standing alone.

Demyan, Lilia, Anya, and Alexi held hands as they looked at the warehouse they'd be sleeping in. Pyotr inched over, and Alexi offered his hand to him. The boy took it gladly.

Edmund scoffed. "Come on, the bunch of you. Let's go see what's in store for us." Igor patted Pyotr on the back as everyone headed into the warehouse.

There were no other people in the warehouse when they entered, but the building was filled wall to wall with cots. Stairs led to the second and third floors that wrapped around the perimeter of the building, also filled with cots. Most of the cots were taken, as evidenced by undone sheets and stacks of books. Anya walked over to the nearest cot and picked up one of the books.

"'The History of Vernulaia: The Greatest Nation in the World'," she read aloud. She picked up another one, and another. All boasted of the power and superiority of Vernulaia.

"Propaganda," Gotfrid said. He looked between Lilia, Anya, and Demyan. "I bet you've seen the same in Morozhia?"

GRIGORY'S GADGET

"At least in Lodninsk we had proper apartments," Demyan said.

"Hey, we'll figure this out," Anya replied. "This is just a setback. It's temporary."

"We need to get out of here," Lilia said. "We need to find Zoya."

"You're the new refugees?" A soldier entered the warehouse holding a clipboard.

"Yes, sir," Pyotr said.

"Follow me," the soldier told them. He led them out of the warehouse and down the dirt road toward the water. They walked through a shipyard, filled with metal, wood, and ship hulls in various stages of completion.

"This is where you will work," the soldier said. "Gotfrid and Igor will report to Officer Brish. Pyotr and Demyan will report to Officer Sherikov. Anya, Lilia, Alexi, and Edmund will report to Officer Patsayeva."

"Hurry up!" one of the officers shouted at the group. She wore an olive green jacket and matching pants. Her hair was tucked up into an unadorned hat. Anya assumed she was Officer Patsayeva, and that her identically dressed comrade beside her was Officer Sherikov. "You have work to do!"

Lilia, in spite of herself, ran to hug Demyan. The soldier grabbed her and shoved her forcefully back toward Anya, Alexi, and Edmund.

"Report to your supervisors, now!" the soldier said, displaying the pistol on his hip.

The group split up. Gotfrid and Igor were immediately sent to bring more lumber to the yard, while Pyotr and Demyan were directed to a near-complete ship by the water to begin welding its hull. The rest were handed hammers and screwdrivers, and instructed to work on the frame of another ship's hull.

"Get to work!" one of the supervisors demanded, pulling out a whip. He cracked it once in the air as a warning.

Anya and Alexi worked tirelessly in the shipyard, driven mercilessly by their supervisors.

Blisters formed on Anya's hands as she worked, hammering nail after nail after nail into the ships' frames. She put down the hammer, clenching and unclenching her fists. The hot sun burned her skin as well.

"Are you alright?" Alexi asked, moving toward her. His skin was flushed, his hair matted with sweat.

"I'm fine," Anya replied with a weak smile. "Just tired."

"Hey!" Officer Patsayeva shouted. "Back to work! No socializing!" Alexi's face turned redder than it already was.

"We need a break," he shouted back at the supervisor. "We've been working nonstop for hours. We just need a rest."

GRIGORY'S GADGET

Patsayeva marched over to Alexi, staring at him angrily.

"You need to mind your place here, boy," she warned. "You don't belong anywhere, but our great nation of Vernulaia has been generous enough to take you in. The least you can do is work dutifully for her."

Alexi scoffed. "Generous?" he asked. "Have you seen where we've been assigned to sleep? I bet that building was condemned before your precious government decided to turn this area into a refugee camp."

Officer Patsayeva punched Alexi in the face. Before Alexi could recover from the blow, he was dragged away by another group of supervisors.

"Alexi!" Anya shouted. Officer Patsayeva moved toward her, brandishing a whip. Anya picked her hammer back up and began working again. The supervisor nodded and smirked, turning to follow the other supervisors.

Anya looked up to see where Alexi was taken. She saw him strapped to a pole with his back to the supervisors. Officer Patsayeva walked toward him, raising her whip. Anya turned away, trying to focus on the sound of her hammer instead of Alexi's yells.

"You're new here?" Anya heard a low voice, just loud enough for her to hear. She looked up again, searching for its source.

"Put your head back down. Don't draw attention."

Anya did as the voice commanded, pretending to adjust a nail.

"Yes, we're new," she said. "Who are you?"

"My friends refer to me as Chameleon. We must be wary here, not everyone *is* a friend. Are you?"

"A friend?" Anya asked. "I suppose that depends. What makes a person qualify as a friend?"

"How do you feel about this nation, Vernulaia?"

"I think it's the most wretched place I've ever been," Anya replied, "and I'm from Morozhia."

"Good. Then you are a friend. I will refer to you as Cuttlefish until you are ready. We will speak more later."

"Speak more about what? What do I need to be ready for?" The voice didn't respond. Anya looked up and around, catching the eye of another officer. Her face flushing, she returned to work.

GRIGORY'S GADGET

Patsayeva marched over to Alexi, staring at him angrily.

"You need to mind your place here, boy," she warned. "You don't belong anywhere, but our great nation of Vernulaia has been generous enough to take you in. The least you can do is work dutifully for her."

Alexi scoffed. "Generous?" he asked. "Have you seen where we've been assigned to sleep? I bet that building was condemned before your precious government decided to turn this area into a refugee camp."

Officer Patsayeva punched Alexi in the face. Before Alexi could recover from the blow, he was dragged away by another group of supervisors.

"Alexi!" Anya shouted. Officer Patsayeva moved toward her, brandishing a whip. Anya picked her hammer back up and began working again. The supervisor nodded and smirked, turning to follow the other supervisors.

Anya looked up to see where Alexi was taken. She saw him strapped to a pole with his back to the supervisors. Officer Patsayeva walked toward him, raising her whip. Anya turned away, trying to focus on the sound of her hammer instead of Alexi's yells.

"You're new here?" Anya heard a low voice, just loud enough for her to hear. She looked up again, searching for its source.

"Put your head back down. Don't draw attention."

Anya did as the voice commanded, pretending to adjust a nail.

"Yes, we're new," she said. "Who are you?"

"My friends refer to me as Chameleon. We must be wary here, not everyone *is* a friend. Are you?"

"A friend?" Anya asked. "I suppose that depends. What makes a person qualify as a friend?"

"How do you feel about this nation, Vernulaia?"

"I think it's the most wretched place I've ever been," Anya replied, "and I'm from Morozhia."

"Good. Then you are a friend. I will refer to you as Cuttlefish until you are ready. We will speak more later."

"Speak more about what? What do I need to be ready for?" The voice didn't respond. Anya looked up and around, catching the eye of another officer. Her face flushing, she returned to work.

CHAPTER THIRTEEN

"That's quite the adventure you've had, Snezhana," Boris said as he sipped from a mug of grog. "I always knew that brother of yours was trouble. But you say the Bronnerush is real?" The two old friends sat in the middle of a tavern that was hidden away underground through a myriad of tunnels. A couple of Boris's comrades sat nearby, guarding the door. The walls were covered in maps of Mirgorod and other parts of Vernulaia.

"I saw it with my own eyes," Snezhana said. "I even saw it in action. Boris, it's everything I was afraid it would be."

"Well," Boris replied, "you say your brother is in custody? If he's not hanged for piracy, he'll likely be sent to those so-called refugee camps. Seems to be a favorite punishment around here lately."

"My brother isn't the only thing in custody," Snezhana went on.

"Oh," Boris replied, gulping down the rest of his grog. "Well, that is a problem." He stood and poured himself another cup.

"Boris," Snezhana started, "The last time I saw you, I asked you to look for Grigory Orlov's lab."

"You said it might hold some secret to unlocking the Bronnerush's power," Boris recalled.

"I think it also holds the secret to destroying it," Snezhana said. "Please, Boris, have you found where it is?"

"Well, yes and no," Boris replied. "I'm afraid this is all bad news. The government uncovered the lab last year. No one knows this, of course. Not officially, not publicly. But the government knows where the lab is, and has been keeping it under strict surveillance."

"And now they have the Bronnerush, too." Snezhana leaned back in her seat, sipping grog.

"The girl with purple hair, Zoya?" Boris started. "They're not going to send her to the camps."

"Why do you say that?" Snezhana asked.

"Because they'll know exactly who she is," Boris replied. "Haven't you ever heard why that family has purple hair?"

"Are you going on about genetics again?" Snezhana asked. "I never understood your fascination with alchemy."

"It's not alchemy, it's science," Boris said. "And genetics are why the trait passed on but not why it turned purple to begin with. Grigory Orlov, when he grew fearful of his gadget's power, created a safety so that no one could use it."

Snezhana stared at Boris, waiting as he took a sip of grog.

"No one, except himself," Boris went on. "The rumor is that he created some sort of genetic lock on the device. In the process, the Bronnerush itself altered Grigory, and his hair began to grow purple."

"Sounds like a load of bull to me," Snezhana snorted. Boris shrugged.

"Some people hypothesize that the Bronnerush contains strange elements," he said, "which changed Grigory's genes. Some say it's magic. Quite honestly, Snezhana, it doesn't matter what it is, or if it's true."

"Because they have Zoya," Snezhana stated. "They have their genetic key."

"Exactly."

Snezhana leaned on the table, smirking.

"Sounds like we need to perform a rescue operation," she said.

Boris laughed. "Looks like our revolution will be coming early."

"Finished," Demyan announced, lifting his welding goggles. "I think that's the last one." He stood and looked around. The other refugees had finished their welding as well and were heading up the stairs, out of the ship's hull. Demyan followed.

"Alright," Officer Sherikov yelled. "Let's set her out to sea."

The refugees obliged, grabbing ropes and beginning to pull the ship upon rows of logs. Demyan grabbed a rope next to Pyotr, whose arms were shaking.

"It's ok," Demyan told the boy. "There are plenty of us pulling. Just hold the rope, give your arms a rest."

Pyotr looked at Demyan and nodded. His grip on the rope loosened slightly, and he simply held on. His arms still shook, but less violently.

The ship began to roll toward the water slowly at first then more quickly. The refugees jogged to keep up with the ship.

"Pyotr, be careful," Demyan warned, noticing the boy struggling to keep up. "Pyotr!"

The boy tripped, stumbling on the edge of a log. He didn't let go of the rope as he fell, and swung to and fro. His body slammed against the hull of the ship, knocking his grip free and sending him flying directly into the ship's path. Pyotr fell to the ground, landing on the row of logs only a few feet in front of the ship.

"Pyotr!" Demyan shouted again. He let go of his rope and ran ahead of the rolling hull. Without thinking, he jumped and grabbed Pyotr, pulling the boy to his feet.

"Come on," he urged. He pulled Pyotr to the side, jumping just out of the way of the ship.

GRIGORY'S GADGET

"Thank you," Pyotr gasped. He grabbed Demyan and hugged him, panting.

"You're welcome," Demyan replied, hugging him back. "You're ok."

Lilia worked furiously, driving nail after nail into the hull of the ship. She worked through the stinging pain of blisters. Her mind was a rush of emotion, and only the continuous hammering held back exasperated tears.

"You can probably take a break," Edmund said, working next to her.

"No, I can't," Lilia replied. "We can't take breaks unless we're told otherwise."

"Relax, Lilia," Edmund said. He waved his own hammer lazily in his hand. "What's the worst that can happen if you just rest for a minute? Now, I always appreciate hard work, but you need to pace yourself."

"You!" Officer Patsayeva pointed her whip in Edmund's direction. "Back to work!"

Edmund grinned at Lilia then turned to face the officer.

"Or what?" he asked, placing his hands on his hips. "That's a mean looking whip you've got. Doubt you know how to use it."

"Bring that worthless dog to me!" Officer Patsayeva shouted then turned her back and walked toward the pole on which Alexi had been whipped the day before.

"Who's going to bring me to you?" Edmund asked, raising his arms boastfully. "I'm sure everyone here hates you. No one is going to do your dirty work for you!"

Even as he spoke, a horde of refugees began moving in his direction. They grabbed him and pulled him off the ship hull, dragging him toward the whipping pole.

"What the hell is wrong with you?" Edmund asked, kicking and writhing against the refugees. "Let me go!"

The refugees threw Edmund at the foot of Officer Patsayeva, who lifted him up and slammed him against the pole. As she stepped back and readied her whip, the refugees ripped the back of Edmund's shirt open.

Lilia felt a confused anger when she saw his back. She had expected to see scars, marks from where Edmund may have been whipped years ago, or from battle wounds. Instead, apart from a patch of hair near the top, Edmund's back hadn't a single blemish.

Then Officer Patsayeva cracked the whip.

Edmund cursed through a scream of pain, glancing back to glare at the officer. She cracked the whip again, this time dangerously close to Edmund's face. He turned back around, swearing again.

Lilia smiled and continued her work.

GRIGORY'S GADGET

Anya worked deep within a ship, welding support beams. Tiny burns riddled her hands from flying sparks. There hadn't been any gloves for her to wear.

"Do you notice anything odd about these ships?"

Anya paused her welding and looked around.

"Chameleon?" she asked. A figure emerged from around the corner, its face shielded by a welding mask.

"One of many, Cuttlefish. Now, the ships?"

Anya examined the ship in which she stood. Much of its interior was unfinished, but its metal hull was complete. Steel beams framed the levels of the ship, outlining rooms and halls to be built.

"They're large," Anya said, guessing. "I suppose they do seem a bit different than the ships I've been on. But I've only been on three in my entire life, and all within the past few weeks."

The figure was silent. Anya frowned and glanced around. Then her breath caught in her throat.

"They're metal."

"Yes, they're steel."

"I've seen metal ships before," Anya said, remembering. "On the horizon. They were warships."

"Yes."

"But Vernulaia isn't fighting in the war."

"Not yet."

Anya stood with a hand braced against the hull, her head spinning.

"We're building their fleet, so they can go to war," she said. "To join Morozhia? Against Starzapad?"

"Yes."

With a rush of anger, Anya threw down her welding torch and slammed her arms against the steel hull. Arms aching from the impact, Anya picked her torch up again and moved toward the wall. The Chameleon grabbed her by the arm.

"No. This is not how we rebel."

"We have to do something," Anya said. "Have you seen how many ships have been built, are being built? This fleet will be huge! The war would be over in an instant. I don't know much about Starzapad, but Morozhia must be on the wrong side of this war!"

"The time is coming. You will know when to act."

"How?" Anya asked. The Chameleon didn't respond, instead turning and walking away, he left Anya alone in the hull of the warship.

The air was hot and humid in the warehouse, with large bugs zipping around between the cots. Some stung or bit, resulting in a near-constant echo of hands swatting skin.

"How is everyone doing?" Anya asked as she and her friends settled onto their cots.

GRIGORY'S GADGET

"As good as can be expected," Demyan said. He glanced at Edmund, who had curled up silently on his side. His back was covered in bloodied bandages. Alexi followed his gaze then muttered something unintelligible under his breath.

"We should get some sleep," Lilia said, lying back.

"Why, so you can try one of your famous escape attempts?" Gotfrid asked, mocking.

"You're confusing me with Zoya," Lilia said, her eyes fixed on the ceiling. "She's not here to formulate an escape plan." Tears pushed their way into Lilia's eyes, but she fought them.

"To be fair, I don't think Zoya ever did a lot of formulating," Anya said with a weak smile. "Her plans were more like whims." She turned on to her side and reached over to Lilia. "Zoya will be ok. It's a good thing for her that she's not here. Right?"

Lilia nodded, but rolled to turn her back to Anya.

As exhausted as they were, the new refugees tossed and turned, unable to fall asleep in the uncomfortable warehouse. The other refugees around them coughed and wheezed, and many made regular trips to the so-called bathroom: a rusted bucket surrounded by a moldy curtain.

"This is ridiculous," Gotfrid said, getting up from his cot. "I can't live like this."

"Where do you think you're going?" Alexi asked him as he walked away. Gotfrid didn't answer.

As Gotfrid approached the door of the warehouse, two guards stood in his path.

"I just need some air," Gotfrid said.

"No one leaves the sleeping quarters after lights out," a guard said.

"Sleeping quarters?" Gotfrid replied. "Have you seen this place? Do you see anyone actually getting sleep in here?"

"Return to your cot," the other guard demanded.

"Just return to your cot," a nearby refugee shouted. "Sleep comes easier after a while."

Gotfrid looked the man over. His skin was pale and streaked with sweat. His clothes were stained, likely with vomit and other bodily fluids.

"Your sickness is what's making sleep come more easily for you," Gotfrid told him. "Why don't you just shut up and let yourself die? You'll be more comfortable then."

"You think you're so tough?" Another refugee stood up from his cot, towering over Gotfrid. "Get back to your cot and shut up yourself, before I make you." He was soon joined by other refugees, all glaring at Gotfrid.

"Why are you aiming your aggression at me?" Gotfrid asked. "If you think you're so big and tough, why don't you kill the guards and lead us all to freedom?"

The tall man punched Gotfrid in the face.

"Talk like that is what starts trouble," he said, grabbing Gotfrid by the neck. The guards stood idly by, smiling.

GRIGORY'S GADGET

"People have tried getting out of the camp," a young man said, coughing. "You can't leave the camp before your reformation is complete."

"Reformation?" Gotfrid asked, spitting blood out of his mouth. "You bastards are all insane."

Gotfrid wrestled himself away from the tall man, and stomped back to his cot. A woman grabbed his arm, digging her fingers in.

"You need to learn some respect," she told him. Gotfrid slapped her. The woman hardly flinched at the strike and grabbed his other arm. She pushed him through the rows of cots until he stumbled and fell backward.

"This one needs to learn respect!" she shouted at the other refugees.

Chaos erupted throughout the warehouse. Anya, Demyan, and Lilia exchanged worried glances. Alexi only sighed.

"Just keep your heads down," Alexi said, still lying on his cot. "Don't draw attention."

"Shouldn't someone help him?" Demyan asked.

"He deserves a good beating," Igor said.

"He betrayed all of us," Pyotr said. "I don't care what happens to him." The boy crossed his arms, but the sad expression on his face betrayed his conflicted emotions.

A scream brought the group's attention back to the chaos. A young, emaciated man charged at Gotfrid with the waste bucket, and smashed him over the head. The contents of the bucket spewed out, drenching Gotfrid's head and torso.

Gotfrid screamed.

"You vile bastard!" he yelled. He grabbed the man by the throat and began to squeeze. The man gasped and clawed at Gotfrid's hands.

With a yelp, Gotfrid let go. He looked down to find a rusty blade sticking in his side. The elderly woman who had put it there pulled it out and jabbed it into his torso again. The other refugees cheered her on.

"Oh my god," Lilia gasped. She rolled on to her back and pulled out Pavel's pendant. Closing her eyes, she gripped the pendant tight, willing her mind to focus on anything but what was happening in the warehouse.

A moment later, the warehouse was quiet again. Gotfrid's body lay limp on the floor, a pool of blood surrounding him.

"He's dead," Anya said. "They...they just killed him."

"Got what he deserved," Igor said.

Anya's gaze darted around the room, her eyes wide with fright.

"Chameleon?" There was no answer.

"Why are you looking for chameleons?" Igor asked. Anya glared at him then turned to face Lilia.

Another refugee was talking to her and holding Pavel's necklace. Or was it another, identical necklace? Anya listened, but their voices were too low to hear. After a few moments, Lilia and the stranger hugged. There were tears in Lilia's eyes.

As the stranger stood, he looked at Anya and winked. Then he turned and left.

"Lilia," Anya whispered. "Who was that?"

"He recognized Pavel's charm," Lilia replied. "He follows the same religion. It's called Drevnih. He said he'd tell me about it." A small smile formed on her lips.

"What was his name?" Anya asked.

"He said to call him Chameleon," Lilia replied. "What an odd nickname."

"Yes, it is."

The night continued on in sleepless silence. The time dragged by, and the buzzing of bugs became progressively louder around the fresh dead body. Shortly before sunrise, Anya heard another sound. She sat up on her cot, trying to hear where it was coming from.

"Chameleon is here, Chameleon is ready," Anya heard a voice whisper to her left. She turned, only to hear the words again, this time behind her. As Anya listened, she realized it wasn't a single whisperer, but dozens throughout the warehouse. She smiled.

"Chameleon is here," she whispered. "Chameleon is ready."

After her friends were carted off to the refugee camp, Zoya was sent down to the holding cells. She spent the night alone, in silence, without food or water. She paced the cell all day, focusing on the stone and dirt beneath her feet to keep her thoughts from wandering to darker places. What waited for her friends in the refugee camp? Was Nikolai ok? Where is the gadget? What were they going to do to *her*?

Eventually, Zoya collapsed in a corner, unable to keep her hysterics at bay. She sobbed and hyperventilated, pounding the wall and floor with her fists until they were sore. Then, finally, she fell into a fitful sleep.

In the morning, two officers arrived to fetch her. Zoya was taken outside, surrounded by police officers, and placed inside a windowless carriage. The officers followed her then closed the door.

"Where are we going?" Zoya asked. None of the officers replied. The carriage started moving, and they traveled in silence. Zoya's hands fidgeted as she gazed at the floor.

When the carriage stopped, the police pushed Zoya into another elaborate building. The lobby of this building was vast and open, with marble floors and statues between each of its tall windows. They led Zoya down a hallway, down two flights of stairs, and into a large bathroom. Three women stood in the bathroom, and the police handed Zoya over to them.

Without warning, the women stripped Zoya of her clothing. Zoya objected with a yelp as they threw her

GRIGORY'S GADGET

into a hot bathtub and began washing the soot and mud from her skin. Zoya cringed at the pain as they scrubbed bruises and scabs on her body. One woman dunked Zoya's head under the water. Zoya sputtered and spat when she came back up, wincing as the woman then combed tangles from her hair.

"What's happening?" Zoya asked. The women ignored her.

The women then pulled Zoya out of the bath and wrapped her in a towel. She was dragged to an adjacent room, where a wardrobe was filled with dresses and gowns. One of the women picked a dress out: a teal gown with a golden-embroidered bodice and high collar. Another woman dressed Zoya in black stockings, drawers, a chemise, and a corset. The corset was pulled tight, squeezing painfully against Zoya's ribs. She could feel fresh bruises forming on her ribcage from the constriction. Over the underclothes, the women pulled a camisole and petticoat. Then, finally, they fastened the gown around her.

The women brought Zoya to a vanity, and pushed her down onto a seat. The women pulled her hair up, twisting and fastening it.

"What's going on?" Zoya finally asked. She felt lightheaded, her vision blurry. "What is all of this for?"

"You're to be presented before the High Council," a decorated soldier announced as he entered the room. He turned to the women. "Is she ready?"

"Yes, sir," one of the women replied, her gaze fixed on the ground.

"Good." The soldier smiled and looked at Zoya. "Miss Orlova, I'm Colonel Truten. Won't you please follow me?"

Zoya glanced at the women who had dressed her then back at Colonel Truten. He held out his hand to Zoya. Taking a deep breath, unsure what else to do, she took it.

"This is certainly an exciting day," he told her. "It's a great honor to be seen by the High Council."

Colonel Truten led Zoya through magnificent halls and rooms with sparkling marble floors and walls covered in elaborate carvings. Paintings on the walls depicted notable people from Vernulaian history, some of whom Zoya recognized from textbooks.

Finally, Zoya and the colonel reached a grand wooden door in which a scene had been carved showing the rise of the Vernulaian state. It depicted images of agriculture, industrialization, war, and finally the glittering city of Mirgorod. Zoya and Colonel Truten stood in front of the door and waited.

"Why do they want to see me?" Zoya asked.

"By now you must realize how special you are," Colonel Truten replied. "I'm afraid I'm not at liberty to say more. But the Council will explain."

The grand door opened, pulled by a boy in a bright blue uniform. Inside a large, open hall with

GRIGORY'S GADGET

stained glass windows that reached from the floor to the high ceiling. Zoya and the colonel stepped inside. Zoya's heart was racing, and she felt her face flushing.

At the back of the hall, thirteen men and women in fine clothing sat behind a long desk situated upon a dais.

"You must be Miss Zoya Orlova," one of the women announced. "So pleased to meet you."

Zoya looked to the colonel then at the Council.

"Thank you," she said meekly.

"Come closer," one of the men told her. "Some of us are hard of hearing or hard of sight."

"Or both," another man said.

The colonel ushered Zoya closer to the Council.

"Has Colonel Truten been kind to you?" another woman of the Council asked.

"Yes," Zoya replied.

"Yes, what?" the woman asked, leaning forward on her desk.

"Yes…ma'am?" Zoya tried. The Council laughed.

"I'm sorry," Zoya told them. "I'm not familiar with what sort of courtesies are expected. I didn't know—"

"Calm down, child," the same woman said. "We know you are foreign. The proper way to address a member of the High Council is 'Your Righteousness'."

"Yes, Your Righteousness," Zoya said.

"Very good," one of the men proclaimed. "I can tell you have a good attitude."

"Yes," a woman agreed. "You respect our authority. You're a smart girl, indeed."

"A smart girl such as yourself is probably wondering why you're here," a man stated.

"Yes, Your Righteousness," Zoya replied.

The man who sat in the center of the desk pulled out the Bronnerush, placing it on a metal stand in front of him. "This is yours," he stated.

"Yes, Your Righteousness," Zoya replied.

"And you know what it does," he continued.

Zoya glanced around at the members of the High Council. "No, Your Righteousness."

"Now, Miss Orlova," a woman said. "Smart girls do not lie. Especially to the High Council."

Zoya's legs felt weak, and the corset made it difficult for her to breathe. "I don't," Zoya started, thinking. "I don't know exactly what it does, Your Righteousness. But I saw it, felt it…" Zoya realized she didn't even know how to tell the truth if she wanted to.

"You've activated it before," one of the men said.

"Yes, sir, Your Righteousness," Zoya replied.

"And how did it feel?" he asked.

"It felt dangerous, Your Righteousness," Zoya replied. She took a deep breath, remembering. "It felt…exciting, liberating." She caught herself and glanced up at the High Council. "But it is very dangerous, Your Righteousness."

GRIGORY'S GADGET

Every member of the High Council was writing on the pieces of paper in front of them.

"If I may," Zoya started, "could I ask: where are my friends? Your Righteousnesses?"

"The other people you were with?" a woman asked. "They've been sent to the refugee camp outside of the city. With any luck, they're as smart as you, and will prove their loyalty and usefulness to Vernulaia very quickly."

"What does that mean?" Zoya asked before she could catch herself. "Your Righteousness."

"Our fears are realized," a woman whispered to the rest of the High Council. "This one is too bold."

"An easy fix," a man replied.

"Colonel Truten," a woman called. "Please escort Zoya to the training facilities. She'll need to be conditioned before we can trust her with the gadget."

"Conditioned?" Zoya asked as the colonel began to pull her away. "What do you mean conditioned?"

"You ask too many questions," a man told her. "And you feel entitled to their answers. Such questioning is a danger to Vernulaia and to yourself. The fine men and women in our training facility will put your mind at ease."

Torture, Zoya thought. Are they going to torture me?

Zoya struggled against the colonel, who held her tight.

"Let me go!" she shouted. "Please! Let me and my friends go! Just let us leave Vernulaia, we'll never come back! We won't cause any more trouble for you!"

"How rude," one of the men grumbled.

"Sorry dear," a woman called. "We need you."

The colonel dragged Zoya out of the room, where a team of doctors in white lab coats stood ready to take custody of her. Zoya continued to struggle until a sharp pain hit her leg. Within seconds the room spun, dimmed, and turned black.

Down the hall from the underground tavern, radicals and revolutionaries gathered around a large table, speaking in frantic tones. Snezhana paced the room, skimming over all the maps, plans, and papers that hung on the walls. She turned to a large map of Mirgorod spread upon the table in front of her. She pointed to one corner.

"This is the refugee camp?" she asked. Boris glanced to where she pointed.

"Yes," he said. "That's likely where they took their captives. Your crew, Zoya's friends, your nephew, your brother…"

"This tunnel," Snezhana observed, tracing a line on the map with her finger. "Do you have access to it?"

GRIGORY'S GADGET

"Yes," Boris replied, "but we really must focus on rescuing Zoya first. Time is of the essence now that the government has her and her gadget."

"Once we take her and the gadget, the government will retaliate," Snezhana replied. "Won't they? They'll send out their troops to recapture the gadget and quash any sign of rebellion." Boris glanced around at his comrades, who had all stopped speaking to listen to Snezhana.

"She has a point," one man said. "Our effort may be for naught if we don't plan well enough."

"So what are you suggesting, Snezhana?" Boris asked.

Snezhana smirked. "I think we need to free the refugees," she said. "Your numbers are impressive, but not impressive enough. Setting the refugees free will give us more manpower and a distraction to split the government's forces."

Boris nodded, looking at the map.

"Alright," he said. "We'll have to work quickly. Perhaps a refugee rebellion will stall the government from unleashing the gadget's power, but we can't count on that." He smiled at Snezhana. "I knew I liked having you around. You'll have a highly respected position in our ranks if you stay."

"You know me," Snezhana replied. "I can't stay put in one place for too long." She winked. "But don't worry, I'll be sure to visit your new utopia to sell my loot."

Lilia sat up, wiping sweat from her brow, making sure not to rest for too long. She glanced at the nearest supervisor, who was preoccupied by a group of new refugees walking into the site. Among them was Nikolai.

Lilia forgot herself and dropped her hammer. She rushed down from the scaffolding where she was working and sprinted to Nikolai.

"You're alive!" she shouted, wrapping her arms around him. Hard metal slammed into Lilia's armpit. She yelped in pain and stepped back, looking at Nikolai's arm. Metal and leather extended from his shoulder to his fingertips. Every joint was a metal hinge. Nikolai touched Lilia's face with his other arm.

"You're alright," he said, smiling.

"What did they do to you?" Lilia asked, gesturing to his mechanical arm.

Nikolai sighed and glanced at it. His mechanical hand clenched and unclenched, hissing quietly as it did. "They had to amputate my arm," Nikolai explained. "I remember arriving at the hospital and hearing someone mention infection. When I woke up, I had this." Nikolai raised his arm, watching it. "I don't even know how it works. I can move it just like I'd move my real arm. But I can't feel it."

"It's like the mechanical hands Olya and Oleg had," Lilia said. "Only yours is an entire arm."

GRIGORY'S GADGET

"Hey!" One of the supervisors pointed toward Lilia and Nikolai, raising a whip. "Get back to work. Now!"

Lilia glanced at Nikolai then back at the ship she'd been working on.

"I really need to go," Lilia said. "They're very strict. I'm sorry."

"It's alright," Nikolai said. "We'll be alright." He grabbed her hands. Lilia's hand fidgeted in his metal grasp.

A supervisor approached quickly from behind Nikolai with what looked like a small dagger. He shoved the object into Nikolai's metal arm. Nikolai yelled out in pain, grabbing his shoulder. His mechanical arm went limp.

"Now you'll work all day without this arm," the supervisor told Nikolai. "I'll reactivate it once you've earned that privilege." Nikolai breathed heavily.

"Yes, sir," he growled. He glanced toward Lilia, who was already running back to her work. Then he followed the supervisor to his own assignment.

Anya stopped working for a moment to wipe sweat from her brow. She looked over at Alexi and watched as he stretched and winced. The back of his new shirt was stained with blood.

Suddenly, the metal of the hull of the ship they were on vibrated as a loud boom sounded outside.

"What the hell was that?" one of the supervisors demanded. Alexi and Anya ran up and out of the ship. Smoke rose from a nearby building.

"What's going on?" Alexi asked Igor, who stood nearby.

"Damned if I know," Igor replied. Another explosion went off, this time closer to the shipyard. Anya heard the sounds of yelling and screaming echoing through the air. A moment later, a flood of people rushed into the shipyard, attacking the supervisors.

"It's time to rebel," Anya said, looking around.

"What did you just say?" Alexi asked with a forced laugh.

"It's time to rebel, just like Chameleon said! This is our chance. Come on!" She grabbed Alexi by the arm and started running down the ramp to the ground. Igor followed, obviously confused but unwilling to be left behind. When they reached the ground, Demyan and Pyotr ran to them.

"It's Snezhana!" Pyotr told them happily. "It must be. Snezhana and her rebel friends!"

"Rebel friends?" Igor questioned. "What rebel friends?"

"You never heard her mention Boris?" Pyotr asked.

"Her drunkard ex-lover?"

Pyotr frowned. "Yes, him. But he's a rebel leader, remember? The Order of the Chameleon?" Igor

GRIGORY'S GADGET

shrugged. Anya's mouth fell open as she tried to piece together the new information.

"We can figure out Snezhana's love life later," Alexi said. "Now is the time to get the hell out of here."

Igor looked toward the water where the freshly finished ship was docked. He looked at Pyotr and grinned.

"But we don't have Gotfrid," Pyotr said sadly, eying the ship as well. "There's only two of us."

"To hell with Gotfrid," Igor spat. "The man was a traitor. He deserved what he got."

"You can't sail the ship by yourselves," Anya said.

"You're welcome to join us," Pyotr said. Anya looked at Alexi.

"Seems like the best option right now," he said. "Let's find Lilia and go."

"And Nikolai," Demyan added. "We need Nikolai."

"Aw, I knew you missed me." Nikolai appeared behind Demyan, grinning. Lilia ran up next to him.

"Oh my," Anya said as she looked Nikolai over. "What did they do to your arm?"

"Story for another time," Nikolai replied. "We need to get out of here."

"To the ship, then," Anya said. The group turned to head back to the ramp. They were intercepted by Edmund, smirking wickedly.

"Ah, there's my crew," Edmund said. "I see we had the same idea. Good!"

"We're not your crew," Alexi told him. "And you're not welcome on our ship."

Edmund laughed. "Your ship?" Edmund challenged. "You're not even on her yet and you're calling her yours? We'll see about that."

"Edmund!" Snezhana shouted her brother's name from across the yard. She ran up to the group, a pistol in each hand.

"Edmund, Alexi," she greeted. "All of you. We need your help."

"Why on earth would I help you?" Edmund asked. Snezhana ignored him.

"We don't have time for particulars," she told the group, "but the government has taken custody of Zoya, and plans on using her to activate the full power of the Bronnerush—the gadget. We need you, and the others in this camp, to help us fight. We need to fight our way to Grigory Orlov's lab, that's where they're taking her. We need to get there and stop them, and destroy the gadget."

"You can't destroy the gadget, Snezhana," Edmund protested.

"Please, go," Snezhana pleaded. She pointed to Boris across the yard. "That's Boris, he'll direct you."

"Alright," Demyan said. "Let's go."

Igor and Pyotr looked at each other, at Snezhana, and at the ship.

"Having a rebel force at sea would be useful," Snezhana said as she followed their gaze. "Grab a handful of refugees and make your crew. Quickly!

GRIGORY'S GADGET

Just do me the courtesy of firing on Mirgorod's navy as you sail away."

"Aye, Captain," Pyotr and Igor replied in unison, running off to the ship. Snezhana walked to where Boris stood.

"Snezhana!" Edmund yelled. Snezhana turned and sighed. Edmund stood red-faced with a sword pointing at her. She laughed.

"Where on earth did you get that?" she asked.

"One of these so-called supervisors had it," Edmund replied.

"You know they carry guns as well."

Edmund ignored her. "I won't let you destroy the gadget," he said. "I've worked too hard. I've come too far."

"You've sacrificed too much," Snezhana told him. She strode up to him until his blade was poking her in the stomach. "You sacrificed me. Your own sister. So I'll be damned if I don't see that gadget destroyed. After what you did to me, I want to see you watch as it crumbles into dust. All you did, all you sacrificed, all for nothing." Snezhana spat on the ground in front of Edmund and turned away.

With an angry yell, Edmund lunged forward. He drove his sword into Snezhana's back until it protruded out of her stomach. Snezhana gasped for breath, looking down at the bloody blade.

"Oh, Eddie," she choked. "So old fashioned. Always reaching for your sword instead of your pistol."

Snezhana coughed up blood as she faced her brother. Edmund's eyes were wide, his gaze flitting from the wound he'd inflicted to his sister's face. He was frozen, breathing heavily. Snezhana raised her pistol.

"Goodbye, baby brother," she said. She pulled the trigger, hitting Edmund square in the forehead. He fell to the ground, and Snezhana collapsed. Tears streamed down her face as she clenched her stomach.

"Snezhana!" Alexi ran over to her and pressed on the wound to try to stop the bleeding. His eyes filled with tears as his gaze darted between his dead father and dying aunt.

"Alexi," Snezhana said. "I'm sorry."

"No, no," he told her. "It's alright. I'll get Boris over here. We'll get you to a doctor."

Snezhana grabbed her nephew's hand. "Alexi," she whispered. "It's alright. You're free now. Just promise me…"

"What?" Alexi asked. "Anything."

"Destroy it," Snezhana coughed. "Destroy the gadget." Alexi nodded.

"I will," he said. Tears rolled down his cheeks. "And you'll be there to witness it."

Snezhana smiled. "You're a good boy, Alexi," she said. "Your mother would be proud."

"Alexi, we have to go," Boris said. He bent down next to Snezhana and kissed her forehead.

GRIGORY'S GADGET

"Do it," Snezhana said to Boris. He nodded, sniffling.

"What?" Alexi asked him. "Do what?"

"Alexi, go," Snezhana said. "Go destroy the gadget and live your life."

"Snezhana," Alexi pleaded.

"Go."

Alexi backed away, looking at Boris, who raised his pistol. Anya ran to Alexi, wrapping her arms around him and directing his face away from his aunt. Boris shot Snezhana between the eyes then bent down and kissed her hand. Alexi held Anya tight, his body heaving.

"I'm so sorry, Alexi," Anya whispered. "But Boris is right. We have to go."

Alexi nodded and wiped his eyes. "We need to complete her mission," he said. "Let's go destroy that damned gadget."

CHAPTER FOURTEEN

Boris led a group of rebels through the underground tunnels toward Grigory's lab.

"Unfortunately, we don't have direct access via our tunnels. But, we can get close, and then we'll have to move quickly above-ground to get there," he had told his comrades.

"Didn't you say it's heavily guarded?" Alexi asked.

"That's why we made sure you're all armed," Boris replied.

"Speaking of arms," Nikolai said, "you don't know how to reactivate mine, by any chance, do you?"

Boris walked around to look at Nikolai's back.

"Ah, yes," he said, pointing to a small hole in Nikolai's mechanical shoulder blade. "There is a special key to activate or deactivate mechanical limbs. The Vernulaian government wants their citizens strong and able to work, but they don't want to lose control. So, at the first sign of insubordination, they disable any mechanical parts."

"So, is that a yes, or no?" Nikolai asked.

Boris smiled. "I just so happen to have one of those keys," he said. He instructed one of his close comrades to fetch the key.

"Thank you," Nikolai said. "I assume these types of mechanical limbs are common here."

"Relatively so, I suppose," Boris replied. "It's standard procedure to affix a prosthetic when a limb is lost."

"In Lodninsk the prosthetics couldn't move," Nikolai said.

"That sounds very inconvenient."

"Is Zoya going to be ok?" Demyan asked Boris. "What are they doing to her?"

"If we're lucky, we'll get there before they've done anything to her," Boris replied.

"And if we're unlucky?" Lilia asked.

"Have your guns ready."

"Absolutely not," Demyan said. "We're here to save Zoya, not hurt her."

"You're mistaken, boy," Boris replied, getting gruff. "We're here to stop the terror of the Vernulaian government, by whatever means necessary."

"I'm sure we'll be lucky," Nikolai said to Demyan. "She'll be fine."

Boris's comrade approached Nikolai then, a dagger-like key in his hand.

"I've heard this hurts," the comrade warned. He stuck the key into the hole in Nikolai's shoulder blade. Nikolai let out a surprised yell then inhaled deeply. His mechanical arm began to move.

"Thanks," Nikolai said. He took the key and put it in his pocket.

The rebels continued along the tunnel until they came to a door that led to stairs they followed up to street level. The sun was setting, casting long shadows between the buildings outside.

"There it is," Boris said, pointing to a small, innocuous brick building surrounded by soldiers. "The lab was unearthed in the basement of that building."

"You expect us to fight through all of those soldiers?" Alexi asked.

"Of course not," Boris replied. "We've got distractions coming any minute now."

"Distractions?" Anya asked.

"The refugees?" Demyan said. "You're going to send those poor people in as a distraction?"

"Those poor people are also armed," Boris explained. "And they have it in for this government as much as any of us. We didn't force the refugees to do anything, if that's what you're thinking. They know full well what they're doing."

"It's not right," Lilia said. "You sent them on a suicide mission."

"And when we gave them their mission, we made that clear," Boris said, bristling. "This is war. This is

GRIGORY'S GADGET

our rebellion. This is how we overthrow this government. This is how we rescue your friend."

The yells of the refugees echoed through the streets, faintly at first, then louder and louder. The soldiers guarding Grigory's lab readied their weapons, but were soon overwhelmed by the sheer number of people attacking them. A continuous rain of bullets fell upon the refugees, taking out a dozen at a time. But still more people came. They tackled the soldiers to the ground, ripping away their weapons and slaughtering them.

"Now!" Boris yelled. "Let's move!"

The rebels hurried toward the brick building. They leapt over the corpses of soldiers and refugees and burst through the door. Immediately, more soldiers ambushed them, but the rebels far outnumbered the platoon. Within seconds, they shot the soldiers down.

"Go that way," Boris instructed Zoya's friends, pointing to the stairs. "She'll be down there, go! We'll guard up here."

The friends ran down the stairs then raced down a long hallway.

They saw no soldiers, but the hall was lined with wooden doors. They kept their weapons raised.

"Which one?" Lilia asked, glancing back and forth. A scream rang out toward the end of the hall.

"That's Zoya!" Demyan yelled, sprinting toward her cry. The others ran after him.

"I think it came from in here," Demyan said. The friends held up their weapons and barged in.

The front half of the room was made up of clean, simple lines. It had a white marble floor and pastel striped wallpaper. The back half of the room, however, was made of old, half-rotted wood. Shelves of antique bottles and scientific instruments lined the walls.

A group of doctors in lab coats stood in the center of the room, hunched in a circle. They turned when the door opened. One doctor pulled his mask off of his mouth and smiled.

"I'd put those guns down if I were you," he said. "She doesn't want to see us being threatened." The doctors stepped aside, revealing Zoya in the center of their circle. She lay on a wooden table that had been raised so that Zoya was nearly standing. She wore only rags that may have once been a dress; teal and golden strands hung across her body. The gadget was on her arm, its armor growing and enveloping her. She looked up at her friends.

Her gaze was blank at first, as though she didn't see them. Then her eyes snapped to Demyan.

"You," she said, her voice slow and scratchy. "You're here…" A sweet smile formed on her lips. One of the doctors grabbed her face and directed it toward his own. In his other hand he had a yellow pendant on a chain. He held the pendant between his and Zoya's faces and its jewel began to glow.

GRIGORY'S GADGET

"You serve the Great Nation of Vernulaia," he said "You are our sword of justice. You will stop any and all rebellion."

Zoya nodded, her expression blank, and looked back at her friends.

"Rebel scum," she said to them. "You think you can undermine this great nation? You have one chance to surrender."

"Zoya, what are you talking about?" Lilia asked.

"Do you surrender?" Zoya asked. The gadget had enveloped her torso and legs, and was making its way down her other arm.

"Zoya, whatever they've done to you, fight it! Fight back!" Demyan said

"So, you won't surrender?" Zoya said to her friends. Her voice was flat and emotionless. The gadget folded over the top of her head, coming down to cover her eyes with goggles. All but her nose and mouth were covered in metal plates, wires, and gears. She raised her right hand. "Then you will be annihilated."

"Run!" Alexi shouted, pulling Anya out of the room. The others ran as well, barely avoiding a ball of light that exploded on the opposite wall in the hallway.

"After them!" the doctors instructed Zoya. "Crush their rebellion!"

Zoya's friends sprinted up to the main floor of the building. Boris and his comrades locked in a swordfight with a new wave of soldiers.

"Run!" Alexi shouted at them. "Run now!" Boris and his comrades didn't hesitate. They followed the friends out of the building. A ball of energy struck the corner of the building, which began to crumble. Nikolai looked back and saw Zoya had reached the main floor. She raised her hand.

"Ready your weapons," Boris shouted at his comrades.

"What?" Lilia protested. "You can't shoot her!"

"I'm sorry," Boris said. "Unfortunately, you were too late. She isn't your friend anymore; she's a weapon of the Vernulaian government."

"Rebels!" Zoya shouted as she exited the building. "Lay down your weapons now, and you will receive mercy. Continue to fight, and you will lose, and die."

"We will never surrender!" Boris shouted. He raised his gun, as did his comrades.

"No!" Demyan shouted. The rebels began to fire.

The bullets bounced off of Zoya's armor. She didn't flinch. Zoya raised both of her hands and shot two blasts of energy toward the rebels. The force of the blasts sent the rebels flying in all directions. Zoya's friends were knocked to the ground, covering their heads. Then they stood and ran into the nearest building.

"We need to find whatever it is that stops the gadget," Anya told her friends.

GRIGORY'S GADGET

"You go back to the lab and look for it," Lilia told her. "I'm staying up here. There must be something we can do to bring Zoya back to reality."

"They're controlling her with that pendant," Nikolai said. "I've never seen something like that before. I don't know how it works, how are we supposed to figure out how to stop it?"

"We have to try," Demyan said. "I'll stay up here with Lilia. Go and look for anything that might help."

The friends peeked out of the doorway. Zoya was marching down the street, surrounded by soldiers. Dozens of corpses now littered the ground behind her. Some rebels fled down the road, others had run back into their tunnels.

"Are you sure about this, Lilia?" Nikolai asked, watching Zoya.

"If we can make Zoya remember that we're not the enemy, then she won't use the gadget against us and we won't have to destroy it. To destroy her. You remember what Snezhana said," Lilia said.

Nikolai nodded. He, Anya, and Alexi waited until the soldiers had moved past their building. Then, they sprinted across the street and into the building containing Grigory's lab.

The doctors were still in the basement. They smiled as Zoya's friends approached.

"How do we stop it?" Nikolai demanded, raising his gun.

"There is no stopping it," one of the doctors replied.

Nikolai grabbed the doctor's throat with his mechanical arm and slammed him against the wall. "That's a lie," he growled. "We know there's a way to stop it. Tell us how!"

"Nikolai," Alexi said, keeping his gun pointed toward the other doctors. "They aren't going to tell us anything."

Anya raised her pistol and shot one of the doctors in the kneecap.

"How about now?" she asked.

The doctor fell to the ground, squeezing his wounded knee.

"We will tell you nothing," he told her. "Except that you are rebel scum and you are going to die."

The third doctor charged toward the friends, a syringe in his hand. Alexi shot him in the head, dropping him instantly. The other two doctors began laughing hysterically.

"What's wrong with you?" Nikolai asked the doctor he held against the wall. The doctor continued to laugh, bubbles and foam pouring out of his mouth. Nikolai let go of his throat in disgust.

"They've poisoned themselves," Alexi said. "Come on, we'll just have to look through the lab ourselves."

Lilia and Demyan watched from afar as Zoya and the soldiers proceeded down the streets of Mirgorod.

GRIGORY'S GADGET

"Do you have any sort of plan?" Demyan asked.

"Some sort," Lilia replied. "Probably not a good sort."

"What does that mean?" Demyan asked. Lilia didn't answer. Instead she darted out of the building.

"Lilia!" Demyan called after her then followed.

"Zoya!" Lilia yelled. Zoya and the soldiers turned, taking aim at her.

"Wait! I surrender!" Lilia shouted. She raised her hands and fell to her knees. "I surrender."

Demyan ran into an alley and watched. He held his gun at the ready.

"You are making the right choice," Zoya told Lilia as the soldiers grabbed her.

"Wait, Zoya!" Lilia yelled as the soldiers began dragging her away. "It's me, Lilia! We've been friends since before we could talk."

"I am not friends with rebels," Zoya replied.

Lilia laughed. "Of course you are," she said. "Because you're a rebel yourself. Zoya, they're controlling you. But you have to remember! Remember me and Demyan and Anya and Nikolai!"

Zoya stood silently for a moment, looking at Lilia then somewhere off in the distance. For a moment, Lilia thought Zoya might remember...

"Take this one away," Zoya told the soldiers, her body becoming rigid. "Her treacherous ways have obviously driven her mad."

"Stop!" Demyan shouted, stepping out of the alley. "You would never let anyone hurt Lilia or any of us." He walked slowly toward Zoya, lowering his gun. The soldiers moved toward him, forgetting Lilia. They stopped as Zoya raised her hand, her open palm aimed at Demyan.

"Another rebel," Zoya said.

"Six years ago," Demyan went on, still walking toward Zoya. "Lilia lost her mother after already having lost her father. The authorities were going to take her away, out of Lodninsk. They were going to send her to her aunt that we all knew was horrible."

"What are you talking about?" Zoya asked. Her hand was still aimed at Demyan.

"No one ever challenged the authorities," Demyan continued. "No one dared make a fuss. Except for you. You found the loophole in the law that would allow her to stay in Lodninsk with us." Demyan smiled and laughed. "I remember you walked right up to a guard who was planning to take Lilia away. You recited the exception verbatim in his face. He was so mad, his face turned bright red. But the guards conceded and let Lilia stay." Zoya's hand began to lower. Demyan was just a foot from her now, looking into her eyes.

"Back away from her!" a soldier shouted.

"You were so brave," Demyan said. "That was the day I fell in love with you."

He moved toward Zoya, grabbing her and pulling her into a kiss. The soldiers began to rush toward him and Zoya, but stopped as Zoya raised her arms. A wide arc of energy knocked the soldiers away.

GRIGORY'S GADGET

Demyan stepped back, his eyes wide. Across his torso, red and black burns scorched his skin. He collapsed, struggling to breathe.

"Demyan!"

Zoya sank to her knees, reaching toward Demyan. She stopped an inch from his skin, afraid to touch him.

"Demyan," she said, her voice croaking. "What have I done? I'm so sorry."

Demyan closed his eyes and fell on to his back. Zoya let out a sob.

"No," Demyan said, his voice low and raspy. "I'm sorry. I'm sorry I was weak."

"No," Zoya replied. "You were never weak. Never."

"Yes, I was." Demyan opened his eyes, gazing up at Zoya through tears. "I've always been weak, but you've always been strong. Zoya, you need to—"

Demyan's body writhed with pain, taking away his breath. He closed his eyes again, but his mouth continued to move.

Fight, he mouthed. Fight it.

"Zoya?"

Zoya looked up, through a wall of tears fogging her goggles, to see Lilia sitting up. Lilia put her hands to her mouth, her own eyes swelling. "Is he…"

Zoya looked at the ground. She dug her fingers into it; cobblestones crushed and turned to dust in her hands. With a scream, she threw an arc of energy toward a nearby building, and another into the sky. Then she turned back to Lilia.

"Run," she said through gritted teeth. Lilia didn't move.

Zoya stood, her eyes fixed on her friend. Then she screamed.

"Run!"

"This is it," Nikolai told Anya and Alexi, pointing to a hand-drawn figure in an old notebook. The drawing depicted a long, thin dagger. The words *kill switch* were scribbled in the upper corner of the page.

"That looks like the key they used on your arm," Anya said.

Nikolai took the key out of his pocket and held it up to the drawing. "You're right," Nikolai said. "Is it really that simple?"

"Grigory Orlov was an inventor," Alexi said. "It's possible he invented those keys in the first place."

"Of course," Anya said, "we have no idea where the lock for this key is located. Is it on her foot? Her shoulder? How are we going to get close enough to figure it out?"

"I guess we'll just have to hope that Demyan and Lilia were able to get through to her," Nikolai said. "This is the best shot we've got."

"Then let's go," Anya said, turning to leave.

Nikolai grabbed Alexi's arm before he could follow her. "Alexi," he said softly. "I'm sorry about your aunt and your father. I didn't like either of them, but I know they were your family."

Alexi grasped Nikolai's non-mechanical arm and nodded. "I appreciate that, but there's no time for sentimentality now. Let's go save Zoya."

As the three of them exited the lab, Lilia came running down the hall. She ran straight to Nikolai, wrapping her arms around him and sobbing.

"Lilia, what happened?" he asked. Lilia shook her head, burying her face into Nikolai's shoulder.

"She…" Lilia sobbed. "She…he's…" Lilia stepped back, wiping her eyes and taking a deep breath. "Demyan's gone."

"Gone, like disappeared?" Anya asked.

"Gone like dead!" Lilia covered her face and wept.

Nikolai clenched his fists.

"Who killed him?"

"Zoya." Lilia's body shuddered with another sob.

"So, Boris was right," Alexi said. "We were too late."

"No," Lilia said. "It was an accident. She didn't want to—"

"We can stop her," Anya said, anger burning through her as tears ran down her face. "Whether we are too late or not, we can stop her. We found the key."

Lilia stood, nodding. With a deep, shaking breath, she said, "Let's go."

Zoya staggered down the streets of Mirgorod, toward the line of soldiers sent to stop her. She raised her arms, shooting clouds of energy toward them. Her arms tingled when she did, a sensation that made her blood rush faster and faster. Zoya watched as the soldiers ran away from her.

Looking around the city that should have been her new home, Zoya was filled with rage. That rage seemed to fuel the gadget: the more anger she felt, the greater the tingling sensation in her arms felt.

You serve the Great Nation of Vernulaia, voices commanded in her head. *You are our sword of justice.*

Zoya held her head, wracked by a pounding headache.

You are our sword of justice. You will stop any and all rebellion.

Zoya shot a cloud of energy at a nearby building, reducing its facade to rubble. The residents of the building screamed as they fled out the back door.

The mine collapsed, Anya's voice said. *They're trapped inside*. Zoya looked up, seeing Anya's specter standing in the rubble of the building. Tears streamed down her face.

I can't do anything, Anya sobbed. *I can't help them*.

"It's ok," Zoya said, reaching out her hand. Another cloud of energy came out of it, further devastating the building.

More soldiers rounded the corner of the street, raining bullets down on Zoya. She hardly felt the impact.

GRIGORY'S GADGET

You are our sword of justice, the soldiers seemed to chant.

"Leave me alone!" Zoya shouted, sending out more clouds of energy.

Nikolai's coming to live with us, Zoya heard Demyan say. *We'll only be in the orphanage another year. Then we'll find our own place.* Zoya looked around, searching for him.

"Demyan?" she called. She began running through the city. The stone roads were charred in her wake.

I'm sorry, Zoya. Zoya saw her father sitting on the stoop of a building. Viscous black fluid flowed from his forearms and thighs. *I didn't want you to see me like this.*

"Daddy," Zoya cried. "Please don't leave me, you can't abandon me." Zoya's father vanished, replaced by flock of black birds.

You are our sword of justice.

Please, I have nothing you want. Zoya looked down an alley, spotting her mother at the end.

Yes you do, Edmund told her, holding a sword to her throat. *You know you do.*

"Mom!" Zoya shouted. She heard her mother scream in response.

But why? A young girl with frizzy purple hair stood next to Zoya, her face streaked with tears. *Why would anyone kill Mom? She never hurt anyone.*

You are our sword of justice.

"Get out!" Zoya screamed as loudly as she could. A pulse of energy emanated from her, spreading out in every direction. The buildings surrounding her were charred and ruined.

"She's over here!" she heard Nikolai shout. "Hurry!"

"No more," Zoya muttered, collapsing to the ground. "Please, no more."

"Zoya!" Anya shouted, running up beside her. "It's alright, we found it."

"I said no more," Zoya replied, refusing to look at her friend. Sparks of light tingled at her fingertips.

"Nikolai, hurry," Lilia urged.

"I don't know where the lock is," Nikolai replied.

Zoya stood, turning toward her friends with her hand raised. She let out a scream, intending to send out another blast of energy. But then she stopped.

In the center of the palm of her hand, a skinny dagger protruded from her armor. The metal began to glow red hot, burning Zoya's hand.

"What did you do?" Zoya screamed. The pain in her palm spread, turning her armor bright red. The pain spread to her neck, and her vision grew dark as Zoya lost consciousness.

You are our sword of justice.

Zoya's eyes opened to blackness. She could feel the room she was in rocking steadily back and forth, accompanied by the sound of creaking wood. Her body was stiff, and her skin felt tight and raw.

GRIGORY'S GADGET

Zoya tried to move her arms only to realize they were bound tightly to the bed on which she lay. Her heart began to race.

"Hello?" Her voice croaked. She swallowed then tried again. "Hello?"

A door opened, letting in a stream of orange light. Lilia appeared above Zoya, smiling hesitantly.

"Zoya? It's me. It's Lilia." She stepped back, staying several feet from Zoya and fidgeting.

Tears welled in Zoya's eyes. "Lilia," she said. "You're alright."

Lilia's smile became more confident as she inched closer to her friend. "Yes, and so are you. At least, physically. We think." Lilia's smile faded slightly, her hands fidgeting more intensely.

"What happened?" Zoya asked. "And why can't I move?"

"Nikolai found the kill switch for the gadget. When he used it...We thought at first it had killed you..."

"It feels like it almost did," Zoya replied.

"But it didn't, you were still breathing," Lilia continued. "But we weren't sure if, when you woke up, you'd be yourself."

You are our sword of justice.

"Am I myself? I can't tell."

"The doctor says it will take time," Lilia said. "But we're here for you."

"Doctor?" Zoya asked.

"Yes, we have a doctor. He was one of the refugees who decided to come with us."

"Refugees?" Zoya's body tensed, her arms and legs pulling at their restraints. "They attacked! They're the rebels!"

Lilia backed away, her eyes wide. Zoya took a deep breath, trying to relax her body. She closed her eyes and breathed, sorting through her thoughts. *Was the rebellion just a dream? Was the rebellion good or bad?* She couldn't remember.

"I'm sorry. It's a lot to take in. You should be resting." Lilia moved toward the door.

"We're on a ship," Zoya said, her eyes darting around the small room. She could smell salt in the air. Lilia turned back toward her.

"Yes, we are," Lilia replied. "There's some good news for you. We've got our very own ship, now."

"And a new Captain." Anya walked into the room then, standing just behind Lilia and giving Zoya the same hesitant smile. "How are you feeling?" she asked.

"Terrible," Zoya replied, trying to sound humorous. "Captain?"

"By unanimous vote," Lilia said. "Even Igor agreed. I would have thought he'd want to be captain himself, but it turns out he's not one for giving orders."

"Unlike you," Zoya said, this time managing a chuckle.

"That's right," Anya said with a wink.

GRIGORY'S GADGET

"So where's Nikolai and—" Zoya's voice caught in her throat as she remembered. *Demyan.* Tears pooled in her eyes as her breath became labored and painful.

"What have I done?"

"It's not your fault, Zoya," Anya said. "You weren't in control of yourself." Though her words seemed sincere, she didn't move any closer to Zoya.

They're afraid of me, Zoya realized. *And why shouldn't they be?*

Anya and Lilia stood in silence, their heads bowed, as Zoya cried. Tears began streaming down their faces as well.

"She's awake?" Nikolai entered the room, rotating his mechanical arm as if stretching a sore muscle. A bespectacled man followed him, regarding everyone with a solemn expression.

"I told you to try not to upset her once she awoke," the man said.

"How could she not be upset?" Anya asked. "She remembers, Doctor."

"Ah," Nikolai said, staring at Zoya.

Unlike Anya and Lilia, Nikolai strolled right up to Zoya's bedside and sat next to her. He grabbed her hand, still bound to the bed, with his mechanical one.

"Zoya, it is not your fault," he said, looking her straight in the eyes. "Alright? No one blames you. What the Vernulaians did to you was horrible. This is their fault."

"But—" Zoya said.

"No," Nikolai said. "No buts. Demyan was killed by the Vernulaians. End of story."

Nikolai untied Zoya's bonds, releasing her arms and then her legs.

"Are you sure about this?" the doctor objected.

Nikolai glared at him. "She's our friend," he said. "She just lost the man she loved because she was being controlled by some tyrannical psychopaths. She doesn't need to be tied up like some monster."

Anya rushed to Zoya's side as she sat up. "I'm not sure if she's ready, though," Anya said, a worried expression on her face.

Zoya brought a hand to her forehead. When she pulled the hand away she gasped. Zoya's hand and arm were covered in metal, the only bare skin she could see was at her joints. She examined her other arm to find the same condition. Then she checked her legs, her feet, and felt around her abdomen. All covered in metal.

"I'm still…" she said. "I thought you said you found the kill switch?"

"We did," Nikolai explained. "Some of the gadget armor fell off. Most of what was on your head, elbows, knees…but a lot of the metal seemed to, sort of, melt into your skin."

"That's why we thought it had killed you at first," Lilia explained, sitting on the bed next to Zoya. "The metal turned bright red, yellow in some places. It was burning so hot—"

GRIGORY'S GADGET

"You appear to be stable, though," the doctor said, staying near the doorway. "Though I'll admit, I don't have much experience with this sort of situation."

"So, I'm stuck with this metal," Zoya said, still examining her arms. "Forever?"

"Welcome to the club," Nikolai said, flexing his mechanical arm. "Personally, I like it."

Zoya smiled. "I suppose I'll get used to it."

Lilia shifted uncomfortably next to Zoya.

"There's one more thing we need to tell you," she said. "We found Demyan, after…when we were fleeing the city."

"We took him, his body, with us," Anya said. "We're planning to give him a proper funeral tonight."

Zoya nodded. "Good."

Zoya grunted as she stood with help from Lilia and Anya. She looked out the nearby window to see the twilight-blue of the sky and ocean.

"How long was I unconscious, anyway?" she asked.

"About a day," Anya replied. She glanced out the window then back at Zoya, biting her lip. "Do you want to see something that might make you feel…" She paused, looking for the right word. "Vindicated?"

Curious, Zoya nodded. Her friends led her into the dimly lit hallway. Easing her up the stairs, they brought her to the main deck. A large crew bustled about, manning sails and scrubbing the floors. Upon seeing Zoya, each member of the crew froze, their faces either blushing or blanching. Zoya cast her eyes to the floor, heat rushing to her own cheeks.

Zoya's friends, ignoring the awkward pause of the crew, brought her to the stern. A red-orange glow illuminated the horizon. Anya pointed to it.

"What, the fading sunset?" Zoya asked.

"No," Anya replied. "That way is south not west. That's Mirgorod."

Zoya's mouth fell open. She could feel anger bubbling up inside of her, conflicted by a wave of relief.

"Did...did I do that?"

"You helped start it," Nikolai replied. "But that's between the Vernulaian government and the rebels."

Zoya grabbed the railing of the ship, digging her nails into the wood. She took a deep breath to calm herself.

"More and more war. She stared at the horizon for another moment. "So, where are we going?"

"All over," Anya replied. "Everyone on our crew had been in the refugee camp. Some weren't really refugees and have homes to return to. So, we're bringing them home."

"And then what?" Zoya asked.

"Assuming the world is still at war? We live as pirates."

"Pirates?" Zoya shook her head.

"Don't sound so surprised." Alexi chuckled, leaning on the railing of the ship. *Had he been there the entire time?* "You've been pirates for the better part of a month now."

"Not by choice," Zoya said. "Only because of your bastard of a father and your crazy aunt."

"Both dead," Alexi said, his face solemn. "We don't have to worry about their games anymore."

Zoya fixed her gaze on the glowing horizon. "And when the war is over?"

"We'll find a nice place to settle down," Anya said. "We'll do more research next time." She smiled despite herself.

Zoya was silent for another moment, deep in thought. "I want to see Demyan," she said at last. Her friends nodded and led her to the captain's cabin.

Demyan's body lay upon the desk inside, a white sheet covering all but his face. Zoya's vision blurred with tears when she saw him, her mouth twitching into a pained frown. She covered her face with her hands then jerked them away again, disgusted by the smell of copper and burned flesh.

"I'm so sorry," she cried, placing a hand on his cold face. "I'm so sorry." She sank to the floor, sobbing.

After a few moments, Lilia said, "We're going to give him a Drevnih funeral."

"Drevnih?" Zoya asked.

"That's what Pavel's religion is called," Lilia said. "Some of the refugees follow it. They told me about the funeral rights, and they just seem—"

"They seem like what Demyan would have wanted," Nikolai said. "Unlike in Lodninsk where his body would have been thrown into an industrial furnace."

"So we won't burn him?" Zoya asked.

"We will," Lilia said. "But, with more dignity. With more respect."

Zoya and her friends remained in the cabin, silent, for half an hour, at which point Zoya stood and nodded. She and her friends lifted Demyan's body, gently, onto a nearby wooden plank. Then, they carried him out to the main deck.

The rest of the crew had already prepared a dinghy for him. The small boat was filled with cloth and broken wood, soaked in oil and tar. The crew parted so Zoya and her friends could place Demyan into the boat. The friends stepped back, joined by Alexi, who grabbed Anya by the hand. Then, Lilia grabbed a bottle of Kraken Ink and soaked Demyan's clothing with it.

Lilia looked to a member of the crew, an elderly woman with long, gray braids, who nodded and smiled.

"If I'm not able to get through this," Lilia said, "Alisa will take over. I am new to Drevnih, so please pardon me if I don't do this entirely correctly. However, Demyan was my friend, so for him, I'll try my best."

Lilia shifted her weight, staring at Demyan then out over the ocean. She nodded again to Alisa, who instructed other members of the crew to begin lower Demyan down to the water.

"May Vozh give his soul courage on his journey to the afterlife," Lilia began, tears running down her face. "May Vestnik guide and protect him on that journey. May Dimka burn away any pain he suffered in life, and may Zhelena bring him to his peace."

As Lilia finished speaking, the dinghy finished its descent to the water. Alisa handed her lit torches, which she passed to each of her friends.

"With this fire, we end your bondage to this world and free your spirit."

Lilia nodded to her friends. They each dropped their torches into Demyan's boat. As the fire spread across his body, catching the soaked cloth and wood, Alisa released the dinghy from the ship. By the time the fire consumed the entire tiny vessel, it was behind the stern. Zoya and her friends moved to watch it float away.

"That was really lovely," Nikolai said to Lilia. "I think Demyan would have appreciated it."

"Me too," Zoya said. She took a deep, shuddering breath and looked at Anya.

"I realized I hadn't asked," she said. "What's the name of this ship of ours?"

"*New Life*," Anya replied, smiling slightly. "I thought it was appropriate since it's what we were looking for when we got into this mess."

"It's perfect," Zoya said. "So what's our first destination?"

"A bad idea," Alexi said, giving Anya a stern look.

"We've discussed this," Anya said to him. "We have to bring them home, and better to do it now, before the war gets even worse."

"Maybe we'll find their princess while we're there, and the war will end," Nikolai said, shrugging as Lilia shoved him.

"Starzapad?" Zoya asked, her eyes wide.

"Yes," Anya said. "We're going to Starzapad."

Zoya Orlova's mind was a manic, swirling fog, but she knew what lay ahead would be new, exciting, and better.

THE END

Thank you so much for embarking on that adventure with me. I hope you enjoyed my book. You can look forward to its sequel coming soon! Want to be the first to know when it will be available? Sign up for my newsletter at:

www.eahennessy.com

Please consider leaving a review on websites such as Amazon, Goodreads, your blog, or any other site you like. Reviews like yours can help other readers find my book.

 E. A. Hennessy is an author of fantasy and science fiction novels. Since childhood, whenever she happened upon a wishing well or other wish-granting object, her wish would be the same: she wanted to go on an adventure. And so, she wrote the types of adventures on which she'd like to embark. E. A. Hennessy lives in Buffalo, New York where she works as an environmental engineer. When she isn't writing or working, she can be found dancing and making nerdy-themed candles.

Connect with E. A. Hennessy:

Website: www.eahennessy.com

Facebook: facebook.com/eahennessy

Twitter: twitter.com/ea_hennessy

Made in the USA
Middletown, DE
27 May 2016